Kenneth Arant

A Snake's Path

A Snake's Life – Book 2

PROLOGUE

A YOUNG ELF WOMAN OPENED HER EYES TO SEE what appeared to be a computer screen floating in front of her.

ထထထထထထထ

Welcome back to the land of the living, Hero!

ထထထထထထထ

"About time," she said aloud as the inky blackness she'd found herself trapped in began to disappear and the image of an ocean superimposed itself over it.

ထထထထထထထ

As a [Hero] you have an obligation to your patron and must fight her enemies as if they were your own.

You have been transported to [Uathea, an earth elemental world. Home of massive forests and the "guardian" of the druids.]

Would you like to see your information?

ထထထထထထထ

"Sure." She shrugged.

The elf had already known most of this information from her talks with the so-called "goddess." She'd already had the basics, why she was brought here, and what was expected of her. But if the goddess thought the elf was going to be a slave to her whims just because she brought the elf back, then she had another thing coming to her.

The only reason the elf accepted the deal in the first place was that she wanted to make a difference in this world. She wanted to help people, to save lives, and to protect the innocent.

And since she'd managed to weasel the knowledge that her home world, Earth, was connected to the "World Tree," she could see her family again. So regardless of what the "goddess" thought was going to happen, the elf was going home to her family.

With her mind made up and her resolve set in stone, the elf re-opened her eyes and looked at the new windows floating in front of her.

∞∞∞∞∞∞∞∞

Because of your past actions/deeds, you are eligible to keep your previous skills as well as receive a few new ones!

Name: Reina

Race: High Elf

Primary Class: Hero

Sub-Class(es): Surgeon, Soldier

Skills: Limit Breaker, Surgeon's Scalpel, Numbing Touch, Simple Weapon Proficiency, Ranged Weapon Proficiency, Minor Stamina up, Minor Strength up, Minor Speed up, Monster Slayer, Spell Creator, Death Defying

Spells: Heal; [Tier 1 healing spell], Regenerate [Tier 2 healing spell]

∞∞∞∞∞∞∞∞

"Hmm... Interesting," Reina mumbled as she reached the bottom of the window.

Before she could spend too much time in thought, the ground started to violently shake, and she heard an ear-splitting roar.

"What on earth was that!?" Reina yelled. The ground beneath her tilted as an earthquake hit, causing her to stumble backwards and fall on her butt. However, her question was soon answered. She looked up and saw two colossal creatures apparently locked in a battle to the death.

The first was an honest-to-god living, breathing dragon! It had brownish yellow scales with spikes covering most of its back and on the back of its head rested four horns with a fifth on his nose... And did she mention that it was the size of a freaking mountain!?

The other creature was a truly gargantuan serpent. It had dark green scales with a gray underbelly, massive wings, and a large red gem in the center of its forehead.

Suddenly, and without hesitation, the serpent slammed the dragon onto the ground and the true battle for dominance began. Grievous wounds were inflicted on both sides as the serpent fought to contain the dragon while a red light danced through the air and occasionally attacked the beast.

"What in the world did I get myself into?" Reina asked herself. Turning and fleeing from the two battling behemoths, she ran until she could run no more. When she turned around and looked back the way she had come, she saw something that would stick with her for years: the serpent and the dragon locked together in a struggle for dominance as a transparent white shell closed around them, preventing prying eyes from witnessing the end of their fight.

Just before the two disappeared from sight, a window appeared and blocked her vision.

∞∞∞∞∞∞∞∞

Do you see now, Hero? These are your lady's enemies and just some of the creatures you must defeat in your lady's name.

∞∞∞∞∞∞∞∞

She rolled her eyes at the screen's dramatic words and waved it away. "They might be *your* enemy, Goddess, but they sure as hell ain't mine."

≁ ≁ ≁

THE NEXT MORNING

Reina pulled her "borrowed" cloak closer to her body in a vain attempt to keep warm. Ever since arriving in this strange world, she'd been almost constantly harassed by the cold wind. Of course, this was made all the worse by the fact that she was naked. That damnable goddess dropped her on an unfamiliar world with little more than the hair on her head and a smile. So, while she did feel guilty for taking the clothes off of a dead elf and essentially becoming a grave robber, at least she was decent now.

She'd been walking almost nonstop since her encounter with the serpent and dragon. She'd only stopped to rest for an hour before dawn and to wash her face in a shallow river. Incidentally, that's where she found her "borrowed" outfit. It consisted of a green woolen cloak, a brown cloth tunic, matching pants, and a pair of dark leather shoes. They were slightly too large for her petite frame, but she tied a knot in the tunic's excess material and wore it like a crop-top. She couldn't do much with the pants or boots, so she had to put up with them being uncomfortable.

The snapping of a twig pulled her out of her thoughts. Her head involuntarily swiveled toward the sound. She shifted her center of mass to make fleeing easier, should the need arise.

"Easy, elf girl." A tall human male stepped out from behind a tree with his hands in the air. "I'm just fleeing the battle. Same as you."

"I don't recall asking what you were doing."

"Okay," he said, drawing out the "kay" sound. "Look, I'm not going to hurt you." He stepped closer to her.

Reina's eyes narrowed and her hypersensitive hearing picked up someone attempting to sneak up behind her. "No? That must be your friend's job, then."

"Ha! Not bad elf. Not bad at all." Another man stepped out from behind a tree. Where the first man was tall and skinny, this one was the complete opposite. "How'd you know I was there?"

"I heard your fat ass jiggle."

The man scowled and pulled a club out from beneath his gray cloak. "You should watch your mouth, elf girl."

A metallic sound caused Reina's eyes to dart back to the first man. He'd pulled a small dagger from somewhere and was gripping it tightly in his left hand.

Hmm—I could use that little trinket. Reina's eyes slowly returned to the fat man. "I'm guessing that fleeing story was bullshit. Anything else you'd like to tell the class?"

"Oh, no, we are fleeing from those monsters," the fat man admitted. "Our camp was near an elf village when that serpent burst from the ground and attacked the dragon." As he was talking, he and the tall man began to approach her.

She backpedaled to keep them at a distance. "So, what, you just get a kick out cornering defenseless girls in the middle of the woods?"

"Of course not," the fat man said with mock sincerity. "However, we recently lost most our 'shipment,' and we need to resupply."

"Oh? What kind of shipment? Maybe I could help you find it if I know what I'm looking for."

"Why don't you come back to our camp and I'll show you?" The man flashed her a crooked grin.

Reina's back bumped into a tree and she internally cursed. "Sorry, but you'll need to buy me dinner before I go home with you."

"Is that a fact?" the tall man whispered as they closed in on her.

"Yep, I'm a classy woman, after all."

"Well, you're certainly a pretty one. I'll give you that." He reached out and ran the back of his hand over her stomach.

Before the man could react, Reina's left palm shot up and slammed into his nose, while her right grabbed and twisted the hand holding the dagger until she heard a painful ***crack.*** She ducked under his arm to avoid the fat man's club and danced out of the way of his follow up attack. While the tall man was holding his wrist and screaming in pain, Reina scooped up the fallen dagger and held it out in front of her body.

"I don't want to hurt either of you. However, if you continue to harass me, I'll show your bodies what kind of week I've been having."

The tall man continued to scream in pain, so he didn't respond to the threat. But the fat one did. He glanced at the dagger in Reina's hand, then yelled at the tall man. "Oh, be quiet, you idiot!" The tall man dropped to his knees and began whimpering. He bit his lip until blood ran down his chin but didn't make another sound.

"You know how to use that blade, elf girl?" the fat man asked.

"Only one way to find out."

"S'pose that's true." He snorted. "Tell you what. You give me that dagger and we'll forget this meeting ever happened." He held out his hand. "How about it?"

The fake smile on his face and the anger behind his eyes made Reina want to shiver, but she suppressed it. "Sure, that sounds fine. Where do you want it?"

"In my hand, elf girl."

"Alright, if you say so," she agreed.

He reached out to take it… Reina grabbed his arm to steady it, then slammed the blade through the back of his hand and ripped it out through his fingers. The man began to scream, but she held it up to his throat.

"Make one more sound, and I'll give it to you again."

He swallowed the sudden overflow of saliva in his mouth and shakily nodded.

"Good. Now, here's what's going to happen. I'm going to go about my day and pretend that I found this knife on the ground, and we never had the—pleasure— of meeting. If you follow me or otherwise hamper my ability to do this, I will gladly introduce my "found" blade to the side of your throat." She pressed the blade against his neck for emphasis. "Understand?"

"Mm hm."

"Excellent. Now, back the hell up."

Fat man followed her orders and stepped away. The rage in his beady black eyes made a cold chill run down her spine, but she once again suppressed it. She backed away from the two men until she felt it was safe to turn and run into the cover of the forest. But, when she was just three-hundred feet from the two men, she made a sharp right turn and circled around behind them.

She'd made the decision to follow them after the fat man had mentioned a "shipment." She hoped she was wrong, and they were just creeps. But she somehow doubted she was that lucky.

The two men stumbled through the forest, eventually finding their way to a campsite about a mile from where she'd met them.

"My luck sucks," Reina sighed. She could hear the sound of the two men whimpering in pain from the nearby tent.

She saw a seven- by eight-foot cage in the back of a wagon. The horse meant to pull said carriage was tied to a post outside the tent. Inside the cage, she saw three men, two women, and a handful of children, all elves, and all wounded in some way. Luckily for her and the elves, the men had only tied the cage shut with a thick piece of rope. While it was thick enough to keep the elves from easily untying it, it held up no better than any other rope under the sharp edge of her new knife.

She made short work of the rope, then popped open the cage door. Once all the elves had climbed out, the largest and most imposing male stepped forward and pointed at the knife.

"May I borrow that?"

"What for? You're free; you can leave."

"These "men," he hissed, "tortured a friend of mine to death to send a message to the rest of us."

"And?"

"I'd like to return the favor."

"You know that won't bring your friend back?"

"I do."

"And you'll do it with or without the knife."

"Yes."

Reina sighed and handed the blade to the elf. "Just— don't forget to return this to me. It's a good knife."

"You have my word." Or so he'd said. All but one elf walked into the tent, leaving a lone woman to tend to the children. Then the screams began. Reina and the elf woman covered the children's ears as best they could while they waited for the other elves to return.

Two or three hours passed before the elves exited the tent looking none too happy, but at least they seemed relaxed now.

"Didn't turn out as you expected?"

The "leader" shook his head and handed the suspiciously clean knife to Reina hilt first, along with a small scabbard he'd taken from the tall man.

"No, Halfar was tortured for five hours before he died. These humans are pathetic, each one barely lasted an hour before they fled this world with their tails between their legs."

Reina quietly inspected the blade for any specks of blood, then sheathed it inside the scabbard and tied its leather strap around her waist. When she turned her attention back to the tall elf, she noticed he was holding out his hand.

"My name is Toross, captain of these men and former member of the Grand Veil tribe of Uathea."

Reina cautiously took the elf's hand and shook it. "Reina, and I'm just passing through."

Toross' ear twitched at her words, but he said nothing on the subject.

"Would you like to come with us? We are preparing to leave this place and could use another pair of hands."

Reina thought it over for a moment, then nodded her head. "Sure, it beats getting lost in the woods again." And so, Reina joined her first adventurer party and with their help, she left Uathea for the worlds beyond.

Chapter One

*D*O YOU WANT TO HEAR A STORY? THE mischievous voice of a young girl asked. *Well, boy, do I have a story for you.*

I wanted to grumble, but I couldn't speak… Not yet.

This, like most stories, is the story of a sna—man. The owner of the voice corrected herself. *I traveled with this man for ten years, and during that time I saw him do things I never imagined possible. He explored the deepest valleys and climbed the highest peaks on five different worlds. He fought off invading armies and slayed monsters no other man could have in defense of the innocent. Commoners and kings alike stood in awe of his power. A few even worshiped him as a deity. But to me… He was just Torga: my adoptive father.*

However, the voice turned harsh. *This man was also an idiot who routinely forgot to watch his back.* The girl sighed. *Nine months and sixteen days ago we were off world on the planet of Alabos, a planet two bridges from here. We found ourselves doing some mercenary work for the king of the small island country of Asta. An unknown monster was reportedly sneaking into the port city of Orsira and destroying the homes of its citizens. In return for finding and eliminating the monster, and ensuring the city would remain unmolested, the king would give us an item that would supposedly enhance Torga's power.*

So, we staked out the city one night and awaited the expected attack. As it turned out, the king was right. An attack did come a few days after we began our stakeout. But it was no monster that was attacking the city. Merely a group of humans dissatisfied with those in power and taking out their frustrations on the unsuspecting populace.

We engaged them, the girl continued. I prayed to Yggdrasil for the strength to help my father in the upcoming battle, and used a bit of my druidic magics— an enchantment on the stone beneath their feet that returned it to its natural state—that of loose soil. The rogues initially lost their balance and gave Dad the opening he needed to ambush them. He magically enhanced his body before leaping into the air, his powerful legs carrying him thirty feet through the air, before landing in the center of the distracted group.

Dad's hand whipped out and decapitated a large man in dull gray plate mail with an almost casual backhand. Before the large man's head could touch the ground, Dad's fists blurred, and three more men were killed. That was as far as he got before the group reacted and began to fight back.

A fireball shot out of a robed man's sleeve and narrowly missed Dad's back as he twisted around it. A large silver axe whipped through the air, causing Dad to make a choice: dodge or get his head torn off. He opted to duck and step into a leather-clad man's chest. Without a chance to dodge Dad's return strike, the man could only watch as my father's fist slammed into his breastplate and sent him stumbling back." The girl sighed. "I could tell from the lack of strength in the blow, Dad's body enhancement spell had worn off. Now was when the danger truly set in because without that enhancement spell, Dad's body was nothing special to a group of heavily armed rogues.

I used magic to turn one of the surrounding walls into a hail of stone spikes that hit the enemy in the back. One lucky spike perforated the robed man's back and tore a gaping hole through his chest, disrupting the spell he'd been about to cast and causing it to misfire. A wave of blue fire left his closed fist and sent everyone, Dad included, flying.

Dad rotated his smoldering body mid-air to land on his feet, but the rogues weren't so lucky. Those that survived the misfire ended up on the ground groaning in pain as loose soil and dust stuck to their fresh second- and third-degree burns.

Dad brushed debris and soot from his white shirt and gave me one of those 'I'm okay' smiles. He walked over to one of the less injured men and grabbed him by the collar of his ruined shirt, as I headed over to join him. I could see the man's mouth move, but couldn't hear what he was saying. Dad could, though. His eyes widened, then his head whipped in my direction.

Get away! he yelled. He dropped the man's collar and sprinted at me faster than I'd ever seen him move outside of combat. The next thing I knew I was lying on my back. The smell of burnt flesh surrounded me, soaking into my clothes and skin like dirty water.

Are you okay?

My eyes snapped open at the sound of my dad's voice. I found him crouched over me, half the skin and muscle on his legs and back had been melted away until only charred bones remained. But Dad yet lived. Neither his face nor tone betrayed a hint of pain, but the fear in his voice was obvious to anyone that had taken the time to get to know him.

I'm fine, I told him. Just shaken up a bit… How about you? That looks pretty bad.

Yeah, he sighed. It is. The asshole had a firebomb tucked away inside his belt. I don't think I have enough magic power to regenerate this level of damage.

That's what I'd been afraid of. You see, Dad's body was essentially just a puppet formed from the remains of a corpse. Without returning to his original body every few months to absorb his own magic, or "fill up the tank" as he so eloquently put it, his puppet body couldn't heal itself… And we'd failed to make the trip back in time for his twice-yearly appointment.

What do you want me to do? I asked, trying my best to keep my emotions in check. No sense in letting him see me cry now, was there?

Lena and Fenris were supposed to meet us here in a few days anyway— Dad's body suddenly collapsed to the side. I managed to get my legs under his head in time to cushion his fall and prevent his head from hitting the stone floor, which he thanked me for. He wouldn't have felt the pain from smacking his face on the ground even if his body hadn't been burnt to a crisp, but it was the thought that counted.

Thanks. Anyway, make sure you find them, and stick with them until it's time, okay?

I nodded.

His right arm slowly came up and rubbed my hair… Good girl… The hand fell listlessly to the ground, and my father wasn't with me anymore."

Ding

∞∞∞∞∞∞∞

Your evolution is complete!

∞∞∞∞∞∞∞∞

My eyes flared, muscles tensed, and a massive crack appeared in the egg-shaped dome surrounding me.
Ding,* *Ding

∞∞∞∞∞∞∞∞

Because of your fusion with the dragon, you have lost your "Store/Release" energy ability and the jewel on your forehead has been turned into mana for your use.

Because of your fusion with the dragon, you have gained the skill Energy Breath.

Energy Breath: Like the dragons of old, your very breath can topple mountains. You can fire pure magical energy from your mouth.

∞∞∞∞∞∞∞∞

Because of your fusion with the dragon, you have unlocked one of his traits.

Magic Eater: With every breath you take, you passively consume the ambient magic in the air.

Warning! Due to the Gluttonous trait, this trait can prove fatal to those around you.

∞∞∞∞∞∞∞∞

I twisted my body and the "egg" split in twain, causing fresh air to flood into my nostrils for the first time in a decade. A pleasant fruity smell entered my nostrils as the dome dissolved into mist, revealing a young woman in her late teens, and I would recognize her anywhere. standing on the highest branch of an obscenely tall tree. However, even that only brought her to the tip of my nose now that I was no longer curled into a ball.

By the young woman's side was a pair of slightly older women. One had fair skin and short red hair; this was Hali. The other had ebony skin and waist-length black hair: and her name was Findral. The two were standing behind Ayla and were having a hushed conversation.

I recognized both, but another pop-up appeared before I could greet them.

ᴔᴔᴔᴔᴔᴔᴔᴔᴔᴔ

Name: Torga

Race: Gluttonous Elemental Serpentine Dragon

Classification: Tier 7

Skills: Minor Stealth, Heat Detection, Superior Gluttony, Supreme Durability up, Supreme Strength up, Superior Growth, Minor Mental Resistance up, Greater Petrifying Gaze, Greater Acid Venom, Detect Concealment, Energy Breath, Superior Elemental Resistance, Fly, Puppet Maker, Body Possession, Magic Enhancement, Elemental Manipulation

Traits: Gluttonous +5, Growth +10, Strong Willed, Venomous, Aquatic, Winged, Immunity to Mind Control, Magic Manipulator, Magic Eater

ᴔᴔᴔᴔᴔᴔᴔᴔᴔᴔ

"It's about time, old man!" Ayla yelled. "Do you have any idea how long I've been waiting in this boring ass forest?"

"Language," I replied instantly. She knew how I felt about her using that kind of language at her age.

"Oh, piss off with your 'language' crap," she grumbled. She folded her arms across her chest and began tapping her foot.

I could barely hear what she was saying, being that my ears, or whatever passed for ears in this new form, were over forty feet away from her. I directed mana towards amplifying my hearing until I could hear faint giggling from the pair behind her. She shot them a dirty look, which only intensified the giggling. *Glad to see their relationship hasn't changed.* I lifted my body out of my giant, egg-shaped prison and shook myself. My scales were stiff, my eyes burned from the light of the sun hanging overhead, and I was hungrier than I'd ever been… But I was *finally* free.

"Hey, Ayla?"

"What?" she snapped.

"Were you serious about some dumbasses worshiping me as a god?"

"Yeah," she snorted, "serious as a goddamned dragon attack."

Ding

∞∞∞∞∞∞∞∞∞

Survive for 100 years: Magical Hydra

Consume 5 different dragon breeds, at least one of which must be 1,000 years old: Legendary Dragon

Consume a Mana Storm & 600 Naga: Draconic Naga

Consume a spark of divinity: ???

∞∞∞∞∞∞∞∞∞

I sighed at the pop-up. *You just had to say dragon, didn't you? As if being a giant snake wasn't bad enough, now I've got this crap to deal with too. And what the hell is a spark of divinity?* The pop-up saw fit to ignore my question… *Alright, whatever, and what happens if I pass them up?*

∞∞∞∞∞∞∞∞

If you pass up the Magical Hydra evolution, you will get: Supreme Regeneration

If you pass up the Legendary Dragon evolution, you will get: Shapeshifting

If you pass up the Draconic Naga evolution, you will get: Supreme Mana Control

If you pass up the ??? evolution, you will get: ???

∞∞∞∞∞∞∞∞

It just couldn't be simple, could it?

჻ ჻ ჻

"Oh," I sighed as I stretched out my body. After unfurling myself from the annoying ball I'd been in for the last decade, I was long enough now that I could only see a vague outline of my tail in the distance.

"Hey, are you listening to me?" Ayla whined. The three of them were riding on top of my head, and Ayla was in the process of regaling me with tales of her exploits since I'd last seen her.

"Yes, Brat. I'm listening," I said. I continued moving where Ayla directed. I brushed trees aside as if they were blades of grass, and the light from the early morning sun cast the forest in a beautiful orange and purple glow.

"Good," she huffed. "Anyway, as I was saying. So, there I am, surrounded on all sides by bandits with nothing but my wits and Granny's staff to see me through." Ayla told her story with all the excitement and energy of a kid on a sugar rush, and I couldn't get the smile off my face. She told me of her adventures with Lena, Fenris, Hali, and Solon: How they fought off bandit raiders, explored a cursed dungeon, and saved the third prince of a powerful kingdom from being kidnapped by a race of giants.

"Wait," I interrupted. "You fought giants?" The only "giant" I'd seen was a *huge*, monstrous man-thing that even I'd hesitate to square off against.

"Well, Fenris said they weren't the same race as the Titan you ate on Iorus. These were called jötunn," she explained.

"Jötunn? I don't think I've ever seen one of those," I admitted.

"Well, jötunn is their name in the local dialect. The actual race is jötnar, which loosely translates to "Frost Giant" in our tongue. And I'd never met one either until we drove off the one attempting to kidnap the prince. They're apparently on the verge of extinction after some war a few millennia ago."

"Millenia? Surely, they would've repopulated by now."

"Not necessarily, old man. You're forgetting that the longer a species lives, the less likely they are to have kids. According to Fenris, jötnar aren't known for dying of old age so their birthrates are even lower than that of the elves."

"You've been hanging around Uriel too much. Your lecturing voice is starting to sound like him," I grumbled.

I felt a weak thumping on my head and assumed Ayla was venting her frustration by stomping her feet.

"I agree, master," a sultry voice interjected. "She is beginning to sound like an old woman."

"Oh, definitely," a boyish voice agreed.

"Findral, Hali, zip it. No one asked for your opinion," Ayla scolded. Even though her words were harsh, there wasn't an ounce of fire behind them.

The three of them had grown close over the years, although Ayla and Hali started out as rivals. Both were high-elf druids of similar skill, if not power. But Hali's lesser power wasn't exactly her fault. Her half-Warg parentage gave her a stronger, healthier body at the cost of her magic supply. While Wargs were inherently magical creatures, they weren't exactly known to be spellcasters. Unfortunately, this created a hard limit to the amount of power Hali would be able to use as she grew older.

Which is why she supplemented it with the sword sheathed on her side. The girl was scarily good with that blade.

Meanwhile, the ever loyal Findral remained at Ayla's side and acted as her older sister, confidant, and bodyguard, just as I'd asked her to all those years ago. Even after the other goblins asked to leave my company and start their own nest, she'd remained. I never asked why she didn't wish to join the other goblins and to be honest, I didn't care. I was glad she remained by my side.

An hour or so after I'd been freed, we arrived at a small clearing littered with tents. The campsite was currently void of people, but I assumed that was because it was early and most would be out doing their morning rituals. I slowly twisted my head to the side, allowing the girls to get as close to the ground as possible before they jumped off.

"We're back!" Ayla hollered. "And we've brought a guest!"

"Yeah yeah, we know. Heard his fat ass coming from several miles away," a shirtless man grumbled as he left the tree line on the far side of the camp and headed over to us. The man wasn't all that tall, but he was solidly built, with wild black hair that flowed freely over his shoulders. Long pointed ears, lava red eyes, and sharp teeth told me exactly who this was. I recognized the demi-elvan form of Fenris immediately and gave him a quick nod, which he returned. A few seconds after he entered the clearing, a mass of people began to trickle in.

"Thanks for looking out for Ayla, Mutt. I owe you one."

"Nah." He immediately shook his head. "I owed you plenty. Looking out for Ayla doesn't begin to repay my debt to you." He finished with a troubled look on his face.

"Even so, thanks." I glanced around at the crowd forming around us. Judging by the matching robes half of them were wearing, and the upper-class outfits the other half wore, I assumed we were dealing with two separate groups of people. "So, what's with all the people?"

Fenris made a show of looking around at the onlookers. "Escort contract. A merchant caravan from Odessa and the priests of some goddess from Phoria. They were going to the same place as us, so we figured we'd bring them along."

"Oh? Where are we going?" I asked.

Fenris' lips went tight, and he stiffened.

Before I could ask what was wrong, someone drew my attention away from him. I watched as a young man stopped beside Fenris. The young man looked to be about twenty. He was taller than Fenris by a couple of inches but wasn't quite as solidly built and looked like a swimmer or marathon runner. He too had wild black hair and lava red eyes, though his hair was short and barely hung over his ears.

"Solon," I greeted him with a nod. "It's good to see you again."

"Hello," Solon said in his usual stoic tone.

"Hi, little brother," Hali said as she moved to his side. He gave her an annoyed look before promptly ignoring her.

"How was your nap?" he asked me.

"Long and uncomfortable," I grumbled. "From the way my back is hurting, you'd think I'd just spent the last decade inside an egg or something," I finished, my voice dripping with sarcasm.

"Aww, poor baby," Hali cooed before she took a few quick steps forward to stand next to me. She patted my scales and tut-tutted at me.

Guess she also picked up some bad habits from me...

"I need to make sure the camp is ready to leave soon, so I'll leave you kids to bring him up to speed and..." Fenris paused, shooting Ayla an odd look, "explain some things." He turned on his heel and quickly walked away. I watched as he made his way over to a thin elf with red hair and a young girl: That would be his wife Lena and daughter Talia.

"What's up with him?"

"Well," Hali cleared her throat, "there have been some changes since you decided to take a nap."

Findral and Solon snorted in unison and Ayla looked decidedly uncomfortable with the change in subject.

"That wasn't my fault," I protested.

"Sure, it was." She instantly shot down my protest with an irritatingly confident smirk. "Anyway, your incompetence aside, Dad's been going through a lot lately," Hali explained.

"Which leaves him in a foul mood," Solon added.

"Right," Hali agreed. "He's getting close to evolving, and that's weighing on his mind a lot. If he evolves successfully, he'll be the first Warg in a hundred years to pass the tier 4 wall."

"But no pressure," Solon muttered.

"He's basically a diamond at this point," Ayla quipped.

I snorted in amusement at the byplay between them. I'd missed conversations like this. "So, he's worried about the usual suspects: Lena, his kids, and not being strong enough to protect them."

Hali nodded, Solon shrugged, and Ayla sighed.

"Welcome to the club, Fenris. We have meetings once a week and commemorative alligator skin jackets." The three teenagers stared at me with varying levels of confusion on their faces, which almost made me burst out laughing. As it was, I sighed to hide my amusement and looked away so they wouldn't see the humor behind my eyes. Unfortunately, I'd turned towards Findral by accident. She watched me with a mischievous grin on her delicate face. She shot me a wink, which I decided not to think about. "I'll have a talk with him," I said. "Maybe I can do something to ease his worries."

"That may not be the best idea, master," Findral replied with that same mischievous grin plastered on her face. "After all, I'm pretty sure you're one of the things he's stressed about."

"Is that true?" I asked Hali after a moment.

"I mean, yeah—" she trailed off, shooting a glance in Ayla's direction.

"O…kay." I also looked at Ayla, who seemed like she was simultaneously trying to imitate a tomato and a ghost. "Is there something you'd like to tell me, Ayla?"

"Not especially—"

"Ayla's engaged to be married, master," Findral chirped.

"What's that?" Solon loudly exclaimed. He pantomimed listening intently to something. "Sure, Mom. Be right there!" He took off without another glance in our direction.

I hardly noticed. Findral's words captured my complete attention and my eyes shifted back to Ayla. This action was accompanied by an involuntary hiss. "Isss. That. So? And just when was I going to be informed of this, Ayla?"

"Um—Well," she nervously laughed. "You did leave me alone, so it's not my fault that you didn't know."

"Hmm, even so. Where I come from, it's impolite to ask for a woman's hand in marriage without meeting the parents first. So—Where is the rude little bastard?" I growled.

"Ayla refused to bring him along. He's waiting for us on the other side of the portal," Hali chimed in with a smirk on her lips.

"Then we'd best not keep my future sn... son-in-law waiting, should we?" I turned away from the girls and began eyeing the people I didn't recognize briefly, but I was still too rocked by the recent revelation to care. *What else did I miss in eighteen months?*

Chapter Two

When the group was ready to move, Fenris, Solon, and Findral helped everyone climb onto my back—a not insignificant feat, considering my current size—and I began to move.

Soon, various groups formed from my companions. Findral, Ayla, and Hali headed away from the others to do some light combat practice. The relative newcomers to the group headed off on their own to set up tents and a campsite, after asking Fenris to make sure I didn't mind. Solon and Talia went off to help wherever they could, and Lena and Fenris were sitting on top of my head and trying to have a conversation with me. However, my mind was currently preoccupied by something far more interesting.

∞∞∞∞∞∞∞∞∞

Survive for 100 years: Magical Hydra

Consume 5 different dragon breeds, at least one of which must be 1,000 years old: Legendary Dragon

Consume a Mana Storm & 600 Naga: Draconic Naga

Consume a spark of divinity: ???

∞∞∞∞∞∞∞∞∞

There's always been a "hidden" evolution to accompany the others. An evolution of much greater difficulty than the rest, so... Where was it?

As if summoned by my words, a new pop-up appeared.

∞∞∞∞∞∞∞∞

Kill the old Serpent King: Serpent King

Consume a planet: ??????

∞∞∞∞∞∞∞∞

I sighed aloud and dismissed the pop-up.

"Torga! Have you been listening to me?" Lena yelled into my ear.

"Not really, no," I admitted without thinking.

"Why do I even bother with you sometimes?" she sighed.

"Because you're a busybody who has a soft spot for strays."

She went silent at my words and left without replying. I split my focus between where I was going and thinking about the evolutions. My plan was to keep my attention divided so I wouldn't accidentally think about the fact that I now had a soon-to-be son-in-law—I shook my head and hissed away the thought.

What do I get if I reject these evolutions?
Ding

∞∞∞∞∞∞∞∞

If you pass up the Serpent King evolution, you will get: *This is a special evolution that cannot be passed up should you unlock it. Once you embark on this path, you will either succeed and become the Serpent King or perish in the attempt.*

If you pass up the '?????' evolution, you will get: *Note: There is not enough information available at this time.*

∞∞∞∞∞∞∞∞

That's... ominous. And what in the nine hells is up with that one evolution? There's no way I can eat a planet. A flashback of some of my past meals raced through my mind: A giant deer, an army of Kobolds, a literal mountain, the Titan, the Leviathan, the Kraken... And, more recently, the dragon. *Okay—Maybe I could eat a planet if I was given enough time.* I stopped moving and dropped my head to the ground, then banged my forehead against it several times. Even though I did it gently, my colossal weight caused minor earthquakes to rattle the area with every hit, knocking over a few trees and startling the remaining animals away.

I thought I heard Fenris yell something like: "It's alright everyone. It's just the Fatass being weird. Return to your business." But I wasn't sure.

"What's the matter Torga?" Lena asked once I'd stopped.

"Just my luck being shitty as usual, is all," I replied, then began moving again.

"Want to talk about it?"

"I'd rather talk about the little prick that decided to ask for Ayla's hand." That made both Lena and Fenris decidedly uncomfortable.

"Well, what do you want to know?" Lena asked after a moment of thought.

"Who is he?"

"He's a prince, actually."

"That doesn't answer my question. I said 'who' is he, not 'what' is he."

"As far as I know, he's a son of the Asgardian royal family."

Asgardian? Why does that name sound familiar? Lena must've mistaken my silence for anger, because she quickly assured me that he was Ayla's age and wasn't some old man. I shook my head at her words. "Good to hear. I'm curious about the name, though. I know I've heard it somewhere before, but I can't seem to place it."

"Understandable. The Asgardians are certainly… memorable," she allowed. "Thankfully, Thor doesn't seem to be like the rest of his family."

"Thor, so that is his name. Is he strong?" *If the little shit is going to marry my daughter, adopted or not, he damned well better be able to protect her.*

"They say he's an accomplished warrior. Supposedly killed a number of giants, though I can't attest to the accuracy of the story. "

I stopped moving at her words and twisted my head around until I could see her. "By 'Giant,' do you mean the Jötnar?"

She nodded her head. "And though it may not seem like it to you, for a normal person that's an incredible accomplishment."

"Are you saying I'm not normal, Lena?" I quietly laughed at her blank expression.

"Do you want an honest answer to that question?" she finally asked.

I thought over her words for a few moments, then turned around and started moving again.

"Probably not," I admitted.
"I didn't think so."

CHAPTER THREE

ARLY THE NEXT MORNING, WE ARRIVED AT THE branch and settled in for breakfast. Lena wanted to use the free time to formally introduce me to the newcomers, but I wasn't interested in meeting them since they would be gone soon. Besides, I had other stuff on my mind.

"Will you calm down already?" Lena asked for the third time in twenty minutes.

"I am calm," I replied while staring into the portal.

"Torga, I know you're eager to meet the kid, but if you don't calm down, you're likely to do something you'll regret."

"I appreciate your concern, Lena. But I. Am. Calm."

Lena growled in frustration and used her magic to raise the land around her until she was staring me in the eye.

"You're acting like a child."

"Am not," I muttered without looking at her.

Lena hopped down from her perch, and had just begun to storm off when I asked, "Did Uriel manage to acquire a jewel for me? I meant to ask him earlier, but I haven't had the chance yet."

"Oh, so now you want to listen to me?" she sneered.

"Look, I apologize for being difficult. Truly, I do." I sighed. "It's just, I'm, well I'm—"

"You're, what?"

"I'm *hungry,*" I hissed. "It's been ten years since I had a good meal and all of you smell so damn delicious, it's driving me crazy," I growled. I slammed my head into the ground to calm myself down.

"Oh—Oh!" She exclaimed as my words registered in her mind. "Why didn't you say anything?" she hollered.

"What exactly am I going to say? 'Hey, guys? Mind if I eat a few of you?' Oh yeah, I'm sure that would've gone over soo well," I snarked.

"Well, no. But you could've stopped to eat something, at the very least!"

I was quiet for several seconds. My eyes landed on each member of my party in turn, then moved on to the newcomers. As I looked from person to person, my hunger grew until—"Alright, new plan. Everyone out. Get your asses over to the other planet. Anyone, and I do mean anyone, still here in thirty seconds is getting *eaten.*"

"Torga, you can't just—" Lena began, but I quickly cut her off.

"Twenty-five."

"Hey Fatass, don't you threaten my—" Fenris yelled, but he too, was interrupted.

"Twenty."

The group stood around in shock for another ten seconds before they saw the truth of my words, and they realized I wasn't kidding around. Once this realization hit them, they left behind their equipment, and all but Findral practically dove into the portal.

"Master, do you remember which planet we're going to?" she asked while slowly backing towards the portal.

"Asgard. Six."

"Okay, just checking!!" After confirming, she dove into the portal and I was left alone.

"Finally, I can finally let go—" It started out small, a leaf here, a blade of grass there. But eventually, the full weight of my hunger made itself known. The monster buried just beneath my scales, always so close, yet kept at bay by my will, was finally set free.

Like a man dying of thirst, the monster began to rapidly pull the surrounding magic towards me and gulped it down again and again.

Not five minutes into this cycle of consumption, the surrounding forest was completely drained of magic. The plants had lost their previous bright green color and were now a sinister black. Not even the animals were saved from this fate as they too were quickly drained of their life-giving magic and were left as mere husks of their former selves. Their bodies exsanguinated from the loss of magic, not even the strongest among them lived for more than a few seconds under the assault of the monster's insatiable appetite.

Soon the destruction spread beyond its immediate surroundings and stretched further into the forest, where more and more plants and animals were drained of their magic until they too died.

The monster continued to feed for thirty minutes and in that time, over ten miles of forest was drained completely dry. The plants killed; the animals turned into husks. Death permeated the area long before the monster receded, and I returned to my senses... For the first time, I was forced to face what I was truly capable of—and it terrified me.

Trees were felled under their own weight, their leaves missing or blackened. The grass and other such plants were also reduced to shriveled husks. As I turned my head towards the portal, something caught my eye: It was all that was left of a deer after its magic was sucked out. Its fur had fallen off leaving it bare, its eyes were missing, and its bones were showing through its skin.

Ding* Ding*Ding*Ding*Ding—

Pop-up after pop-up appeared before my eyes, each detailing a creature I'd consumed in my madness. I couldn't bear to look at them, at the evidence of my loss of control, so I dismissed them almost as soon as they appeared.

My jaw tightened as I began to scan the area for a sign—any sign of life. I found none. After scanning the area for a few minutes and seeing exactly what I'd done, I shook my head and let out a defeated sigh. *Thank god. If I hadn't forced them all to leave when I did, that would've been them lying on the ground instead of a deer.* I gazed at my surroundings for a few minutes more, then my eyes narrowed. *Let's see if I remember how to do this.*

I closed my eyes and thought back to all the times Lena had tried to teach me to use my Magic Manipulation skill. I could almost hear her say...

~ ~ ~

"Focus, Torga. Bring forth that colossal amount of energy inside you and push it into your surroundings. Bend it to your will. You are the master of your energy, not the other way around." Lena said.

"What about the magic that's around me; the magic I don't create?"

"In that case, you need only to push your will outside yourself. Then the magic in the air will be yours to command as well."

"Outside myself?"

Lena shrugged, "It didn't make sense to me at first either, but you'll understand it eventually… Probably."

～ ～ ～

I opened my eyes and did exactly as Lena said. Reached deep within myself and pulled my magic to the surface, or at least I tried to. What actually happened was I accidentally tapped into a slightly different skill. The ground beneath me began to violently shake as I used the elemental manipulation skill to reach deep into the planet and pull the earth towards me. The result was me being bodily thrown into the air by a massive pillar of stone and sent flying.

I crashed into the ground, slowly rolled over, and lifted my head into the air. I glared at the pillar. I opened my mouth and activated my energy breath skill and released a blast of energy that easily disintegrated the pillar.

"Stupid magic." I grumbled, then tried again. This time, however, I was prepared and directed the earth to flip over the deadlands; fresh soil was exposed and the deadlands were buried deep beneath the ground, where they would serve as nutrients for new plants to grow.

I grunted in satisfaction and nodded my head. *That should do it. Now to get out of here. I've wasted enough time on this planet as it is.* I lowered my head to the portal and allowed it to suck me in.

∞∞∞∞∞∞∞∞

Welcome to the Bi-frost

Please select your next destination from the available branches.

∞∞∞∞∞∞∞∞∞∞

I ignored the choices and blurted out my destination.

∞∞∞∞∞∞∞∞∞∞

In order to reach Asgard from this location, you will have to make 4 transitions. Do you accept?

∞∞∞∞∞∞∞∞∞∞

"Yes."

∞∞∞∞∞∞∞∞∞∞

Understood.

∞∞∞∞∞∞∞∞∞∞

The kaleidoscopic lights flashed brightly for a moment, then the first transition began. A flash of red, a flash of blue, a gaping maw of darkness I didn't want to think about, and then I was ejected onto a world as different from Uathea as lava is to an ice field: The ground was covered in blades of grass so green, it looked like they'd been individually painted. The golden leaves of the trees swayed in a gentle breeze.

However, what truly distracted me was the sky: It was pitch black, save for a bright rainbow that split it in half and radiated light. The rainbow somehow projected enough light that I could see as if it were daytime on any other planet. After I finished gaping at my surroundings, the first thing I noticed was that very few people were waiting for me. The priests from Phoria were noticeably absent from the group.

Findral was the first to make her way over to me, so I asked her what happened.

"The head priest and Fenris had some kind of falling out; you'd have to ask him for the specifics. But it ended with Fenris giving them half their money back and kicking them out of the group."

"I see… Thanks, Fin. I'll ask him about it later."

"Of course, master," she cheerfully replied.

"By the way, where's Uriel?"

"I think he's over with the merchants. Would you like me to go get him?"

I twisted my head and glanced back at my body, then looked down at her. "That'd be helpful, yes."

She nodded her head, then walked away with an obvious sway to her hips. The sound of someone clearing their throat caused me to look away from her. Lena was standing next to me.

"See something you like, Torga?" she asked in a sickly-sweet tone.

"Not especially. I was just reminded that she was a three-foot tall goblin a few years ago, and now she looks like—"

"A succubus?"

"A dark elf," I replied with more intensity than I meant.

Lena quirked a brow at me but didn't disagree. "She's a good girl, Torga. And she reveres you. It would be understandable if you were to—"

"Finish that sentence, Lena. I dare you," I hissed.

Her mouth closed with an audible snap.

"I may have only adopted Ayla, but I think of Fin as my daughter too. I dare you to say otherwise."

Lena went stiff for a moment, then she relaxed and sighed. She shrugged her shoulders and gave me a half-hearted smile. "Sorry, Torga. I sometimes forget where your heart lies. My bad."

I grunted and decided to let it go. I knew Lena didn't mean anything by it. She was as protective of the girls as I was. Sometimes even more so.

"By the way, what happened to the priests?" I asked. If anyone would know what happened, it would be her. Fenris always told her everything.

"The head priest Samuel was—uh—upset about your involvement in our travels. I won't repeat what he said so don't ask, but he had some rather distasteful opinions about you and Findral."

"Shame," I sighed.

"I know. I never thought a priest would say such things—"

"Oh, no. I meant it was a shame Fenris kicked him out before I could eat his soul and devour his body."

Lena went silent for a long moment. "Torga, sometimes, you scare the hell out of me."

"I do believe Torga scares the hell out of everyone with half a brain, Lena."

I snorted and turned my attention to the newcomer. He was an older male dark elf. He wore what passed for nobleman's finery to the dark elves, which consisted of a regal set of maroon robes. His hung loosely off his wiry frame. Black silk trousers peeked out from beneath the hem of his robe with every step he took. His shoulder length silver hair was intricately braided through with bands of gold. And, like most druids that spent their lives in the forests of Uathea, his feet were bare.

"Hello, Uriel."

Uriel took a long drag from his pipe, then nodded his head. "Hello, Torga. I was wondering when we'd have a chance to talk."

"On that note, I'll leave you two to it. I have some merchants to wrangle..." She trailed off while looking at the crowd of people in the distance. I could tell from her body language that she didn't want to deal with them.

"Tell anyone that gives you trouble that I'll eat them if they don't behave."

"There's an idea," she snorted. She walked away after offering her thanks, leaving the two of us alone.

Uriel looked up at me with a blank expression on his face. He took another long drag from his odd smelling pipe. When he exhaled, smoke came out of his nose in a wave of white and the odd smell grew stronger. "You've gotten bigger."

"Not by much—"

"I've seen mountains smaller than you. Like, seriously, what the hell is up with your growth?"

"Good question—though, that is why I wanted the jewel."

"Ah, right." He moved his robe to the side and pulled a small pouch out for my inspection. He opened it and poured three stones into his palm. "While I'm positive the enchantment will work as its meant to, I'm less sure of how long it will last. That's why I'm going to fashion these three into one and use that. Hopefully, that will keep the enchantment from breaking down."

"Good idea. It would be very inconvenient if I suddenly returned to my normal size when I'm inside a city or something."

"The explosion would be bad too."

"Yeah, that would also be bad—wait, what explosion?"

"Oh, just the instantaneous release of your entire mass in the form of compressed magical energy."

"I see. And, do these explosions happen often?" I asked, a feeling of dread settling into my stomach.

"No, of course not. Only one out of ten stones will explode. Truthfully, I'm curious how big the explosion would be. The last time a stone detonated, it destroyed some castle back on Rhan. Really pissed off the royal family, it did. Of course, yours is ten times bigger than that stone." He patted my scales and smiled at me. "But worry not, I'm sure that won't happen to your stone."

Then why mention it? I sighed internally and began to wonder if I genuinely wanted the stone after all.

Chapter Four

"YOU DO KNOW THE GIRLS AREN'T GOING TO want to leave you alone after so long apart, right?" Lena casually said whilst preparing her bag for the journey.

"What they want is, unfortunately for them, not what I'm concerned about at the moment," I somberly replied. We were approximately twenty miles from the town of Sheehan, and this would be the last town for a thousand miles where we could resupply. The girls had their own equipment to see to, and I'd be damned if I would be the reason they were using subpar equipment.

Lena finished pulling her bag strap tight, then looked up at me. "Whatever, but they're not going to like this."

I gave her a dry chuckle and my approximation of a shrug. "They'll get over it. Besides, I'll have my hands full dealing with Uriel."

"Alright, I understand your point."

"I figured you would—"

"Yeah? Well, maybe you can explain it to me because I sure don't understand." Ayla came out of nowhere and spoke in an annoyed tone. "Why is it that every time we get together, you always send us away?"

I turned my attention to her. "You know that isn't what's happening, Ayla."

"Do I? Wouldn't be the first time you sent me away without caring about what I wanted."

I narrowed my eyes at her. "Is that so?" I looked back at the rest of our group. "And do the rest of you think the same?" I looked at each of them individually and, to my surprise, most of them nodded in the affirmative with only Fenris replying negatively.

"You do what you do because it's what you believe to be best." He shrugged. "While most here have faith that you could protect them from just about anything, I know otherwise."

"You're not helping, Dad," Hali muttered.

Fenris rolled his eyes and looked at his daughter. "Despite your opinion of the Fatass, Hali, the fact remains true that he isn't invincible. The fact is never truer than when he's around us... Isn't that right?" Fenris asked while meeting my eyes.

"Surprisingly, Mutt. In this instance, you are correct," I admitted.

Hali and Ayla spun their heads to stare at me. "Are... Are you saying we're a burden to you?" Ayla whispered.

"No, that's not what I'm saying."

"Sure, sounds like it. Fine, if you want us to leave, then we'll go with Lena."

"But Ayla—," Lena began.

"No," Ayla interrupted her. "Father has made his decision. Let's not argue with him about it."

"Ayla is right. Arguing with master is not the way to change his mind," Findral said quietly.

Hali looked between the two for a couple of seconds. "Fine," she sighed. Hali and Ayla then split off from the group to prepare themselves for the journey.

"That could've gone better," Fenris muttered.

"Yeah," I sighed. "What ever happened to the days when they would do as I said without throwing a fit about it?"

"Those ended the day they grew up and got engaged," Fenris snorted.

I shot Fenris a blank look and stared him down.

"What? I'm just saying you still see them as little girls, that's all."

"Are you trying to say you don't?" I asked.

Fenris smirked and turned his head in the direction the girls had left in. "Of course, I do. I probably always will see them as the little girls that used to beg me to race them around on my back," he admitted.

"When will the two of you get it through your heads that they aren't those little girls anymore?" Lena asked in an exasperated tone.

Fenris and I looked at each other, then back at her. "Never. Not in this lifetime," was our simultaneous response.

Lena groaned and cupped her head between her hands. "I truly pity those poor girls. With you two guard dogs around, they'll never get married," she muttered, though said "guard dogs" heard her all the same.

"Hey, I resemble that remark," I chuckled.

"Eh, you've called me worse," Fenris mumbled, then he and Lena walked off to finish their preparations, leaving me alone with my thoughts.

I am sorry for my words, girls... But... I don't know what I would do if something happened to either of you. I internally sighed. I laid my head down and closed my eyes while I waited for Uriel to arrive so we could get started. Unbidden memories of the past rapidly appeared and disappeared until I eventually dozed off.

~ ~ ~

The sound of sobbing echoed throughout a darkened inn. I followed the sound to a door across the hall from where I'd been sleeping. Lifting my hand, I tentatively knocked. "Ayla?"

The sobbing quieted down, though I could still hear the occasional sniffle through the door.

"Ayla, are you okay?" I asked quietly.

"Go away..." Her voice sounded raw, like she'd screamed it hoarse. "I'm fine; sorry for waking you."

I pressed the button on the handle and pushed the door open. Ayla was lying on her side with her arms wrapped around her body and her knees pulled close. Her damp eyes reflected the light from the candle sitting on her end table as she stared at me. I found myself staring back. How could someone make something this pure, this innocent cry? What kind of monster did it take to cause this much grief in a little girl?

Not for the first time since coming to this world, I felt completely and utterly powerless.

I walked over and sat down beside her on the bed. "It's okay to cry, Ayla," I said quietly. "Everyone does."

"You don't." She sucked in a breath, causing her snot filled nose to rattle.

"Of course, I do," I told her quietly. "And for the same reasons you do."

She was quiet for a while, but I didn't mind. I just sat with her in the darkness. At some point, my hand had begun rubbing her back, much in the same way I'd done for my own daughters all those years ago.

"I miss her..." she cried. I didn't need to hear the name to know who she was referring to.

~ ~ ~

My eyes snapped open and I looked around to see if anyone was nearby. Once I was satisfied, I laid my head back down. *Your safety will always come first, Ayla... So long as you and Sarah live, I'll do anything to protect you... even from the monster inside of me.* I looked around at the dead plants surrounding me, and the darkness that was spreading out from me as I unconsciously sucked in ambient magic. *And if that means I have to keep sending you away until I learn to control this? Then that's a sacrifice I'll gladly make time and time again.*

CHAPTER FIVE

A FOUL ODOR FILLED MY NOSE AND I CAME TO with a violent cough. I glared down at Uriel, who was even now puffing on his pipe. "How can you smoke that crap? It smells like an ogre's ass."

Uriel ignored the question in favor of smiling around his pipe. He pulled a large red stone; about the size of a grapefruit, out from beneath his robe and held it out for me to inspect.

"Have you decided where you want it?"

"I have."

"Then get comfortable, Master Torga. This is going to take a while."

"Of course, it is," I sighed. I laid my head back down and closed my eyes, while Uriel got to work digging a large magic formation into the ground.

An hour or so later, I watched as Uriel finished carving a symbol into the ground around my head. Though there were no words involved in his making of the symbol, Uriel would often stop to mumble something to himself before continuing. After a while, I could no longer contain my curiosity. "What's the symbol mean?" I asked while looking at the various lines and curves. There were nine in total, with each line ending in a circle around my head.

"It represents the original nine worlds" was Uriel's distracted reply.

"What do you mean?"

"Well, if you believe the humans, the gods created the worlds for the various races to inhabit." Uriel walked over to a circle on the top right of the symbol. "Niflheim, the world of ice and birthplace of dragons." He drew an upside-down triangle in this circle. He moved to the opposite side and pointed at the circle opposite of Niflheim. "Muspelheim, the world of fire and birthplace of the giants." He drew a square here, then moved to the next circle down. "Alfheim, the birthplace of the elves." He drew a small swirl inside the circle. Again, he moved to its exact opposite. "Svartalfheim, birthplace of the dwarves." Here, he drew a diamond. He moved down to the next circle and drew a leaf inside it. "Jotunheim, birthplace of the Titans." He moved to the next circle and drew two straight vertical lines. "Midgard, the birthplace of the humans." Then he walked to the three circles in front of Torga's head and drew from left to right: two horizontal swivels that looked like a river, a sideways eight, and three interconnected circles inside the remaining one. "Helheim, the final resting place of the dead," he said, motioning to the one on the left. "Vanaheim, the first world of magic." He motioned to the one on the right. And finally, he pressed his cane into the ground in front of the last circle and looked into Torga's eyes. "Asgard, The home of the gods."

"And, just how accurate is this?" I asked.

Uriel shrugged and started moving again. "No idea. These legends are so old, I don't think anyone actually knows the truth."

My eyes glazed over for several seconds as I thought about my few interactions with a "god" and I began to believe in the story, if only slightly. "You said this is what the humans believe, right?"

Uriel just nodded as he walked over to his bag and started rifling through it for something.

"What do the elves believe?"

At my words, Uriel paused and looked up. "We don't believe the gods created the worlds at all." He reached into his bag and pulled out a five-centimeter-long, by two-centimeter-wide metal stake and walked over to Torga.

"We believe that the lady—the being you know as Yggdrasil—is the first and it birthed the gods to be its caretakers. They, in turn, created the gods we know today for much the same reason."

I wanted to ask more questions, but Uriel silenced me with a shake of his head. "The time for talking is over. We must begin or we won't finish before sunrise," he said while indicating the moon above.

"Very well, proceed."

"I will and I apologize in advance, Torga."

"For what—AGHH!!"

Uriel had waited for the moment I opened my mouth to stab the stake as far as he could into the bottom of my jaw. The stake pierced in between two scales and then extended to dig itself even deeper into my hide. With every second that passed, the stake wormed its way deeper until it reached my jawbone. Only then did it stop and begin to return to its normal size. Uriel yanked the stake out and began to clean it off while he inspected his work. "You know, Torga, I'm impressed you managed to stay conscious through that."

Though I was still in a lot of pain from having the jewel inserted, I managed a glare at him. "Don't underestimate the willpower of a guy who willingly jumped into lava, Uriel."

He nodded his head in agreement. "Fair point. Even so, I'm surprised you didn't ask for the anesthetic." Uriel walked back over to his bag and began to put everything back into its place, then he turned back to me.

"There was an anesthetic?" I hissed.

"Yep." He pulled a pen-sized cylinder out of his bag and walked over to me. "You should get some sleep. The jewel has to sync itself with your magic before it'll be of any use to you."

Before I could react, Uriel slammed the cylinder into the spot where the jewel was located, and I immediately felt like someone had dunked my head into a bucket of ice water. However, by the time Uriel pulled the cylinder out of the wound my eyelids felt like they were fifty times heavier than they were a minute ago. Before I knew it, my eyes were closed, and I was fast asleep.

~ ~ ~

"Hey, Fatass, wake up," Fenris shouted into my ear.

I peeked through cracked eyelids at the sound and glared at Fenris. "Must you always be so loud, Mutt?" I grumbled as I lifted my head off the ground and looked around. I counted off each of his friends as they entered the clearing, but... Someone was missing. Actually, a lot of people were missing as the trader's caravan was also gone, but I couldn't see Ayla, Findral, or Hali anywhere.

"Hey, Mutt, where's—"

"Damn Fatass, I knew you must've been hungry, but did you have to eat so much of the forest!?" Fenris yelled while staring with his mouth agape at the several miles of forest that'd been turned into a wasteland. The trees were gone, large swaths of grass were missing, and even the nearby stream had disappeared.

"You should've returned sooner, then!" I barked. However, my anger at Fenris' question soon evaporated as I once again tried to find the trio.

"Hey, Lena? Where's A—" Again I was interrupted, this time by Talia and Solon running up to Fenris.

"Hi, Torga!" little Talia squeaked. Her long black hair bounced as she ran into my side and proceeded to hug me where she could. "Did Uriel finish helping you?" she asked.

Unlike Hali and her mother, Talia was told around her eighth birthday that she just didn't have the magical power to become a full druid. Because of this, instead of being trained by her mother, she was trained by Fenris in the ways of martial combat. And by the gods was she ever good at it. She was blessed with the thin body of an elf, the strength and speed of a beast-man, and the instincts of a Warg. Once Talia matured a little bit, she would be a force to be reckoned with.

"Yes, he did." I couldn't help but chuckle at her exuberance.

"Sorry, Torga. She slipped away from me," Solon said by way of apology. He took Talia by the hand and led her off.

Deciding to look around for any other interruptions, I raised my head and glanced around at everyone. Lena, Solon, Talia, Uriel, Fenris, and Lena's chosen elf bodyguards were all I could see.

"Lena, where are the girls?"

Lena, who'd been in a rather animated chat with her daughter, froze at the sound of my voice. "Who?" She asked without turning to look at me.

I narrowed my eyes into thin slits as a low hiss began at the back of my throat. "Let me rephrase the question. Where. are. Ayla, Findral, and Hali?"

Lena slowly turned around and nervously chuckled at my question. "I'm sure they're around here somewhere," she finished lamely.

After staring at her for several seconds and getting nowhere, I decided to change targets.

"Fenris?"

Despite the rather obvious glare his wife was giving him, Fenris answered Torga immediately.

"They went on ahead to Asgard."

"Alone?"

Fenris snorted. "Don't give me that look. I didn't know they were leaving either."

"Ah. Well, then. Thank you for telling me."

"Yeah, Yeah. No need to get all 'nice' on me. I just didn't want to hear you whining that 'your little girl could be in danger,' for the next three days." Fenris smirked up at me.

"Your little girl's out there too, you know?" I sneered.

That wiped the smirk off his face.

"Don't remind me," Fenris growled.

I turned my attention back to Lena, who was staring holes through the side of Fenris' head. "Why didn't you tell me about this?" I asked her.

"Because..." Lena paused as she collected her thoughts. "Because no matter what you think, or how you feel about the matter, Ayla is an adult now, Torga. If you're there to solve all of her problems or make all of her decisions for her, then she'll never grow up."

"I see..."

Lena breathed out a sigh of relief. "So, you'll let her do this on her own?" she asked with a smile... that very quickly turned to fear as her eyes met mine. Lena had been looking at everything but my eyes while she explained herself, so she never noticed the atmosphere around her change.

"I see,.." I repeated. "You believed yourself to be right, so instead of simply telling me the truth and trusting that I was mature enough to let MY daughter make her own mistakes, you chose to hide it from me. What else have you hidden from me; I wonder?" I whispered just loud enough for her to hear.

"N... Nothing."

"The funny thing is... I don't believe you. I've known for years that you've kept things from me, and I accepted that because I was sure that it was your business and your business alone. However, do not believe that just because we are friends, I won't destroy you if it means protecting those girls. Am I being clear enough for you?" I hissed.

Lena shakily nodded her head. "C—Crystal."

Fenris placed himself between Lena and me. "I'll forgive you because of the circumstances," he snarled. "But don't you EVER threaten my wife again!"

"You're also my friend, Fenris. So, I'll extend this courtesy to you. If you—if either of you—do something that leads to any of those girls getting hurt, I'm holding the two of you personally responsible." I stared down at them. "Now, help me find our daughters before I lose my temper and do something I'll regret."

INTERLUDE: AYLA'S CHOICE & FINDRAL'S DUTY

OURS AFTER PULLING THEIR DISAPPEARING ACT, Ayla, Findral, and Hali landed in a small clearing outside the village of Millhall, approximately seven hundred miles east of the rest of their group. The reason they were able to cross such a vast distance in such a short amount of time was solely due to Findral's ability to fly while carrying them. This was no easy feat, however, and Findral was currently lying on the ground, panting from exhaustion and unable to move.

Ayla and Hali knelt beside her and used their magic to ease her muscle aches and replenish some of her magic.

"Thanks again for going this far for me, Fin. I know you would've rather stayed with the old man," Ayla said quietly. "You can go back to him as soon as you're able—ouch!" Ayla grabbed her head and glared down at Findral. "Why'd you hit me?"

"Because you're being a prat. I already disobeyed master's orders by taking you away. Leaving you now would be a betrayal of my promise to him, and that's a line I refuse to cross."

"Fin's right," Hali said, interrupting Ayla before she had a chance to speak. "Do you have any idea how pissed

Torga's gonna be when he finds out we ditched mom and dad?"

"He'll get over it," Ayla replied flippantly. "He left me alone for eighteen months, What's a few more weeks? Besides, we're heading to the same place anyway. With Fin on our side, we'll easily beat them to Asgard City and force the old man to accept that we aren't the burdens he seems to think we are."

Hali and Findral gave Ayla a skeptical look.

"Trust me, nothing's gonna happen."

They gave Findral half an hour to rest before they set out towards Millhall. It was what passed for nighttime on Asgard, and the ever-present rainbow in the sky had dimmed considerably. After entering through the main gates, they made their way over to a portly man in a guard uniform and asked for directions to the inn so they could finally get some rest. None of them had had a wink of sleep in almost twenty-four hours and Findral was looking like a stiff breeze would knock her over.

"I wouldn't if I were you, little missy," the man replied immediately.

"Why not? It has beds available, right?"

"O' course, it does. But there's been odd stirrings in the forest lately and talk o' the Jötnar returning has everyone on edge. My advice would be for tha three of ya to either head towards the capital immediately, or hustle back tha way you came. 'Tis not safe 'ere."

"I'm sure we can handle ourselves, but thank you for the warning, all the same. Now, about that inn?"

The guard rolled his eyes but gave her what she wanted and sent them on their way. "'Tis your funeral," he muttered before they were out of earshot.

The three walked until they reached the inn. When Ayla pushed open the old wooden door, she was quite surprised to find the inside packed with people of all races. They appeared to be having a party of some kind, as they were chanting and singing loudly to each other.

She forced her way through the crowd to the desk on the opposite side of the room, where she found a small man standing behind the desk.

"How may I help you?" he asked without looking up from the glass he was wiping with an old cloth.

"I'd like three rooms, or a single room with three beds," she said.

After hearing her words, the man's head bobbed up and down. He pulled out three brass keys from beneath his desk and sat them on the counter in front of him. "That'll be forty silver pieces."

Though she thought the price was steep, she reluctantly pulled out the correct amount of coins and passed them to him. He counted the coins in front of her, then slid the keys over to her side of the counter and led them upstairs to a set of rooms. "Breakfast will be ready when the crimson light brightens," he informed them before turning and returning to whatever party was going on downstairs.

"Goodnight," Findral muttered as she pulled a key from Ayla's hand. She entered her room without another word and locked the door behind her.

"Goodnight, Ayla." Hali also took her key from Ayla and entered her room a few moments later.

Ayla sighed tiredly, then went to bed.

~ ~ ~

A cacophony of screams woke Findral from a wonderful dream involving her and her master. She rolled out of bed naked as the day she was born and approached the window.

Mutilated corpses of the villagers lay strewn about the streets, while other corpses—presumably, those of their neighbors and fellow villagers—consumed the flesh of the living.

Now, on Yggdrasil, it wasn't uncommon to hear stories of undead: corpses brought back to life by some manner of foul magics. Findral had even run into a couple during their various adventures over the years... But never this bad. Sure, a zombie or two here and there wasn't too awful. One on one, a normal villager could take down a zombie, provided they had a weapon and were smart enough to keep the zombie's teeth away. But something told her these weren't normal zombies. For one, they were fast—easily faster than a normal human, and maybe even faster than a horse. And the second thing that led her to believe they weren't normal zombies: They seemed to ooze cold from their very pores. The corpses they were feasting on had turned blue from the chill in the air, and the blood that ran through the streets appeared to be frozen over.

She let out a long, slow hiss of anger at the needless deaths before her, then grabbed her robe from the back of the chair where she'd left it the night before and threw it on, foregoing the usual outfit she wore beneath it. If she needed it, she could always come back for it later.

She exited her room and knocked heavily on the doors to Hali and Ayla's rooms. They each answered after five knocks, and she explained what she'd seen.

"Damn it." Ayla hissed. "Go see if you can save anyone, Fin. Hali and I will join you as soon as we're able—"

"Not a chance in hell." Findral interrupted. "My duty is to protect you two, not the townsfolk. As regrettable as it may be, whether they live or die isn't my concern."

"Fin—"

"No, Ayla," Hali said in a guilty tone. "Fin can't leave us, or she'll be breaking her promise to Torga."

"To hell with that promise!" Ayla hollered. "Get your ass out there and save those people!"

"No," Fin replied immediately. "You want them saved, you better get your elven ass ready and get a move on. I'll be right behind you."

Ayla cursed Findral's name but did move to get dressed and ready for combat. Minutes later, she and Hali left their room and the three of them made their way downstairs.

The first thing they saw upon entering the dining room took Findral's breath away.

The skinny man from the night before was knelt on top of a table with his back to them. In front of him lay a little girl. Her light blue dress was stained with blood, and her brown ringlets created a halo above her head.

The sound of flesh being ripped apart filled the room. The skinny man's head whipped around at the sound of Ayla's gasp. He had a dismembered arm hanging limply from his lips, which he released as soon as his eyes met theirs. His were the color of freshly fallen snow and, now that he was looking at them, Findral could see that his skin had taken on a bluish hue.

He opened his mouth, revealing blood-stained teeth, and hissed at them.

"Fuck off," Findral hissed. A wave of fire exploded out from her outstretched hand, instantly reducing both the man and the child to ashes, along with approximately thirty percent of the dining room.

She swiveled her head to see several undead stumbling through a doorway on the far side of the room, and she tossed a blue fireball in their direction. The ball reduced everything it touched to ashes, even destroying the wall behind the undead. The building began to let out an ominous creaking noise as the fireball tore through another two walls before finally dissipating.

"We need to get out of here." Ayla said quietly.

"What about our bags?"

"Forget them. If you don't have it with you, you're not going back to get it."

Hali grumbled about having to leave her bags behind but didn't protest. She saw the necessity behind Ayla's words, just as Findral did.

As soon as the three girls left the ruined inn, they were swarmed by a mob of undead. An explosion of stone spikes tearing free from the ground slashed an undead to shreds, while a sword of blue fire bisected one at the waist, and a hail of stone daggers ripped through the head of another.

"Remember, don't let them touch you," Ayla told the two of them.

"Yeah? Let them try," Findral replied. She threw off her robe, exposing her voluptuous body to the world. Then she began to laugh as her skin turned to ash when a veil of blue flames engulfed her from head to toe.

"I think you've been hanging around the old man for too long, Fin. You're enjoying this way too much."

"I'll take that as a compliment," Findral replied in a shaky voice.

A plume of blue fire flew from Findral's open mouth, disintegrating the legs of an approaching undead and alighting the ground in front of her. She whipped her head to the side, dragging the plume along with it, and vaporized another group charging them from the shadows of a nearby building.

She turned back to find Ayla and Hali staring at her. "What is it?"

'Since when could you do that?" Hali asked incredulously.

"Dunno." Findral shrugged. "It just came to me."

"Less talking, more killing!" Ayla yelled. She pointed her granny's staff at an approaching undead and forced a mass of vines to erupt from the ground around it. The undead was hoisted into the air as the vine pierced its body until it resembled a pincushion.

Findral and Hali burst into motion without another word and began slaughtering the undead without mercy.

A while later, as Hali and Ayla were resting atop the blacksmith's shop, Findral landed in front of them with an odd expression on her face. "You want the good news or the bad news first?" She asked.

"Bad news first, Ayla replied with a sigh.

"The bad news is the town appears to be completely wiped out."

Hali sighed and rubbed the bridge of her nose. "Shit..."

"What's the good news?"

"Well, it appears someone may have gotten out and alerted the capital, somehow. A group of long ships is headed straight for us."

"What?"

"You're joking."

Findral shook her head. "Nope, you should be able to see them in a few minutes."

Sure enough, approximately ten minutes later a group of ten ships appeared on the horizon. They were made of a dark wood that blended in well with the night sky, though the white sails they used to catch wind and move through the air allowed them to be seen. However, above all else, one thing stood out above all others: The flag the lead ship was flying was that of a horned helmet on a dark green background.

"Well, look who it is. Ayla, it's your lover-boy," Hali smirked.

Ayla stared blankly at the approaching ships and sighed. She hung her head and shook it back and forth.

~ ~ ~

They met the ships outside of town and Ayla stepped forward to greet the sailors as they disembarked. The first man to greet her was a tall man with shaggy red hair and emerald eyes. "Ayla? What're you doing here?" he asked while moving towards them.

"We were heading towards Asgard City and had to stop off for supplies when this crap went down. What about you, Thor?"

"We received reports of Jötnar in the area two months ago. My men and I have been patrolling our eastern borders ever since. Though, I wish we'd returned to resupply sooner; we may have been able to save these people," the man said somberly. "Have you left any for my men?"

"We killed what we could, but you know how undead are."

"Right." He chuckled darkly. "Alright, you heard the lady. Spread out and kill anything that moves. And stab anything that looks like it should be moving."

"Aye!" his men cheered as they flowed around him and entered the village. Ayla watched them go until most of them were out of earshot, then she sighed. "We need to talk," she said.

"Uh oh. Am I in trouble?" he joked.

Ayla allowed a smirk to show on her face. "I think so."

"Okay, I'll bite. Why am I in trouble?"

"Because my father wants to meet you."

"Oh..." He gulped. "He doesn't know about the—"

"Marriage? Yes, yes he does."

"How about the—"

"No, he doesn't know about that yet."

"And the uh... other thing?"

Ayla looked at him in confusion.

"What other thing—" The moment she began talking, Thor seized the opportunity to quickly advance on her and pull her into a kiss. Though she tried to push him away at first, she eventually relaxed and kissed him back. That is, until a loud growl caused the two to quickly separate. Ayla looked over her shoulder at the source of the sound and saw a thirty-foot-tall wolf stalking out of the forest towards them. Fenris was panting heavily and a sickly-looking Solon was riding atop his back. "If you'd like to keep that tongue, I'd suggest you keep it to yourself for the foreseeable future," Fenris growled.

Thor slowly nodded and raised his hands into the air. "Sheesh, calm down big guy—" He was interrupted when Ayla threw a hard right hook into his jaw. The impact knocked him to the ground and caused him to roll around in pain. "Okay," he groaned and rubbed his aching jaw. "I deserved that." He climbed to his feet, then turned back to Ayla and opened his mouth to speak but had to stop to dodge another punch headed for his jaw. "Whoa!" he yelled as he leaned away from the second punch. "Okay, stop!" He raised his arms up to block the punches she was raining down on his arms. Eventually, she tired herself out and he was able to speak. "You done?" he asked from inside his guard.

Ayla slowly nodded her head as she tried to catch her breath.

"Whew," he sighed. "You've got a lot of anger in you for a little wom-UGN!" As he was talking, Ayla swung her right foot and caught him between the legs with all the force she could muster at the moment. The prince dropped to his knees and hung his head as his eyes went cross-eyed. "That..." he wheezed out, "was totally uncalled for."

Ayla bent down to look at his face. "Did you enjoy that kiss?" she asked.

The prince nodded his head, as he was currently in too much pain to speak. "Good, so did I. But I told you before that I hated it when you spring kisses on me like that."

"All done?" Findral asked in an amused tone.

"For the moment."

"Well then we should be getting back to master soon."

"'Tis a bit late for that, don't ya think?" Fenris said as he sat down next to them.

"Hi, Solon. Hi, Dad..." Hali waved nervously.

"Hello, Hali," Solon replied as he slowly climbed off of his father's back.

"Don't 'Hi' me, Hali. Do you have any idea how much trouble you're in? And that goes for you two, as well. What the hell were you thinking?"

"What was I thinking? I was thinking, since Dad didn't want me around, I wouldn't be," she said defiantly.

"Wait, you ran away?" Thor asked from behind her.

"Uh… Kinda? We were coming to see you anyway, so, with Findral's help, I got a head start on them."

"Without telling anyone."

"That's not true. I told Lena."

Fenris frowned at her, then sighed. "For the love of the gods, don't tell the old grumpy ass that."

"Grumpy?" Ayla asked.

"Oh yeah. He was furious when he found out you left."

"I didn't get either of you in trouble, did I? Cause if I did, I'm sorry. I'll talk to him when we get back. I'm sure he'll forgive you."

Fenris just shrugged her off. "Don't worry about it. This isn't the first time Torga and I have gotten into an argument over the years and it most certainly won't be the last. It's basically a game between me and the Fatass, at this point." Fenris looked over their shoulder at the village. "I vote we get this taken care of quickly so I can get you girls back. It's not a good idea to keep him waiting any longer than absolutely necessary right now."

Ayla looked over her shoulder at Thor and half-smiled. "Ready to meet your father-in-law?"

Thor looked between Ayla and the village several times before finally letting out a sigh. "From what I've heard about him, I think I'd rather face down an army of ghouls."

"Good instincts," Findral laughed.

After spending the rest of the day clearing out the remaining undead, Ayla and the others decided to make camp for the night inside the village and begin making their way to Torga at sunrise.

Ayla was standing on the roof of the inn, overlooking the town, when suddenly a hand was placed on her shoulder. She whipped her head around and found Hali standing behind her with a grin plastered on her face. "Trouble in paradise?" Hali asked.

Ayla snorted and motioned for Hali to join her, "If this is paradise, I'd hate to see what hell is like."

"That bad, huh?"

Ayla thought it over for a moment, then shrugged.

"Okay, maybe I'm exaggerating a bit. But it's still pretty bad."

Hali's response was to smirk at her, which prompted Ayla to smirk back.

The two sat in silence for several minutes while they stared out at the empty village.

"I envy you, you know?" Hali suddenly said.

"What?" Ayla laughed, as she believed Hali was poking fun at her again. But when Hali turned to her, the expression on her face told Ayla that this was no joke.

"I'm serious. I honestly do envy you, Ayla."

The smile on Ayla's face fell and was replaced with confusion and concern. "Why envy me? I'm nothing special."

Hali rolled her eyes. "Believe me when I say that I'm very aware of just how 'normal' you are."

"What's that supposed to mean?"

Hali shrugged. "You're not beautiful, not smart, definitely not a powerful druid—"

"Okay, you've made your point," Ayla interrupted.

"You sure?" Hali asked. "I mean, I have a list and everything."

"I'm sure."

"Suit yourself."

The two sat in silence for a while longer, before Ayla asked, "If I'm so 'normal', then why envy me?"

"Because you have something I want," Hali replied while stepping over to the edge of the building and looking down on the Asgardians guarding the front of the building.

"And that is?"

"Torga."

"My dad?"

"Wow... Maybe there is a brain beneath all that hair, after all." Hali smirked over her shoulder at her, then turned away from Ayla.

"Wait!" Ayla jumped to her feet. "You were serious about that!?"

Hali looked back over her shoulder and winked. "Serious as a dragon attack."

Ayla stared after Hali in shock until she collapsed to the ground.

I always thought she said that to annoy me. To think she was actually serious... Ayla suddenly shivered as she recalled the conditions bet they'd made a few weeks ago during one of their usual sparring matches.

"I win, you have to call me Mama Hali," Hali had said, and at the time, Ayla thought she was only joking. But now? Now she was really glad she'd managed to win a match against her for a change.

"Say, how about we go double or nothing on that bet?" Hali asked without looking at her.

Before Ayla could respond, Fenris alerted the group that they were surrounded.

"Okay, we need to come up with a plan," Thor told them after they'd gathered in front of the inn. He unsheathed the sword at his waist and prepared himself for combat. "How many can you smell?"

"Not sure; it's hard to tell from this distance." Fenris quietly said. "But it's at least thirty men."

"Any idea what we're dealing with?"

"That's easy; I smell humans."

"Got anything more specific?"

"If I had to guess, priests from Phoria," Fenris growled.

Ayla glanced around and thought about the present situation. The twins were standing in front of Fenris while Findral stood off to the side. Across from them, Thor and his men stood with weapons drawn as they readied themselves for battle.

"Not including the priests themselves, there were also twenty crusaders and a few magic users hiding amongst them," Fenris said.

"What does that mean for us, exactly?" Thor asked.

"Simple. It means we can easily kill them while suffering only a few casualties. Though, I should warn you that the magic users are conjurors."

"You don't think they can summon anything powerful enough to break our defenses, do you?" Thor's right-hand man Jorolf asked. Jorolf was a powerfully built man who wore more plate mail than you would usually find on an entire platoon of men.

"Most likely not. That would require them to send out their battle mages and that would be an act of war. Surely, they wouldn't do that—" Before Thor could finish speaking the ground began to shake, and a loud roar echoed through the trees. Everyone in camp turned to glare at him. "Okay, maybe I was wrong," he admitted.

"Why would Phoria go to war with Asgard?" Ayla asked.

Well, they have been at odds with us for several months now," Thor explained.

"Why? What did you do?"

Thor looked honestly hurt by her accusation. "I did nothing. It was my muscle brained brother who killed their crown prince in a mock tournament last year. They've been rather cross with us ever since."

Fenris snorted, "I can't imagine why."

Heavy footfalls were among the first sounds they heard coming their way. The second was the twang of multiple bows being fired from the treetops.

"Incoming!" Fenris hollered.

The soldiers raised their shields to block what they could, while Ayla and Hali caused the ground to raise up to meet the arrows in the air. After a few seconds of this, they waved their hands and sent the raised ground rocketing in the direction the arrows had come from. They heard a few shouts of pain and a couple of thuds from something falling to the ground below, but they knew the ground had missed the bulk of the shooters, as the arrows kept coming.

"Fenris and Asgardians, you're up front," Thor barked, causing them to quickly move to obey his orders. "Ayla and Hali, the two of you are in charge of keeping those archers off of us."

"Right!" they said in unison while directing their energy to form an earthen shield above the group.

"Findral, you and I will guard the rear. We can't let them flank us, understand?" Silence was his answer. "Findral?"

"Fin?" They all turned to find Findral missing. The only evidence of her ever having been there was a burnt patch of grass.

"Did she really run away?" Thor angrily asked.

"Findral wouldn't do that!"

"She just did!"

"As much as I hate to admit it, Findral is the last person on this planet that would leave Ayla's side," Hali said.

"Oh yeah? And why is that!?"

"Simple," Fenris interrupted. "Because she would never betray Torga's trust—damnit, incoming!" he growled as four groups of humans came charging towards them. Each group had five people and they all had a glowing yellow shield around them.

"They've been shielded!"

"Damnit!" Ayla yelled as her portion of the earth shield slammed into the ground ahead of them.

"What're you doing, Ayla?" Hali yelled.

"It's not me!" she fought to raise the shield back into the air, but no matter how hard she tried, it wouldn't budge.

"No, it was I." A hooded man stepped out of the darkness of an alleyway.

"I knew you were trouble, ya damned priest!" Fenris growled after seeing Samuel walk out of the alley.

"Oh, come now beast. You didn't actually think you could get away with it, did you?"

"Do you know this guy?" Thor whispered to Ayla.

"He traveled with us for a while. Fenris kicked him out of the group because he was being an asshole."

"What is it you think I've done!?" Fenris asked.

"You've corrupted these beings of light with your foul nature, Warg!" Samuel yelled in a crazed tone.

"What in the nine hells are you talking about?"

"The elves you dull creature!" As Samuel spoke, the wind began to pick up. "Not only did you corrupt the women with your foul presence, but even the children have been corrupted. Look, that one has been so corrupted he's begun to take on your appearance!" Samuel yelled while pointing at Solon.

"That's my son, you daft cunt!"

Samuel was taken aback by the admission, and his previously pitying eyes turned to scorn as he looked at Ayla and Hali. "Have you all been taken to bed by this foul creature?" Samuel whispered. "Have you all become whores of the demon spawn?" Following his words, the wind began to spiral around as multiple loud thuds racked the area. "See, even the gods are so offended by your corruption that they've offered their power!" Samuel's face twisted into one of extreme anger as he glared at Fenris.

"Smite the heretic with your awesome power, Oh mighty God!"

"Gladly..."

As quickly as it appeared, the wind ground to a halt and a deafening silence racked the camp.

"What?" Samuel asked aloud as he turned around to face the voice he'd heard... What he found was a pair of blood red eyes staring deep into his soul.

"You not only called my friend 'demon spawn,' but you called Ayla, Findral, and Hali whores... But, do you want to know what ultimately decided your fate?"

Samuel felt something he'd never felt before travel down his spine... a feeling of complete and total powerlessness as he stared into pools of blood.

"You did all of that, while I was starving." Suddenly, the blood was immediately replaced with a set of fangs and rows of razor-sharp teeth. "Thank you for the meal."

CHAPTER SIX

"WHERE ARE YOU, MASTER?"
I looked up at the sound of Findral's voice, a novel experience since it'd been a while since I had to look up to see anything. I found no sign of her, but I knew I'd heard her.

Once Fenris caught the girls' scent in the village and began following it east, I took to the skies and followed him from a distance. I knew he and Lena wanted me to stay behind and wait for the girls to return on their own, but I was past caring what either of them wanted. A minute or so later, she landed only a few feet from me in a streak of fire that left a trail of burnt ozone in its wake. "Hello, Findral. Good of you to join me. Though I am curious how you found me."

Findral wobbled in place for a moment, then collapsed to her knees. She struggled to look up at me, but once she did, a blinding smile appeared on her face.

"Master? Is that really you?" she asked.

"In the scales. Were you expecting another giant snake?"

Findral's dark skin flushed with embarrassment. She quickly cleared her throat to hide it and shook her head. "No, master. I just didn't expect you to be so..."

"Small?" I asked.

"Close, though that works too."

"What can I say. I didn't like the idea of Fenris bringing you back on his own. Besides, I've finally been returned to a slightly more manageable size, so I wanted to get out and stretch my wings a bit." I looked over my body and once again marveled at the stone's ability. I was still massive by any creature's standards—over sixty feet long from head to tail, not counting my horns. But considering I was now but a fraction of my original size, it was a significant improvement.

"Noticed any side effects?"

"Not to my knowledge."

"That's... good. I'm happy for you, master." She smiled. "Wait, no, we don't have time for this." She struggled to her feet. "Ayla needs your help. They're in danger."

My eyes narrowed and a low hiss came from the back of my throat. "Tell me everything."

Findral quickly gave me a brief overview of what happened since they snuck off and what she knew of the current situation. I responded by ordering her to lead me to this "threat" and then to rejoin the others.

"But, master, what if you need help? When I left there were at least thirty enemy combatants."

I let out an involuntary hiss and bared my teeth. "*Good.* It's been far too long since I've tasted combat and I've been itching for a decent meal ever since we got to this world."

Findral thought over my words for only a moment, then nodded her head. "I will only come to your aid should you need it."

"Lead the way."

Findral quickly blasted herself into the air and took off in the direction she'd come from. She flew far faster than I'd ever seen her move: streaking through the air like a shooting star. After waiting a few seconds for my body to catch up, I wound it into a spiral and used my tail as a spring to launch myself into the air in pursuit of her.

A few minutes later we arrived at the outskirts of a small village. Findral used her mastery of fire to cloak herself from sight and land on the barrier wall. I flapped my wings in a slow but steady rhythm as I passed over the wall and began to circle at a height of about six hundred feet. From that height, I had a great view of the village and its surroundings. I spotted a group of people in a battle formation just outside of a large wooden building.

I thought about landing and joining them, but a strange sight caught my attention. I watched as a man cloaked in a robe I recognized led a small army through the narrow alleyways of the village. Originally, I was going to wait and see how this played out, then drop out of the sky and scare the hell out of him, maybe with some kind of catchy one-liner to throw him off his game.

But any thoughts of playing with him vanished as soon as he ordered his army to attack without so much as a word to them.

I looked down at the ground surrounding the little square my companions were in and saw the other priests and their entourages: a few crusaders, a magic user, and the priest who would act as support for the band. However, their numbers were inflated due to their use of what I knew to be golems. Each golem looked like a human made entirely of granite. They were between twenty and thirty feet tall and supposedly weighed as much as five tons.

That fact didn't stop one of them from turning into rubble after I slammed into it at full speed.

The flashy way I destroyed the golem was a surefire way to alert the others that something was up, which is why I quickly opened my second set of eyelids and activated my petrification skill. To my surprise, the skill activated even before they could turn to face me, and most of the humans were turned to stone within a few heartbeats. I whipped my tail at the two that somehow managed to resist my initial attack, batting them to the side and sending them hurtling through a couple of their company men.

The petrified crusaders shattered like a dropped vase.

I vaguely heard the priest's ranting, but I didn't have time to focus on it as the golem closest to me swung its massive fist in a downward arc towards my head.

I refused to move.

The fist slammed into my head with the force of a cannonball, resulting in a loud boom that echoed off the walls of the nearby buildings. I grimaced: not because of the punch, but because of how loud the sound was. I bit down on the 'golem's fist and twisted my head around, breaking off its arm and pulling the golem close. I ducked my head and coiled my body around it. A few seconds later, the magical construct's waist crumbled to dust under the force of my grip.

At risk of alerting the entire town to my presence, I acted to at least attempt to mask what I was doing by closing my eyes and focusing on the air around me. I pushed my magic outwards, allowing it to saturate the air, then I pushed it into a slow spin around the village that should help keep the sound down.

However, that would do nothing to those close enough to see what was happening—as was the case with the two companies of crusaders and golems that came charging around the corner.

My eyes locked onto the rapidly approaching crusaders, whilst my heat sense went to work trying to detect the magic users. It was a bit like trying to watch two objects while being cross eyed, but I made it work.

I activated my petrification ability just as my heat sense came back with something. As soon as the first crusader turned to stone, I focused all of my attention on the magic users. I forced four large spikes of stone to shoot out of the ground and into the darkness of the forest. Three loud thuds later and one cry of pain let me know they'd hit their mark, so I quickly reactivated my petrification skill and held it until the last crusader turned to stone midstep.

Before I had a chance to celebrate, I felt a terrible pang in my stomach that sent me reeling. I suddenly lost all strength as my hunger reached a level I'd never felt before. *Guess that's what I get for using too much magic.*

Four golems seized the opportunity I'd given them and jumped me. They began beating me into the ground; four sets of massive fists pummeled my scales until their granite hands began to crack and my scales started to ache.

"Have you all been taken to bed by the foul creature?"

My head snapped to the side and I stared off in the direction of my companions. Did he?

"Have you become the demon's whores!?"

My temper flared and the monster within me came to life. The golems were reduced to dust as my hunger drained them of their life-giving essence in less than a blink of an eye. My magic responded to my emotions and briefly ran rampant, causing the wind I was controlling to turn into a roaring twister as too much mana was pushed into it.

I thought I would need to struggle to lift my head, but rage and the ambient magic I was pulling in was fueling me. I wound my way around the stone crusaders and tiny buildings until I reached the edge of the twister, behind the spot where I'd last seen the hooded man. I slowly pushed my head through the heavy winds and stared down at the fool.

"Smite the heretic with your awesome power, Oh mighty God!"

"Gladly..." I hissed. I swallowed the priest whole, taking extra care to chew as many times as I could while he was sliding down my throat. As I felt the weight settle in my stomach, I turned to see everyone staring at me.

Some pretty boy with red hair and a gilded sword tried to take a step back, to push Ayla away from me.

I hissed quietly at the action.

Ayla grabbed the man's hand and pulled him closer to me with a creepy smile on her face. The man looked like he wanted to either plant his feet or run away, but something, presumably his pride, kept him from doing so.

"Ayla, what are—" She clamped her hand over his jaw and slowly turned his head to face me.

"Thor, I would like to formally introduce you to Torga, my adoptive father. Old man, this is Thor, my fiancé."

I stared down at the pretty boy, and he returned my stare with wide eyes.

"P—Pleasure to meet you."

"Sure, it is," I chuckled. "You and I need to have a little chat."

"I really don't think—"

"Either you'll sit down and talk with me, or I'll eat you and Ayla can find another boyfriend."

"I'm her fiancé," Thor replied forcefully.

"I know what I said." I turned away from the pretty boy and looked Ayla up and down.

Ayla watched me watch her for several seconds, then showed me a bright smile. "Hi, Dad. You're looking well. Have you lost weight?"

I narrowed my eyes at her use of the D-word. Despite my going through the process of formally adopting her in the eyes of the other druids, Ayla rarely referred to me as her dad; it was usually either "Old man," "Torga," or "Father" if she was feeling formal. I was only "Dad" when she thought she was in trouble—which she was, and she knew it.

"Don't think you're off the hook, Brat. We will be having a talk after I finish with his highness, Lord pretty boy."

"But, Dad—"

"No, Ayla. I mean it." I glanced over at Fenris and nodded my thanks, to which he returned a nod of his own.

Ayla frowned, but couldn't seem to decide what she wanted to say. She looked like a fish out of water for a few seconds, which made me want to laugh or crack a joke, but I was supposed to be in "angry dad mode." So, I had to keep that at a minimum.

As the jewel had been performing as expected, I had lost about ten percent of my body mass a second before stopping at my current size. I was a far cry from where I wanted to be, but I wasn't about to start complaining. I was enjoying my relatively small size while I could as I made my way over to the stone crusaders and began to eat them.

"Sup, Fatass," Fenris said by way of greeting as he stepped up behind me.

"I'm thinner than you are."

"Hey, just because that jewel is making you appear smaller than you are, doesn't mean I don't know what's in front of me."

"Aw, and after I'd told the doctor to make it look natural."

"What, no—What does that even mean?"

"Don't worry about it," I chuckled. "Now, as much as I like talking to you... Do you mind?"

"Knock yourself out," Fenris blanched.

"Master!" Findral yelled as she came running over to me.

"What is it now?" I whined.

"Ayla's fiancé—er, boyfriend—is requesting your presence," she replied.

I tilted my head. "He's requesting *my* presence?"

"Yes."

"Sir pretty boy, lord of the runway models, is requesting *my* presence?"

"Um—Y-Yes?" she stammered.

"Okay, thanks for passing on the message, Fin," I said happily as I picked up a crusader and started munching on him like he was a piece of hard candy.

"Um—m-master?"

"Mm?" I turned to her with a half-eaten crusader hanging out of my mouth and tilted my head again.

"Never mind, master. I'm sure he won't mind waiting."

Actually, I'm rather hoping he does mind. I smirked at the thought and went back to eating.

When I was finished snacking on my rock candy, I slowly made my way through town until I arrived at the last place I'd seen the group. I found Ayla, the pretty boy, and a militia's worth of men in leather armor unloading wooden boxes from several ships. I found myself staring at the vessels and wondering two things: how they managed to get them into the village harbor, and why they looked so damned familiar.

"Finally, he shows up," Thor said angrily. "What, were you off taking a nap somewhere?"

"No," I replied while staring him down.

He glared expectantly at me, waiting for an excuse that would never come. Ayla began to fidget from the uncomfortable silence that stretched out between us. The pretty boy, on the other hand, looked perfectly calm as he returned my stare.

At least he's brave.

After a few minutes of neither of us speaking, Ayla finally spoke up. "Look, the two of you can compare dick sizes later. Thor, you needed him for a reason, right?"

"Yes," he replied without looking away from me. "But I think I have my answer."

"Do you now?" I laughed. "And what answer would that be?"

"You aren't coming with us to Asgard." His reply was delivered with the confidence of someone used to being obeyed.

"Then have fun returning by yourself."

"Oh, Ayla's coming with me." He grabbed her hand to emphasize what he was saying and tugged her into his side. "The others are welcome to come along if they wish. But you aren't coming."

I looked between him and Ayla: She looked uncomfortable, but wasn't objecting to his words. "I see," I sighed.

"Good, now—Urk!" Thor was interrupted as a slab of stone slammed into his chest, sending him skipping across the cobblestone road like a pebble over water. A few of his soldiers grabbed him before he could skip too far and helped him back to his feet. He was shaken but didn't seem to be badly hurt.

"Let me explain *something*," I hissed. "I don't care who you are, where you came from, or what your title is. Compared to the things I've seen, the things I've killed, you're nothing more than an insignificant whelp who thinks he's tough shit. And yet, you have the gall, the absolute nerve, to order *me* around? To let you whisk my daughter away somewhere I cannot follow?" I leaned down until we were at eye level. "You're even dumber than I thought."

"Care to put your money where your mouth is?" Thor asked, drawing his sword, and stepping towards me. "I'm the first prince of Asgard, brother to the king, and a level seventy-nine magic-swordsman. I've killed giants, dragons, and many others in defense of my kingdom. What makes you so special, what gives you the confidence to take me on?" the prince asked with no small amount of amusement in his voice.

"Because, whelp. I eat heroes like you for breakfast." I looked to the left and twisted my head as if I'd heard something, which prompted the prince to look that way as well. Then I shot forward and lightly headbutted him in the chest. He was knocked off balance, landing on his ass with a heavy thud.

"That was a dirty trick." He scrambled to his feet and picked up his sword. He held it horizontally in front of him. It was about four feet long and three inches wide. The back of the blade was made of a dark metal, while the edge was made of a much lighter metal. A circular guard extended from the bottom edge of the blade to the end of the hilt to cover his hand, and the hilt itself was covered in a dark rubber to prevent slippage.

"Fancy sword."

"My father had it crafted for me. It's enchanted to never dull, never break, and to increase its sharpness upon making contact."

I nodded to show I understood. "Good, then you should have no problem cutting me with it."

"Um—What?"

"Oh, here we go." Ayla sighed.

"Cut. Me."

"Are you sure about this?" he asked cautiously. "This sword has cleaved through a dragon's scales. And despite your attitude, I'd rather not hurt my future snake-in-law."

I narrowed my eyes at him. "Alright, I'll make you a deal. If you can cut me with that blade, I won't protest your taking Ayla with you."

"And if I can't?"

"Losing confidence already?"

He frowned at me, then brought his blade to his side while drawing his body into a low stance and slightly turning to the side. "I'll try not to hurt you too much."

He watched me for a few seconds, then his body sprang into action. He rotated to ensure maximum speed as his arm whipped towards me. The blade struck true and sparks erupted from the place of contact as it grazed my scales. Thor completed his movement and sheathed his sword.

I glanced down and saw a thin white line across my torso: No blood had been drawn, though my scales had been slightly damaged. I looked from the mark to Thor. "Not bad. You managed to cut me."

"Imagine what would've happened if I wanted to kill you."

"Fair enough," I allowed. "Now it's my turn."

"Give me your best shot—" His eyes went wide, and he gasped as the air was knocked out of him. The stone pillar I'd summoned between his legs returned to dust after fulfilling its purpose. Thor fell to his knees, his sword clenched tightly in his hand but useless. "T— That's not—" He tried to suck in a breath, but none would come.

"I'm sorry, I couldn't hear you. Wanna try that one more time?"

He opened and closed his mouth several times before finally shaking his head.

"Are you sure?"

He nodded his head, as he finally could no longer keep himself upright and he collapsed onto his stomach.

I lowered my head until my mouth was inches from his ear. "Now, imagine what would've happened if I'd wanted to kill you," I mocked. "Remember one thing going forward, 'your highness.' The girl you've chosen is a monster's daughter. I'll gladly take any pain you inflict on her out on you, your family, and your kingdom. And I'll enjoy Every. Fucking. Second of it."

I raised my head to my full height and grinned at Ayla, who was scowling at me. "Don't give me that look, Brat. I owed him that one." I left her to tend to his injuries and made my way over to Fenris and Findral.

"Are you sure he's okay?" Fenris asked after seeing the prince lie completely motionless.

"Eh, probably." I shrugged.

CHAPTER SEVEN

ITH THE SUN HANGING HIGH IN THE SKY AND a gentle breeze rustling the trees, I found myself having a rather crappy morning. I hadn't had any sleep in two days since I was trying to keep my hunger under control, then Fenris had informed me that Asgard was one of over a thousand floating islands, all of which were nearly identical if you looked at them from the ground. So, we had two options: I fly us there and risk Asgard seeing it as an attack or hitch a ride on one of the Asgardian ships.

However, now that it was just the two of us, I found myself wondering what he knew about those special evolutions.

"Hey, Fenris?"

"Mm?"

"Have you ever heard of an evolution the system couldn't recognize?"

Fenris had a sudden coughing fit. "Y—You have one of those?"

"No."

"Oh, thank the gods—"

"I have two."

"WHY!?" he yelled. "No, never mind. You're you, of course you would get that evolution." He sighed.

"Is it a bad thing?"

"Bad? Not unless you count being the envy of all of Yggdrasil a bad thing. Everyone who cares about evolving as a way to gain power wants one of those evolutions."

"Why?"

"The system doesn't recognize them because they don't currently exist. You would be the first person in history to evolve into those creatures. You would, for all intents and purposes, become the progenitor of an entire race."

"Oh…" I sighed. I felt like I was sighing a lot lately.

"What about a king evolution?"

Fenris was quiet for a long moment. "Torga, take it from me. Be *very* careful saying stuff like that out loud."

"What? King evolution?"

"Yes. It's dangerous."

"Dangerous? Fenris, I don't even know how to unlock it. All it says is "kill the old Serpent King," but it doesn't mention who that is or where I could find them. What, am I just supposed to search throughout all of Yggdrasil, killing every serpent I find along the way until I get lucky and kill the Serpent King?"

"Torga, I mean it. Stop talking about it," Fenris said seriously. "The path of kings is started by stating that you wish to accept the King's Challenge. Once you say those words aloud, you and every other Serpent King will be whisked away to a private corner of Yggdrasil, in a realm outside of time and disconnected from the outside world until only one remains. There's no quitting halfway, and no giving up. You're stuck there until you either win or die trying, then your body is sent back for your family to deal with. This is usually the fate of those wanting to be a king of beasts. For all your power, Torga. I fear you'll meet the same fate."

"Yeah—" I hesitated momentarily. "But that may not be the worst thing I could do."

Fenris didn't respond, to which I was grateful. I didn't want to explain myself any further right now. My talk with Fenris came to a screeching halt after that, but he didn't leave my side. We began making our way over to the temporary campground we'd set up outside the inn, seeing as I was too large to fit inside any of the nearby buildings, and Fenris joined me since he didn't feel like showing his demi-elf form to a group of strangers. On the way, we circled around one of the ships and I caught a voice I recognized. "Oh, Ayla... You shouldn't have," they mumbled.

I felt my eye twitch as I looked up at the window above our heads. I rose to my full height and peeked through it to make sure what I thought was happening, wasn't. After all, it would be a shame for the whelp to die before the wedding…

Sleeping alone in the room naked as the day he was born, and using a pair of waterskins as pillows, was Thor. While I desperately ignored the telltale signs of the kind of dream he was having, I scanned the room to make sure Ayla wasn't with him, then withdrew my head. As I did, I heard him mumble, "You're cold. I can fix that—"

I felt my eye twitch again.

"Well?" Fenris asked in an amused tone. It was the first thing I'd heard him say in almost ten minutes.

"He's definitely compensating for something with that sword of his. Surprised I managed to hit the thing," I replied as naturally as I could.

Fenris snorted in response and we continued heading for our sleeping area.

As the morning continued to drag on, people started to wake up and get ready for the day. I saw Ayla, Hali, and Findral heading off on their own after breakfast and briefly wondered where they were going. *They wouldn't try to run away again, would they?* That thought ran through my mind a few times. *Maybe I should follow them?* I wondered.

I noticed Thor and another man following after them a few minutes later, and my decision was made.

I let them be.

"You're not going to follow them?"

"No."

Fenris was quiet for a moment, "You feeling okay?" He placed his paw against my forehead and muttered something about my not having a fever.

"First of all, I'm a reptile, genius. My body temperature would be lower than yours even if I was running a fever. And secondly," I jerked my head out from under his paw. "Get your grubby paws off me. Why're you still hanging around me anyway? Don't you have work to do?" I asked, referring to the fact that he was supposed to be getting ready to go collect the rest of our group.

"I'm not leaving for another hour. And besides, I have to finish patrolling the perimeter of the village for monsters."

The mutt had jokes. The most powerful creature I'd seen in the forest was a tier four shaggy deer. Anything below the fourth tier wouldn't come anywhere near the village with me around. Creatures below fourth tier were rarely sentient and lived mainly through their instincts.

They ate when they were hungry, slept when they were tired, and used the bathroom whenever the urge hit them. A truly boring life—at least, to me it was. However, because of this, their senses where heightened to a level no sentient creature could truly comprehend. On some level, these animals could sense danger long before they had anyway of truly knowing what was there. This sense for danger had led to more than a few instances of my having to rely on inorganic material to survive, as every animal for miles had fled for their lives. Which was another reason I'd wanted a smaller body. It's one thing to be a mile-long serpent when my life was on the line and I was fighting against a fellow giant. But it's slightly difficult to procure meat when you're the size of a mountain. Most creatures, unless they're either deaf or stupid, will flee for their lives at the first sign of a creature higher on the food chain than they are.

And I happen to be nearing the top of the food chain. Unbidden memories of the golden being and a laughing skeleton in a top hat floated through my mind at that thought and I retracted my statement. If you counted those *things*, then I was little more than a microbe in an ocean of stars.

"Torga, are you sure about letting them go? What if they run again?"

"Then they run." I sighed. "I made a deal with the whelp. If he could cut me, I'd let them go. Well, he cut me."

"Seriously?" Fenris eyed me up and down. "There's not a scratch on you."

"I never said it was good cut." I smirked at him. "He barely managed to leave a mark on my scales. But that was all he needed."

"Wow—So—You're really going to honor your word?"

"That's what I said."

"I know. I'm just surprised is all. I can't believe you're going to let Ayla run off with some guy to have all the wild sex she can handle. And, you let Findral go with her?"

"I'd watch what you say, Mutt. Hali went with her too." I looked over my shoulder at Fenris' horrified expression and couldn't stop a grin from almost splitting my face in two.

"I'll—uh—I suddenly remembered I had something to do. Talk to you later, Fatass!" He dashed away faster than I could follow and was racing through the trees a moment later.

I waited until he was out of sight before I burst out laughing. Was I happy about the situation? No, of course I wasn't. But I intended to honor my word—and not just the promise to let her leave with him.

~ ~ ~

A few days later, I found myself napping near the campfire. Fenris was sitting nearby watching Lena and Talia play. They'd arrived with the rest of our group in tow yesterday, and he'd stuck to them like glue ever since. He was happily licking a beef-based soup out of a large wooden bowl Lena placed there for him, and periodically gnawing on a large steak.

"You know he's glaring at you, right?" Fenris asked while watching Thor out of the corner of his eye.

I glanced over at Thor, who was sitting on the lowest step of a nearby house, a bowl of his own clutched tightly in his hand as he shoveled the dark colored broth into his mouth. Sure enough, he was glaring at me.

"Yep."

"And you're not worried about him trying anything?"

I looked at Fenris. "I'm counting on it."

"You're plotting something." I knew it wasn't a question. He didn't bother asking for the details because he knew me well enough to understand how my mind worked. If he had a part to play in my plan, then I would've told him by now.

"You're testing him," Fenris muttered.

"I'm sure you're just overthinking things, Mutt."

"No, I know you, Fatass. If you wanted the kid dead, then nothing any of us could say or do would stop you from killing him. So, what makes this kid different from everyone else you've killed?"

"What makes you think he's different?"

"I've known you for over a decade, Torga. Want to know how many people I've seen you give this kind of opportunity to?" Before I could speak in defense of myself, Fenris pressed on. "Not a damn one. I've seen you kill kings without a moment's hesitation. I've seen you kill more people than I care to remember. Granted, most of them deserved it, but even still you did not hesitate to kill when necessary. So, why? Why is he any different?" Fenris stared and waited for the answer to his question.

"Ever since I came to this 'world' I've lived by one creed. It's a saying that I've long since carved into my heart and is the driving force behind almost everything I do." I took a deep breath, then grimaced as magic was involuntarily drawn towards me, creating a static-like effect in the air. "Protect those I care about with everything I have, kill those who stand against me as quickly and efficiently as possible, and under no circumstances allow them to attack first. Strike fast and hard, and kill without mercy has been my strategy in almost every fight I've been in and it's served me well, but it won't work here," I said, gesturing with my head to the girls sitting around Thor. "Not too long ago, Ayla would've tried to follow me anywhere, even to the depths of hell itself if it meant I wouldn't leave her alone. But the whelp is a blessing, an annoying blessing I'd like nothing more than to eat, but that can't be helped. Through him, I can ensure that she's safe."

Fenris stared down at me for several seconds, then he snorted and smacked my head with a paw. "You're an idiot if you think she'll choose to stay with the kid over going with you. If it comes down to it, I have a feeling Ayla would kill him if it meant protecting you. I mean sure, she'd feel like absolute shit later, but you are her dad: the man who raised her, protected her, and always ensured she was taken care of. If your goal in this was to make her stay instead of following you, then I think you've already fucked that plan up." Fenris used his tail to point to an angry Ayla who was currently giving Thor a death-glare. "And if you think she'd pick anyone over you, then you're even stupider than I thought." Fenris grinned.

"And I'm very aware of just how stupid you think I am," I chuckled.

"What's the real reason you're doing this?" Fenris asked in a serious tone.

"I—I can't control myself any longer."

"Control yourself? What do you mean?"

"Every day I suppress my hunger, I grow closer to losing control. It's always there, screeching at the edges of my consciousness like a nail on glass, and I don't know how much longer I can keep it under control."

"Damn, are you going to tell the girls?"

"I haven't made up my mind yet." I sighed. "They already know something's up thanks to my outburst back on Uathea."

"You need to tell them."

"Yeah, I know—"

"Jötnar! Jötnar in the forest! Quickly, they're heading this way!"

Fenris and I looked in the direction the voice had come from and saw a lone Asgardian sprinting down an alley towards us. He was holding a bloody stump where his right arm used to be, and his clothes were heavily stained with blood and other strange fluids. He collapsed to the ground twenty feet from the center of the square and never made another sound.

CHAPTER EIGHT

ANDEMONIUM ERUPTED AS THOSE WHO KNEW what a Jötnar was began to panic. "Alright, alright. Settle down everyone," Thor commanded. For the first time since I'd met him, he was showing the poise and confidence of a true prince, and not just acting like some warrior with an ego. "My men and I will move to eliminate the Jötnar threat immediately. There's no need to panic."

The civilians from the caravan began to loudly rattle off questions to him. People were yelling over each other so much that I could barely understand what they were saying, but Thor seemed to handle it just fine.

I looked over at Fenris, who was grinning at me. "You're going to move, aren't you?"

"Of course. I've been starving for some meat."

"I thought so." He chuckled, took a quick glance around, then motioned with his head to an alley behind the group. "Race you there?"

I pushed as much magic as I dared into my body and enhanced my speed far beyond what my body would normally be capable of. Though Fenris reacted quickly and dashed away, disappearing in a burst of speed that left me reeling, I quickly followed after him by shoving against the ground with my tail and launching myself high above into the sky. I heard the ground detonate behind me as my acceleration destroyed a portion of the cobblestoned streets. Once I was in the air, I unfurled my wings and angled my body towards the barrier wall.

Got ya. A few hundred feet from the village wall, a heavily armored army of four or five dozen oddly shaped humanoids marched. All of them were big. Even from the sky I could tell the smallest among them stood head and shoulders above the Asgardians, while I estimated the largest to be well over twenty feet tall. Their bodies were oddly proportioned and covered in the dull gray armor, complete with a full helmet that hid their faces. Some of them carried the same weapon, but no two were alike. Hardly any of their limbs seemed to fit their bodies. Their helmeted heads were either a tad oversized for their slender frame or much too small for their broad shoulders. Most had two arms and legs, but a few had extras that grew from odd places.

I pulled in my wings and dove towards the ground, mana pooling and condensing into a red sphere a few centimeters from my snout. The mana grew larger, spun faster, and whined like chainsaw as it grew more powerful.

I held it for a few seconds, then let it go.

The force of the magic leaving my snout managed to stop my forward momentum and throw me into a fierce spiral while the ball of energy tore off towards the army of Jötnar.

I grunted from the effort it took to reposition my body so I was facing the ground again. My eyes stung from the wind pressure assailing them, but I kept them open so I could keep an eye on my targets.

The ball struck off center, hitting the ground a dozen or so feet to the left of the Jötnar. However, the explosion that followed more than made up for my crappy aim. A shockwave slammed into me a heartbeat after the ball detonated. The Jötnar that were killed in the initial blast had their bodies torn asunder, while the rest were thrown away from the epicenter of the explosion.

I spread my wings and hovered in place while I surveyed my handiwork: About a dozen Jötnar were dead, though it was impossible to really tell due to the sheer number of pieces their bodies were in. Another ten or so were unmoving on the ground. I wasn't sure if they were dead or just unconscious, so I caused stone spikes to erupt from the ground and pierce their chests.

I caught sight of something moving quickly towards the army and for a brief moment I diverted my attention.

Fenris, having returned to his full size during the jaunt over, raced towards the group of Jötnar closest to the village and pounced on them. Teeth and claws flashed as they shred Jötnar armor and flesh like sheets of paper.

I didn't want to be left out, so I angled my body towards one of the three twenty-foot tall Jötnar at the rear of the group and dove after it. I realized too late that I was too far to the left to hit its center of mass, so I did the next best thing: I bit into its neck as I flew by and dragged it to the ground, coiling my body around its legs to help throw it off balance.

The creature screamed out its death rattle seconds before I snapped my jaws shut, nearly decapitating it, and cutting the sound short. A cooling sensation flooded the inside of my mouth and I felt my tongue go numb. I stared holes in the remaining creatures while I swallowed the throat of the dead giant.

The Jötnar still standing started yelling in an oddly guttural language and pointing at the corpse. As he screamed at me, the words grew more distinguishable by the second until I could understand them, thanks to an odd skill I'd received years ago.

Ding* Ding

∞∞∞∞∞∞∞

You have eaten the following race for the first time.

Frost Giant: Tier 6

∞∞∞∞∞∞∞

"It's here!" "The serpent!" "The devourer!" Three Jötnar exclaimed one after the other.

Their words struck me as odd. Had I met these creatures before? Did they know me? I thought about questioning them, but I didn't have the chance to. A Jötnar with arms as big around as an elephant's leg leaped at me as if it were a large gorilla. *Kill all but one and question it*—The heads of three Jötnar disintegrated as Findral appeared behind them with a sword of blinding blue flames clutched in one slender hand.

Or not. I sighed.

The giant, and every other non-friendly creature near Findral, was decapitated before they even knew she was there. She stepped up with a look of intense fury on her face. Her sword was ready to defend me from any Jötnar stupid enough to come within melee range.

"You dare!" I heard Fenris roar a second before he dragged a brute to the ground by its shoulder. Its panicked scream was cut short as he tore out its throat, bathing himself in its blood.

Fenris let out a pained yelp and leaped off the thing's corpse. To my heat sense, it seemed like he'd been doused in… ice? His body temperature plummeted wherever the blood touched.

I was never more grateful for my superior elemental resistance than I was right then.

"Fin, get the Mutt back to the village and get Ayla and Hali to work on him."

"But—"

"That's an order." I looked into her eyes and saw the fear behind the rage. *She's… worried about me?*

She looked like she wanted to say something but moved to obey my order instead.

"Thank you, Findral."

She dashed over to Fenris, weaving between several Jötnar, and decapitating them as she went. Then the two of them disappeared in a pillar of blue fire as Findral accelerated to her top speed.

I turned back to the too quiet creatures and saw them watching me with looks ranging from intense rage to some form of curiosity.

"Now," I hissed. "Where were we? Oh, yes. You lot mentioning something about a devourer, right? Does any of you have something you'd like to share with the class?"

Judging by the widening of eyes and the opening of mouths, they were surprised that I could speak their language.

Several of the smaller Jötnar raised their weapons and pointed them at me. The larger creatures copied them soon after and I exhaled in annoyance. *Why don't they ever take the easy way out?*

"Alright, just remember, you asked for this." I pushed off with my tail and started the battle anew. I used my mana to temporarily boost my speed and surprise a quadruped Jötnar with the lower body of a big cat. I hit it dead center, crumpling its armor like it was an aluminum can.

A large fist wrapped around my tail a second before I was slung through the air and slammed into the ground a dozen feet away. I twisted out of the way of a giant, misshapen foot and sunk my teeth into the creature's calf. My venom poured through my fangs and entered its blood stream. Acid venom warred against glacial blood as its blood vessels were destroyed.

I fed my tail through the gaps in the giant's armor, then heaved and slammed it onto its back. I swung around until I could reach its head. I took its head in my mouth and bit down, crumpling the thick metal of the helmet and turning the softer skull beneath into putty.

The creatures went wild then, whooping and hollering at me.

"Yeah—yeah. Bring it on you ugly frozen dinners. I'll give you a reason to *scream*." I hissed. I freed my tail from the fist of the dead giant and faced down the army.

I coiled my body like a spring and aimed at another twenty-footer with what appeared to be goat horns on its head. If they wanted a fight to the death, I was all too happy to oblige—but they turned tail and ran instead. Fleeing at speeds that would've turned racehorses green with envy, the creatures disappeared into the dark forest, leaving behind the dead or dying bodies of their comrades.

Oh, no you don't. I launched myself at the back of the last twenty-footer and tackled it. I sunk my teeth into its shoulder, wrapped my tail around its legs, then pulled it to the ground and pinned it beneath my bulk. It tried to fight its way free, but it was in my territory now that I had a hold on it.

I glanced around to make sure the coast was clear and saw the fleeing form of the last Jötnar as it disappeared into the forest. "So," I looked at the pinned giant. "You're going to tell me how you know me, yes?"

"I—I don't—" I sunk my teeth into its shoulder again and allowed a few drops of venom to enter its blood stream. The giant screamed as its veins and muscles were eaten from the inside via the acid.

"Now, while I'm not a fan of frozen dinners as a matter of choice, we do what we have to when we're *starving*," I hissed. "So, either tell me what I want to know, or I'm going to see if you taste better than you look."

It let out a low-pitched whine, then began to talk.

CHAPTER NINE

W E WERE AIRBORNE WITHIN THE HOUR. Clouds parted and the sky trembled as the ten Asgardian airships tore through the sky at two-hundred and sixty knots, or three-hundred miles per hour.

I looked over the side of the ship from my place on the deck and whistled appreciatively at the rapidly moving scenery as the trees of the forest gave way to a flat plain that seemed to stretch on forever in every direction.

"What are we going to do if Asgard has truly fallen?" Ayla asked. It was the first time she'd spoken since I'd delivered the information I'd gleaned from the Jötnar, and we departed. I glanced over at her and saw that she, Fin, Hali, and Thor were sitting at a table near the center of the ship. They were playing some kind of card game while the ship's crew bustled around them.

Because of the size and capacity limitations of each airship, Fenris and I couldn't ride on the same ship. Fenris, Lena, Solon, Talia, Uriel, and the elves that served as Lena's bodyguards boarded another ship, while the caravan was allowed to load onto a couple of ships at the rear of the formation.

"It hasn't," Thor denied.

"But, what if—"

"It. Hasn't," he said forcefully. "Torga was clearly mistaken, even if he was telling the truth about understanding the Jötnar, which I'm not sure he was. The Jötnar are infamous liars and tricksters. He wouldn't be the first, nor the last to fall victim to their lies."

"I would definitely be the last to fall for that particular Jötnar's lies," I calmly replied. Let the whelp believe whatever he wanted to believe. I knew what the Jötnar told me was the truth. It's not easy to lie when your veins were being dissolved from the inside out and you're begging for the sweet release of death. Of course, the smart ones would lie as a final act of revenge against the one torturing them. That's one of the reasons torture was usually hit or miss, depending on several factors. The biggest of which was the one doing the torturing and the one getting tortured. In this case though, I didn't think the frost giant was intelligent enough to plan that far ahead, so his information was probably accurate.

Regardless, if Thor didn't believe me, we wouldn't be racing towards Asgard as fast as the airships could carry us.

After seven hours we came to a sheer cliff face that extended far beyond the clouds. The pilot of each ship shifted the rudders until we were moving parallel to the cliff wall. We climbed for so long, and the magic of the ship made the journey so smooth, by the time we reached the apex and leveled out, I'd almost forgotten we were flying in a vertical line.

As we leveled out, I could see our destination on the horizon. The sky was littered with a thousand black dots of various sizes, and in the center of the mass of rocks floated Asgard: a mammoth city of gold built into the side of a mountain. We flew through the night and into the next morning before Thor informed us that we were closing in on our destination.

I looked ahead of us and saw that he was right—though I was wrong in my earlier estimate. Asgard wasn't built into the side of a mountain. It was a mountain unto itself.

"How far until they know we're here?" I asked.

"Thirty miles, give or take. Depends if Heimdall is working today. If he is, then they knew we were coming since before we entered the howling mountains."

"Good." I nodded my head. "Alright, then. Get your asses over here and get ready for trouble."

"Why?"

"Just do it, Thor," Ayla said. "If Dad believes it's necessary, then I believe him. He rarely leads us down the wrong path."

Thor rolled his eyes, then trudged along behind her. "I'm telling you, he's mistaken. There's no way in hell Asgard was taken by—"

"Incoming!" the captain yelled. A heavy impact suddenly caused the airship to list to one side. The forward mast exploded into splinters as the wood deflected whatever projectile had been fired at us.

Ayla stumbled mid-step and, almost as if I were watching the entire thing in slow motion, fell over the edge of the ship.

"Ayla!" I cried. I dove over the side of the ship and tucked my wings tightly against my body to reduce drag. She screamed as she fell, her body plummeting towards the ground faster than I could follow.

Her eyes widened as she watched me fail to reach her.

With the ground rapidly approaching, I hissed angrily and unfurled my wings. I activated the jewel embedded in my skull and retrieved the mass I'd stored away. My body expanded rapidly, ballooning several tens of feet per second until I was long enough to shove my head beneath Ayla's body.

I felt something slam into the side of my head, just behind my left eye. I involuntarily twitched to keep whatever it was from slamming into my eye, almost dropping Ayla in the process. "Ayla, you need to hang on!"

She didn't respond.

"Ayla—Ayla?" I called out.

"Master?" I heard Findral call out to me.

I rotated my head to see Findral hovering above my head in all her glory. Gone were the thick robes she'd been wearing since I'd woken up from my decade long nap. A thick veil of blue fire covered her from scalp to toe, and tongues of flame would periodically snap off of her naked form and scorch the air around us. She had two massive black wings at her back, which bore a striking resemblance to a bat, baring the veins of bright blue fire that crisscrossed them multiple times.

"Findral, how's Ayla? She isn't answering me."

Findral landed on my head and was quiet for a few seconds. "She's alive, but barely. It looks like she hit her head pretty hard when you caught her."

"Can you take her to Lena?"

"That's—The ship Lena and Fenris were on was shot down."

"What? How'd that—" Another cannonball slammed into the side of my head and my temper flared. "That's it. Fin, take her to Hali."

"What're you going to do?"

"What do you think I'm going to do, Findral? I'm gonna eat them."

"You wanted to play hardball, right? Then let's play." Several cannonballs ricocheted off my scales, only serving to infuriate me further. Findral appeared next to my eye with an unconscious Ayla in tow. She nodded to me, then departed in a flash of blue fire.

With the two of them gone, I no longer needed to hold back. I scanned the skies and noticed a group of black and green airships circling overhead and firing upon the golden Asgardian ships.

I opened my mouth wide and fired a beam of magical energy at the enemy airship on my left, instantly turning it to ash. I quickly swept my head to the side, dragging the beam ninety degrees and slicing any ship unlucky enough to get caught in it. The ship immediately to my rear dropped out of the sky like a helicopter with its rotors damaged.

I hissed at the realization that I'd missed a few ships entirely and they skirted around me in pursuit of the Asgardian ships. I snapped my mouth shut to cut off the beam, then aimed ahead of the ships and fired again. The beam quickly caught up to the fleeing ships, engulfing them in a wave of pure kinetic force.

I cut the beam off after a second and surveyed the damage. Wherever the beam touched, destruction followed. My eyes locked onto a small stream of smoke rising from a spot a few thousand feet away. *Survivors? But from which group?*

"Master?" I turned from the crash site to Findral.

"Find Fenris and the others, Fin. Start over there." I motioned to the crash site with my nose. "And… Pass along a message to Thor for me, would you?"

"Of course, master."

"Thanks, Fin. Okay, here's the message: Take care of them, whelp, protect them with your life or I'll take it from you when I find you."

"Understood, and—be careful, master."

"Don't worry about me, Fin." I turned my head to see the lights of Asgard growing brighter as a golden shield began to cover it. "I'm far too hungry to lose now."

She disappeared in a flash of blue fire, and with a mighty flap of my wings, I began moving towards Asgard.

CHAPTER TEN

THE FLIGHT TO THE OUTSKIRTS OF ASGARD ONLY took twenty minutes, but since I was constantly being bombarded by cannonballs and fighting off airships, it felt like a much longer journey.

I gazed upon the glory of Asgard for the first time, not as an adventurer or the father of the bride, but as an invader.

And they'd brought it upon themselves.

Situated at the direct center of a crowd of mountains that slowly orbited around it, as if it were the sun and the mountains were planets, was Asgard. It shined with a resplendent golden light, illuminating its surrounding like the star it pretended to be.

As I drew closer, small bat-like creatures poured from the gaps in Asgard's armor. At least, I thought they were bat-like until they started exhaling plumes of ice that peppered me like machine gun fire. That was when I recognized them for what they truly were: drakes.

Unlike dragons, drakes were only slightly more intelligent than your average horse. Also, unlike dragons, drakes were pack creatures, and it wasn't uncommon for the beast nations to domesticate and use them as war mounts. I'd visited one such tribe during my stint as an adventurer and seen the creatures up close and personal: A normal drake was usually between eight and twelve feet long, depending on the breed. Earth drakes were usually the largest, while water drakes were the smallest. However, their appearance was normally easy to spot. Their scale and eye colors varied by race, though I'd been told they always had pitch black wings and tails. Fire drakes were a combination of reds, oranges, and yellows. Water drakes were blues, purples, and greens. Earth drakes were browns and various shades of gray. I'd also heard tales of wind drakes being pure white, but I'd never seen one in person.

I mention this distinction, specifically, because none of the drakes I saw were those colors. Every drake flying towards me was black as the abyss and, if my tongue was telling the truth, smelled like a corpse. And for the pièce de résistance, riding atop the drakes' backs were Jötnar in their familiar suits of armor, wielding lances so large I doubted a normal man could even move them, let alone use them in combat.

It would appear the Jötnar have decided to bring the attack to me. Good. I was tired of destroying their ships anyway.

I opened my mouth and let loose a stream of condensed mana upon the drakes and their riders.

I cut the beam short as I felt my mana reserves run dangerously low and my hunger made itself known. *Damn it!* I hadn't eaten since we left the village and it was coming back to bite me on the ass. *I need to run until I can find something to eat—No, I can't do that.* I shook my head and used both sets of wings to arrest my momentum.

I hovered in place and watched as the drakes and the remaining ships began to circle me.

My battle had only just begun. No way was I going to quit now... *Then again, who says I have to?* I closed my eyes, wincing as something stuck into my lower-left wing, but I remained focused on what I wanted to do.

Alright, monster. You're hungry, right? I felt a pang in my stomach as "it" voiced its agreement. *Good, then eat your fill. Eat until nothing remains of this place, and all those who conspired to interfere with Ayla's happiness are nothing but ash!* My eyes opened, and with them, came the door I'd forced over my hunger.

I screamed as the feeling of raw, unadulterated hunger slammed into me. A pain unlike any I'd ever felt erupted inside my mind. I wasn't *just* hungry; I was on the verge of death. If I didn't eat now, then I'd—a drake spat ice at my face. The ice acted as razor sharp daggers, peppering my scales with tiny holes as they punctured, but failed to penetrate deep enough to matter. However, it did shock me out of my mental spiral and help me find my focus.

I released the first wave of my gluttonous aura. It shot out in a circular wave, devouring anything in its path without question or exemption. Drakes, ships, Jötnar, the ground far beneath me, all was devoured as wave after wave of aura poured out of me.

Ding!*Ding.

ꝏꝏꝏꝏꝏꝏ

Due to a combination of traits, a trait has evolved!

Aura of Gluttony: Due to Gluttonous +5 evolving into Gluttonous +7 and your need for sustenance reaching critical levels, the Magic Eater trait and the Gluttonous trait have combined to create the Aura of Gluttony trait.

Note: this is always active

ꝏꝏꝏꝏꝏꝏ

A brackish green sphere surrounded me for an instant before winking out a moment before a hail of ice perforated my scales… Or, it should have. What actually happened was the ice dissolved while it was ten feet from my face.

A feeling of dread came over me as I thought about the repercussions of the aura always active.

Ding.

ꝏꝏꝏꝏꝏꝏꝏꝏ

Name: Torga

Race: Gluttonous Elemental Serpentine Dragon

Classification: Tier 7

Skills: Minor Stealth, Heat Detection, Supreme Gluttony, Supreme Durability up, Supreme Strength up, Supreme Growth, Minor Mental Resistance up, Greater Petrifying Gaze, Greater Acid Venom, Detect Concealment, Energy Breath, Superior Elemental Resistance, Fly, Puppet Maker, Body Possession, Magic Enhancement, Elemental Manipulation

Traits: Aura of Gluttony +8, Growth +13, Strong Willed, Venomous, Aquatic, Winged, Immunity to Mind Control

ꝏꝏꝏꝏꝏꝏꝏꝏ

I dismissed the pop-up, shaking the feeling away for the moment so I could focus on the here and now. I could worry about the rest later.

A barrage of ice and steel came flying at me and I watched in horrid fascination as everything that came near me was dissolved and absorbed by the aura at the exact same distance. As soon as something came within ten feet of me, it was done.

Well, then. No sense in waiting around for the inevitable. Might as well make the best of this crapshoot. I flapped my wings once, then dove towards the ground to build speed. I ignored everything in my path and barreled towards Asgard.

Now, I towered over the drakes, hell, I towered over the mountains around me. I wasn't sure how long my body had gotten since before I evolved, though I was positive I'd grown even larger since the day I'd left the evolution shield. But Asgard was still larger than I was by a factor of at least two.

I beat my wings harder, gaining speed with every passing second as I charged. I heard the roar of cannon fire and the cries of drakes as they moved to stop me from assaulting their ill-gotten prize.

Asgard was a large city with three ascending levels, which served to separate the city into three districts. Although I didn't know which district served which purposes, I was fairly certain the castle at the center was where Thor lived.

The castle itself, while being extremely large in its own right, was nothing compared to the nine towers surrounding it. Each one stretched over five hundred feet into the air and was topped with a glass dome from which light trickled out. They were truly a sight to behold.

Forget the Asgardians, Sarah would kill me if she knew what I was about to do to them.

I twisted my body into a corkscrew and tucked my wings into my side to reduce wind drag and dove towards the center of Asgard. I aimed my head at a circular building with an open ceiling, the kind that reminded me of a baseball diamond from back home, and accepted the pain that was to come as a matter of course. However, I'd forgotten about just how… effective my new ability was. Almost without effort, my aura devoured anything I came into contact with: I devoured the golden building and a dozen or so unlucky Jötnar who happened to be training in the center of the "diamond" in the few seconds it took me to fall past them.

Unable to stop myself before I crashed into the mountain, I braced myself for impact, only to be surprised when my aura moved and devoured the mountain beneath Asgard as I fell through it, creating a perfectly circular hole. I passed completely through the top of the mountain and came out the other side.

I looked back at the hole I'd fallen out of and almost started hyperventilating. The mountain Asgard had been built around now had a gaping hole through the center of it, and the mountain itself was beginning to crack and crumble due to the structural weakness I'd caused. *Okay, note to self: Be extra careful when landing. I don't want to fall through the damn planet.*

Twin roars of epic proportions ripped me out of my thoughts. I twisted my head to face the sound and felt my heart skip a beat. Two dragons, twins in every way except eye color, crashed into the ground beneath me. They were easily over a thousand feet long, with thin cat-like bodies, pale blue scales, and massive black spikes covering their backs. I could guess what they were: If the Jötnar's taste held true, then I was looking at a pair of Ice Dragons.

One of the two dove past me, its birdlike wings allowing it to move faster than I could react. It clung to the underside of the mountain as if it were defending its nest, elegant body hunkered down in a defensive posture with only its head exposed. Its spikes seemed to vibrate as they stood on end, turning the dragon into a giant blue porcupine.

Meanwhile, the other dragon let out a low hiss and charged me.

Shit. I twisted out of the way of its jaws, returning with a bite of my own. It dodged away, dancing out of the range of my fangs.

I took a moment to glance around at the airships and the drakes. They were being too quiet for my liking and I didn't want them ambushing me while I was trying to fend off the dragons. What was left of the airships landed on one of the surrounding mountains and appeared to be watching the fight. Meanwhile, the drake riders seemed to have gone AWOL, disappearing from the battlefield entirely.

A tidal wave of magic and icicles formed in the air all around me. I had just enough time to widen my eyes before the icicles shot towards me accompanied by a sonic boom. I didn't get the chance to react before the ice perforated my scales as easily as a hot knife slices through butter. Though luckily my aura dissolved them just as easily.

Guess that's what I get for letting myself be distracted. I exhaled a breath, making sure to focus on the fire aspect of my mana as I did. I sucked in a deep breath, then exhaled quickly. Fire exploded out of my mouth and shot towards the ice dragon, who was standing on top of one of the other floating mountains.

The dragon danced out of the way, casually leaping over the fireball as if it were an everyday occurrence. For all I knew, it very well could've been. However, I made sure that I was on top of the dragon the moment it landed.

I launched myself at it, sinking my fangs into its left shoulder and slamming my full weight into it. We tumbled through the air for a bit, before crashing onto the ground. I used my length to my advantage by wrapping my tail around the creature's back legs and using my body to pin it to the ground.

I opened my mouth and created a ball of condensed mana. This battle was about to end—but then a pair of blue forelimbs latched onto the upper and lower portions of my mouth and forced it shut. I glanced over at the second dragon in time to get an eye full of ice.

"When we agreed to help the Ice-Kin take this pathetic rock," the dragon beneath me said, **"I never imagined we would run into a creature such as yourself,"** the second dragon said, finishing the first's sentence.

I was wrenched off the first dragon and thrown bodily across the plateau. My aura dissolved most of the rocks as I tumbled over them, causing a relatively smooth crevice to appear in my wake. When I finally stopped sliding, I was lying on my back with my wings pinned at an awkward angle. I cursed as I rolled onto my stomach and lifted my eyes to stare at the dragons. "I'm going to enjoy eating you. It's been a long time since I got a two for one deal."

"That's our line," they said simultaneously.

"God, that's creepy. Does that come from the inbreeding or did it take practice?"

Their spikes vibrated in sync with one another as their tempers flared. **"Watch your tongue, snake,"** the first dragon began.

"I'm going to tear it out and eat it in front of you."

"I wouldn't do that if I were you. Sarcasm and snide remarks are kind of my 'thing,'" I joked. "Besides, I don't think you could. You'd have to take the Jötnar's dick out of your mouth first, and you wouldn't want to disappoint your masters now, would you?"

"You'll die for that!" they yelled. Together they rushed at me.

"Funny." I glanced up at the gaping hole in the center of Asgard. "I thought I was supposed to do that anyway."

They leaped at me with their talons extended. I twisted my body out of the way of the first dragon's talons, but the second's stuck in my side. I wanted to yell at the burning cold that began to permeate my body, but I settled for sinking my teeth into the first dragon's neck.

I lifted the dragon off its feet, then slammed it on top of the one stuck to me, tearing its talons out of my side and temporarily stunning them.

I focused on the earth beneath them, then forced bands of stone to rise out of the ground and wrap around them.

They screamed, and they yelled, but the bands prevented them from moving. I smiled down at them. "Thanks for the meal."

Crack

I stopped moving at the sound of stone being broken. I quickly scanned the bands holding the dragons in place, but they were holding solid… Then I looked up and saw that Asgard was falling apart. A crack had formed around the hole I created, and that hole was beginning to spread outwards and affect the rest of the mountain.

Cursing, I pushed off the ground, leaping up to the mountain and using my wings to hover in place. I focused on the earth element and tried to fill in the cracks before they could permanently damage the structural integrity of the city. My stomach throbbed, and my magic failed to activate. *Damnit, I'm running on empty here!* I sucked in a deep breath, desperately trying to pull in as much ambient mana as I could, but for some reason I was pulling in much less than normal. Then I looked down and saw the problem: The twin dragons were also absorbing mana, and they were doing so at an astounding rate.

I tucked my wings in and dove towards the dragons. I landed next to their heads, then sunk my teeth into the one I'd already bitten and ripped its head off with a single strong pull.

"No!" the remaining dragon yelled. **"You'll pay for that. You hear me? You'll pay!"** It struggled fiercely, thrashing about with its tail and forelimbs as it fought to break free from the bonds that imprisoned it.

Crack

My eyes widened as the stone bands cracked.

Shit. The dragon exploded into motion. Using its sibling's body as a distraction, it threw the corpse at my head, and I ducked out of the way. When I looked back, the other dragon was gone.

It got away, I hissed.

I pushed off with my tail and floated up to the mountain. I briefly entertained the idea of trying to save it again, but why bother? The Asgardians were dead, killed by the Jötnar and turned into ghouls. *I would be doing them a favor…*

I looked around at the hundreds, possibly thousands of Jötnar running around in a panic and smiled. "Hear me, mighty Jötnar," I began. If my words reached them, they didn't show it as they continued running for cover. "My name is Torga. I'm sure some—well, most of you know why I'm here." I saw the mountain shift slightly, which wasn't a good sign. "You have invaded this kingdom, killing its citizens, and raping its culture." I felt my stomach leap into my throat as the mountain began to fall out of the sky. "Well, I hope to god you enjoyed it. Because you're not going to get the chance to do it again." The eastern and western sides of the mountain fractured and fell away from its main body seconds before Asgard itself commenced to tumbling through the sky as it plummeted over six thousand feet to the ground below.

Ding

ᚳᚩᚳᚩᚳᚩᚳᚩᚳᚩ

Congratulations! You have successfully destroyed any chance the kingdom of Asgard has of recovering. As such, you have become known across the planet as the "Destroyer" and are now feared by the inhabitants.

ᚳᚩᚳᚩᚳᚩᚳᚩᚳᚩ

Son of a bitch... I sighed.
Ding!

ᚳᚩᚳᚩᚳᚩᚳᚩᚳᚩ

Name: Torga

Race: Gluttonous Elemental Serpentine Dragon

Classification: Tier 7

Titles: Destroyer of Asgard

Skills: Minor Stealth, Heat Detection, Supreme Gluttony, Supreme Durability up, Supreme Strength up,

Supreme Growth, Minor Mental Resistance up, Greater Petrifying Gaze, Greater Acid Venom, Detect Concealment, Energy Breath, Superior Elemental Resistance, Fly, Puppet Maker, Body Possession, Magic Enhancement, Elemental Manipulation

Traits: Aura of Gluttony +8, Growth +13, Strong Willed, Venomous, Aquatic, Winged, Immunity to Mind Control

∞∞∞∞∞∞∞∞

I stared at the new addition to my personal screen and had to choke back the desire to scream. Just telling me about the title was one thing, but now I had to look at it every time I saw my status?

What kind of cruel bastard would implement that idea?

Interlude: Reunion

"**N**o!" Thor yelled. He was at Findral's side in a second, taking Ayla's body from her and setting her on the deck. "Did she— Is she?" he stammered. Thor hated himself for his weakness immediately.

"No," Findral shook her head. "She's breathing, if barely. She hit her head pretty hard when she landed, but she should be fine once Hali takes a look at her."

Thor felt himself sighing before he knew it. He tucked Ayla's head into his chest and held her while Hali started chanting in the strange language of the druids. As she spoke, Thor found himself reminded of the only druid he'd ever met before meeting Ayla. But the memory passed as quickly as it came, and he focused on Ayla. The entire process took only a few seconds, but it felt like an eternity to Thor. Holding onto Ayla's unconscious form, unable to do anything to help her…

Ayla sucked in a gasping breath and had a coughing fit as she tried and failed to sit up.

"Easy, easy Ayla. You're okay. You're safe, I got ya," Thor whispered into her ear, pulling her head deeper into his chest to ensure she couldn't accidentally hurt herself.

She tapped reassuringly on his shoulder, obviously grateful for the comfort he was giving her. A hand smacked Thor's forehead. "She can't breathe, you twit!" Hali yelled.

He released Ayla's head and she immediately shoved him away and sucked in several mouthfuls of air.

"What, was the concussion not enough for you so you decided to add asphyxiation on top of it?" Hali accused.

"Easy, Hali, he didn't mean it," Findral said.

"Yes, I—I didn't mean it. Ayla, I swear, I—"

"Am a dumbass?" Ayla's eyes were full of tears. She coughed into her hand several times, then tapped on Thor's arm. "Don't worry, dear. I'm well aware."

Thor helped her to her feet, making sure to hold onto her arm to keep her steady.

"How're you feeling, Ayla?" Hali asked. "Any dizziness? Nausea?"

"No, I'm fine. Thanks, Hali."

"Of course." Hali smiled at her.

Thor absently noticed that Hali was incredibly beautiful when she smiled.

"Just make sure not to let the oaf smother you the next time he gives you a hug, okay? You've been through a lot today. You don't need him adding any more trauma on top of it."

"Trauma?" Ayla asked. Then the light of recognition appeared in her eyes and she pushed her way free of Thor's arms. She stumbled over to the edge of the ship and gazed up at the gargantuan form of her monster—Er, father.

When he'd heard that Ayla had been taken in by such an… eccentric man when she was eleven, Thor had originally thought it was a joke. He came to believe otherwise after the numerous stories she spoke of, and the high praise she hoisted upon him. However, looking at him now, Thor was having a hard time picturing Torga as anything but a vicious monster.

It's difficult to put into words just how massive Torga was in his current form. Even from several miles away, his form cast an imposing shadow on the howling mountains: He was easily over two thousand feet long—possibly three thousand, the twin seventy-foot horns jutting out from the back of his skull and the thirty-foot-long horn on the tip of his snout made him look far more dragon-like than Thor was comfortable with.

Dragons were known to be cunning, manipulative, extremely powerful, and vicious enough to use that power at the slightest insult. They weren't "evil," but it wasn't uncommon for them to be described as such. And Torga? He was all of those things and more, because he appeared able to shrink himself at will. Ayla had once mentioned he was a tier seven creature. Thor vehemently disagreed. He'd killed tier sevens before, and Torga—he was no seven.

Boom!

Thor reacted quickly to the sound of cannon fire and dove on top of the three girls. They hit the desk and braced for impact. Those damn Jötnar might damage their vessel, but Thor was confident it could survive a single barrage. And then they would repay those bastards for every splinter.

"Hold your fire, hold your fire! It's one of ours," a familiar voice yelled.

"Eh?" Thor looked over his shoulder. The clouds were too thick at this altitude to see anything more than a large shadow moving towards them. The crew grew anxious. Under the orders of Thor's first mate Jaune, they prepared to defend the ship with their lives, if necessary.

"Bastards!" Hali yelled. She shoved against Thor's chest and fought to get back to her feet.

"No, wait a minute," Thor whispered to the girls. "Hold your fire!" He hollered to the rest of the crew. They were clearly confused. However, they'd long since learned to follow his orders without question.

Thor stood in front of the girls and cupped his hands around his mouth, "Heimdall! Is that you?" A pregnant silence came over them as they waited. A few minutes later, the nose of a colossal airship poked through the clouds on a collision course with their ship. Thor recognized it immediately. At six stories tall and over nine hundred feet long, Gungnir, The King of Asgard's personal ship and the spearhead of his army, appeared as if by magic.

Gungnir slowed to a stop within boarding distance. A heavy thump resounded through the ship as something heavy landed on the deck. That "something" turned out to be a large man with skin so pale, it was almost transparent. He stood to his full height of seven feet and pushed his shoulder length white hair behind his ears. His eyes lacked discernible pupils, but that meant little to Asgard's guardian.

"Ahoy there, Thor. Fancy seeing you here," Heimdall said in a calm tone. He stared unblinkingly ahead, as if he were blind. But nothing could be further from the truth. Thor knew Heimdall was observing anything and *everything* of note within miles around them.

"Heimdall, so you did make it." Thor approached the giant and held out his arm for him to shake. Heimdall ignored it.

"Most of those within the palace survived the initial assault. Your parents and siblings included."

"That's great news," Thor exclaimed. "What of the rest of Asgard? Surely we were able to evacuate them?"

"Some, but not all."

"Well, what're we waiting for? With my crew and Gungnir, we can easily retake Asgard."

"I—do not think that's an option anymore," Heimdall cryptically replied. He raised his hand and pointed into the distance.

Thor slowly turned around and gazed over the railing. Heimdall was pointing in the direction of Asgard, which was clear from the shining light piercing the clouds. But Thor wasn't sure what was stopping them from retaking Asgard. And then it became obvious. The clouds parted for miles ahead of them, no doubt due to Heimdall's magic, allowing Thor to see Asgard for the first time in months. Then he saw Torga and his heart fell.

Torga was floating above Asgard, completely untouched by the Jötnar ships that no doubt continued to attack him after Thor and his party retreated. His red eyes glowed ominously, even as his face and body were illuminated by the golden light of Asgard.

For a brief moment, Torga reminded Thor of one of the old legends: The tale of the serpent god Quetzalcoatl.

Without moving, without so much as twitching, Torga somehow ripped a third of Asgard from the main body. A few moments later, another third was ripped loose… Then, the whole of Asgard plummeted from the sky. Torga remained fixed in place, his eyes shining with a red light and what appeared to be steam trickling from his mouth as he breathed.

It was then that Thor realized how silly he was being. Torga was no god.

He was a demon.

CHAPTER ELEVEN

I SUCKED THE LAST PORTION OF THE DRAGON'S TAIL into my mouth and swallowed. Due to the sheer size of the dragon, my aura couldn't dissolve it fast enough for my schedule, so I finally managed to fill my stomach for the first time in—well, years.

I looked around for a few minutes and spotted a titanic sized airship hovering in the distance. *They haven't started shooting at me yet. Maybe Thor was right, and the Asgardians managed to make it.*

I flew towards the ship at a steady pace. When I was about halfway there, I activated the jewel and shrunk to my more manageable sixty feet. My eyes widened as I noticed a discrepancy. I was longer now, at least eighty feet long in this form. I cursed at the realization that I could grow so quickly now. *Just another thing I need to keep an eye out for.* I sighed.

Ding

ᢒᢒᢒᢒᢒᢒᢒᢒᢒᢒ

You have eaten the following race for the first time.

Ice Dragon: Tier 7

ᢒᢒᢒᢒᢒᢒᢒᢒᢒᢒ

I dismissed the pop-up a few minutes before I arrived at the airship. Originally, I'd planned to blow it out of the sky if it proved hostile: however, my fears were unfounded as I spotted Ayla and the others standing on the deck with Thor and some albino looking guy.

I thought about landing next to them, but remembering my new "gift," I decided against it altogether. I would have to hover until I could have a talk with Uriel about how to control my aura.

I inspected Ayla from a safe distance. Looking her up and down, I didn't spot any obvious injuries, though I was still concerned about internal injuries. I knew from experience that concussions, internal bleeding, and other deadly conditions didn't always have obvious signs. "How're you feeling, Brat?" I asked after a moment or two of no one saying anything. I looked around and noticed for the first time that half the crew weren't even looking at me, and the other half looked—hostile?

Hali looked uncomfortable, as if she wanted to be anywhere but here. While Findral gazed at me with sad eyes.

What's up with them?

"What have you done?" Ayla asked in a tone so low I had trouble hearing her.

"What do you mean? I killed the Jötnar, of course," I said. I was confused about what she expected me to say. I'd killed them for what they'd almost done to her. Wasn't that a good thing?

"No, that's not what you did," she uttered venomously. Tear-filled eyes landed on me, and I found myself almost wanting to move further away. The rage in her eyes was palpable, and for the first time in her life, that rage was directed at… me.

"Ayla, I don't think he understands," Findral muttered just loud enough for the five of us—six if you included the albino—to hear.

"Of course, he doesn't. He never does," she spat. "Where are the other Asgardians? Hmm?"

Thor mumbled something I didn't catch, but Ayla shot him down immediately. "No, I'll deal with this. You go spend time with your family."

"… You sure?" he asked. His voice was tinted with trepidation, but also something else. Anger, perhaps?

Why is everyone so pissed? I wondered.

"Yes," Ayla said, never once taking her hate-filled eyes off of me.

"I don't know what you're talking about—"

"Think about it for a minute. I'm sure it'll come to you."

"Now, Brat. I'm getting sick of your attitude—"

"They were inside Asgard!" she screamed. The fury in her voice made me move back a bit.

"What—No—the Jötnar said—"

"The Jötnar lied, like Thor told you he did. The Asgardians were being held prisoner inside Asgard as a way to draw the survivors into a trap. There are millions of people inside that city—sorry, there *were* millions of people inside that city."

The horrified realization of what she was saying hit me. At first, I didn't believe it—didn't *want* to believe it. But the more I thought about it, the more it made sense. I'd known that torture wasn't the most reliable method of getting information, exactly for this reason. But my own arrogance blinded me to the truth.

"Ayla, I—I'm sorry. I didn't mean for this to happen."

"You're sorry? Sorry won't rebuild their home. Sorry won't help these people survive the winter when this ship runs out of mana. Sorry won't bring their friends and family back." She hissed, growing louder and more irate with every addendum.

"Ayla, that's enough," Findral growled. She placed her hand on Ayla's shoulder and spun her around to face her. "He's apologized and explained what happened."

"Of course, you would side with him. He committed genocide, Fin. At this point, he's no better than the dragon that ate Granny—"Ayla's face was spun to the side as Findral's fist slammed into her cheek.

"Findral!" I yelled. A portion of my aura flared, briefly becoming visible to the naked eye. I forcefully shoved it down and grit my teeth. "That's enough, Fin. I appreciate you standing up for me, but Ayla is right. Intentional or not, I'm personally responsible for their deaths," I said in a softer tone. "And that's something I'll have to live with."

"Master…"

"Hali, any word of your family yet?"

"N—No. Not yet."

"I see. I'm going to go look for them," I told her.

"Thanks, Torga."

"Don't thank me, Hali." I sighed. Without another word, I angled my body away from the ship and dove towards the forest far beneath us.

~ ~ ~

It took several hours, but I finally found the crashed ship on the outskirts of the plateau. I created a platform out of stone and used it to haul them back up to the ship.

Fenris was rightfully pissed about the entire situation. After all, his family could've died in that crash. Luckily, the Asgardians didn't mess around when it came to the safety measures on their ships. The ship was ruined beyond repair, but everyone survived with only some scrapes, bruises, and soiled trousers to show for it.

"Hey, Fenris. Can I talk to you for a minute?" I said quietly.

"Yes, I did notice that you'd gained weight. Look, can this wait for a while? I'm tired and I'd like to take a bath—"

"I'm leaving."

Fenris' mouth closed immediately, and all traces of exhaustion left him. "Are you serious? You're really going through with it?"

"I don't have much of a choice, Mutt."

"There's always a choice to be made," he said emphatically. "You just haven't found the right one yet."

"Fenris—I—I can't touch any of you, not even accidentally." I twisted my tail around and brought it within ten feet of the railing. The wood disappeared in an instant, devoured by my aura. I had to quickly withdraw my tail before I did any real damage to the rest of the ship. A railing could be replaced, the hull—not so much. "That is what will happen to anything that comes within ten feet of me. You think I want that to happen to Ayla, to Findral, or any of your kids?"

Fenris looked uncomfortable at the showing. "There's ways around that. Uriel could whip up some enchantment to hold it at bay, or you could learn to control it on your own. This doesn't mean you have to leave, you fucking idiot."

"And in the meantime, am I just supposed to be extra careful not to accidentally kill one of you?" I muttered derisively. "I could barely control my hunger when I wasn't constantly consuming everything within ten feet of my body, and, newsflash, have you seen me lately? I can't even see my tail half the time because I'm so gods be damned *big*!" I hissed. "Face it, Mutt. I don't have many options, here."

"Are you going to tell the kids?"

"I'll make sure Findral knows. Hali and Solon too."

"But not Ayla?"

"Ayla—doesn't want to see me right now."

"Since when did you care what other people wanted? The snake I know would force her to listen, especially when it was over something this serious. You could die doing this, Torga. Are you really going to let whatever happened between the two of you be the last thing you ever say to her?" he finished quietly. "Think about it. I can't force you to speak to her, but it's the least you could do."

"Alright, I'll think about it." I sighed.

~ ∻ ~

Three hours later, I found myself hovering alongside the ship, since I couldn't land on it for fear of destroying it. I discarded all thoughts of throwing myself a pity party and focused on the task at hand: talking with the king and queen of Asgard and trying to save Ayla's engagement.

The queen, Lady Frigga, was calmly sitting in a chair someone had prepared for her, looking for all the world like some kind of supermodel in a thin white dress that exposed her shoulders. Her golden tresses hung loosely over her chest, while a golden helmet adorned with lifelike bird wings sat atop her head.

In stark contrast to the beautiful queen, the man standing behind her with his hands resting upon her slender shoulders was Odin: King of Asgard. He was a stern-looking man with short gray hair and a long silver beard. His right eye was covered by a strip of leather, though his other eye was the color of storm clouds. The king stood before me in a loose-fitting pair of tan trousers and a black shirt emblazoned with golden script that I had no chance of understanding.

They watched me the same way I watched them: warily, while waiting for the other shoe to drop and this all to blow up in our faces.

"You destroyed Asgard," Odin stated in a controlled tone.

"Accidentally," I corrected.

"Heimdall tells me, and I quote, that you "destroyed the structural integrity of the mountain by diving through it, causing it to fall out of the sky.""

I looked off to the side where Heimdall—the albino from earlier—was standing. He shot me a thumbs up, then went back to staring at nothing.

I've already killed millions of Asgardians. One more won't matter much, will it? I sighed to myself. "Yes, well. I had a moment of insanity." I noticed the way they were looking at me and hastened to add, "Oh, I'm not making excuses. I fully admit that I'm the one responsible, even have the title to prove it." I sighed again, this time aloud. "Look, you don't owe me anything. But don't blame Ayla for my mistakes. She's a good kid who was dealt a shitty hand, that's all."

Odin and Frigga glanced at each other, an entire conversation passing between them with just a series of eyebrow movements. I know this to be the case because Sarah and I were like that. *Sarah, what would you think of me now? Would you love "the Destroyer" or would you despise him for being the monster that he is?*

"If people blamed my mistakes on my children, I would never see them married," Odin said somberly. "You have my word, serpent. She will not be blamed for Asgard's destruction. I'll ensure that, personally."

I exhaled a breath I hadn't realized I was holding. "Thanks…" I released the full weight of my magic upon the ship. "*You know what will happen if you're lying, yes?*" I hissed.

"Of course," Odin replied. He stepped around his wife, placing his body between me and her and squaring his shoulders. The man was unarmed and armor less, but he didn't so much as flinch when our gazes locked. "You'll kill us. I would do the same, were I in your position."

I nodded my agreement. "Glad we're on the same page."

"There is one thing you could do for us, to—help ensure she isn't blamed."

"And what might that be?"

"Leave," Odin said simply. "Leave today, and don't come back."

~ ~ ~

Early the next morning I silently floated away from Gungnir. I'd said my goodbyes to Fenris and his family, and it went about as well as I expected.

I'd thought about biding my time and waiting for the moment I was absolutely sure Ayla was safe before I left. But truth be told, I was the most dangerous person here, and not in a good way. The longer I stayed, the more danger everyone was in. Better I leave now, before I screwed up and hurt someone I actually cared about.

For all the bad my situation caused, I had to admit, it was entertaining in a way. The Asgardian's reactions were especially humorous. While most of them seemed to hate me for destroying their home, a select few would send me slight smiles and nods whenever they saw me. I'd heard from Uriel the Asgardians of old were a war crazed bunch that respected strength and honor in battle above all else. Guess some of them still possessed that mentality, even if it meant throwing praise to the one who destroyed your home and killed your people.

I glanced at the ship, then at my companion and nodded my head. "I'm ready, Fin. Remember, look out for yourself, and for Ayla."

"Yes, master. I will protect Ayla with my life," Findral replied solemnly

"No, Fin. I said take care of yourself and Ayla. The two of you are the closest thing to family I've got in this world. I don't know what I'd do if I lost either of you."

"I—see. I will endeavor to follow your orders, master."

I shook my head. "This isn't an order. You're free. You can do whatever you want from this moment forward."

Findral was quiet for a long minute. So long, I had to turn around to check if she was still there. She was. She looked at me with deep sadness in her eyes. "If I'm free to do whatever I want, then—I'll wait for your return, Torga."

I didn't know what to say to that, so I just nodded my head.

"I… I accept the King's Challenge." I waited for a moment to see what would happen, but nothing—

∞∞∞∞∞∞∞∞

You have accepted the King's Challenge.

∞∞∞∞∞∞∞∞

I stared blankly at the gray box for a moment, then had to shake away my surprise at the pop-up. *That's a new color.*

∞∞∞∞∞∞∞∞

You will now be transported to the Serpent home system.

Goals—If you fail any of these, then your right of succession will be declined by the gods and death will be your only reward.

- Reach the 10th tier before your confrontation with the king.

- Slay the 8 Royal Serpents.

- Slay the king.

- Survive.

Your transmission has begun.

∞∞∞∞∞∞∞∞

I waved away the window and looked back at Findral one last time. "Tell Ayla I'll be back before the wedding."

"You better be. She'll never forgive you if you miss it."

I felt a coldness enter my mind. One minute I was looking at Findral, floating in the skies of Asgard with a gargantuan rainbow as a backdrop. The next thing I knew, I was standing in the middle of nine stone pillars on a planet with an amethyst sky. I couldn't see any stars or moons in the sky, though from the looks of things I didn't need them. The atmosphere was bright enough on its own. A blizzard was raging around me, preventing me from seeing anything beyond the pillars.

I reached out with my tail and pushed past the largest stone pillar, expecting my tail to carve out a path through the storm. However, I immediately felt a searing pain race up my tail instead. I yanked it back inside the circle and inspected it for damage. Luckily, I didn't see any scaring or burns. Just a patch of ice where the storm touched my scales.

My aura isn't working?

∞∞∞∞∞∞∞∞

Warning!
You've entered the territory of Orochi, the Serpent King.

This territory is in a time dilated zone as dictated by the gods. As such, time passes at a rate of 10,000:1.

As you are the challenger, you are henceforth barred from leaving this area until the moment of your death—or your crowning.

You have been deposited inside the only Neutral Zone in the system. All skills and traits have been temporarily disabled. Once you leave this place, you may not re-enter on your own.

∞∞∞∞∞∞∞∞

I groaned after reading the warning, then waved it away. *Well, at least I shouldn't miss Ayla's wedding... Unless I die, anyway.*

Chapter Twelve

M Y NEUTRAL ZONE WAS MARKED BY A CIRCLE of nine pillars: eight small and one large. I assumed this was to indicate the eight royal serpents and the king, respectively. Moving closer to the pillars, I noticed that each one had a name engraved upon its surface in a language I didn't recognize but could somehow read anyway. *Orochi, Amatzin, Naunet, Shabaka, Unger, Sereath, Rajah, Dragar, and Urosh.*

I circled the zone several times before finally settling in front of one of the smaller pillars, the one with the name Urosh carved into its surface. "I guess you're first." I placed my head against the pillar and was instantly teleported away.

I found myself in the Bi-frost with a pop-up in front of me.

∞∞∞∞∞∞∞∞

You have arrived at your destination, Planet Ushillon: Territory of Urosh, the Royal Naga
Goals:

- Find and Slay Urosh.

- Survive.

Rewards: Naga Form

∞∞∞∞∞∞∞∞

Naga?

Though I'd traveled across a fair portion of Yggdrasil, I had never encountered a Naga personally. They were apparently quite rare, as even Fenris and Lena had only encountered a handful in their lifetimes. Because of this, I was somewhat eager to see what they were like and what abilities they possessed.

The portal opened and I was temporarily blinded by the bright light that followed. I clamped my eyes shut and waited for the translocation process to finish before opening my eyes.

A deep musty smell assaulted my senses as I was released from the portal. The air was incredibly humid, and I could feel my lungs struggling to keep me sufficiently supplied with oxygen. Then came the feeling of constantly being dragged down. The gravity on this world was making it slightly more difficult to move, which made me thankful for my body's natural strength. Were I any weaker, I may not have been able to move at all.

I found myself in something of a tropical rainforest, with tall trees approaching two-hundred feet in height with a deep blue bark. Their massive drooping leaves spread out as far as the eye could see and served to shade the ground from the intense light of the twin suns. Flying reptiles dotted the sky as they flew in groups both large and small. And in the distance, I could just make out a medium-sized stone structure carved into the side of a mountain. *Might as well start there.*

Along the way, I decided to have myself a little wildlife safari/snack combo as I passed by several watering holes used by the local wildlife. A twenty-foot-long purple reptile with four short legs that kept it close

to the ground, a long spiked tail, and two large, white horns on either side of its head was the first to be eaten.
Ding

∞∞∞∞∞∞∞∞

You've eaten the following race for the first time.

Horned Croc: Tier 5

∞∞∞∞∞∞∞∞

It was followed by several ten-foot-tall tortoises that walked around on their hind legs. They had thick yellow frills around their necks, two sets of eyes on either side of their noses, and if my observation was correct, they could shoot acid out of the mounds on their shoulders. However, this failed to help them once I had them wrapped up and was crushing the life out of them.
Ding

∞∞∞∞∞∞∞∞

You've eaten the following race for the first time.

Acid Cannon Lizard: Tier 4

∞∞∞∞∞∞∞∞

The creatures on this planet are a little weird. They taste pretty good, though. The acid gives it a nice spicy flavoring, and they have enough meat on them to satisfy me for a little while.

While moving through the forest, I noticed that as I drew closer to my target, the size of the creatures decreased, while the tier increased.
Ding

∞∞∞∞∞∞∞∞

You've eaten the following race for the first time.

Spring Bat: Tier 6

∞∞∞∞∞∞∞∞

A red lizard with a six-foot wingspan, it had eight short tentacles instead of legs, which it used to bounce from tree to tree before opening its wings and gliding through the sky. These creatures were also extremely aggressive. I was attacked several times by swarms of them, though apart from their attitudes, they seemed to be relatively harmless—to me, anyway.

The way they attacked was also interesting. They would use the little spikes that covered the inside of their tentacles to find purchase in the "soft" meat of their prey, then they would use their clawed hands to rip out chunks of flesh.

However, my scales were so tough the bats simply had no way of holding on. I manipulated the air around me to blast them out of the sky, then I'd let my aura deal with them. *It's almost like an all-you-can-eat bat buffet.*

Branches breaking caused me to look up in time to see a mass of silver metal falling towards me. As the metal broke the ten-foot mark, it was ripped apart atom by atom and consumed by my aura.

What the hell was that?
Ding

∞∞∞∞∞∞∞∞

You've eaten the following race for the first time.

Armored Gecko: Tier 6

∞∞∞∞∞∞∞∞

I spent a few minutes scanning the treetops for any other armored geckos, and watched as they hunted. They were four feet long and had dark green scales and a single yellow eye on a two-foot stalk. I assumed they climbed high into the treetops and waited for something to pass beneath them, then did a freefall onto their target, killing or at the very least severely wounding it. However, if it seemed as if its prey could survive the initial impact or somehow dodge it, the gecko was more than happy to leave them alone. Unless they passed beneath them again.

But the creature that most surprised me was actually another serpent.

ᖳᖰᖳᖰᖳᖰᖳᖰᖳᖰ

You've eaten the following race for the first time.

Cursed King Serpent: Tier 8

ᖳᖰᖳᖰᖳᖰᖳᖰᖳᖰ

This two-foot-long blood-red serpent had nine eyes that completely surrounded its hooded head and an oval-shaped mouth that it used to latch onto its prey and quite literally suck the life out of them. But the thing that made me glad my aura had a ten-foot radius and could dissolve them from a distance, was the effect the creature had on the ground as it moved. The ground would turn pitch-black and dissolve into nothing just seconds after the tiny serpent passed by.

Creepy little things. I involuntarily shivered.

Three hours later, I arrived at the base of the mountain and began to scout out the area. I searched in and around the base for any entry points I could make use of, but despite my efforts I found nothing of the sort.

The only way up that I could see was a carved staircase that went up the side of the mountain and to the front entrance of the building, which severely limited my options for sneaking in. *Of course, I could just blast the door down and be done with it.* I tilted my head from side to side as I weighed the pros and cons of each choice. Then I remembered one flaw to my plan: my aura. Even now it was busily dissolving the ground beneath me at such a rate I had to constantly move, or I'd find myself in a hole deeper than I was long.

"Have you seen any sign of them?" a raspy voice asked.

"Oh, yeah I did. I invited them over for tavoa milk and spring bat strips last night—Of course, I haven't! Don't you think I would've said something if I had?" a higher pitched voice asked sarcastically.

I turned my head in the direction of the voice and saw two serpents bickering just inside the tree line. They were between fifteen and twenty feet long, though unlike my own body, they possessed a torso reminiscent of a human.

That's a Naga?

Thin scales covered the visible parts of their body, and two long fangs peeked out from beneath their upper lips. They had different colored scales, one being a deep red, the other a pale green, and while the red naga was completely bald, the other had black hair cut close to the scalp.

I pushed off the ground and started following them through the air, using my wings to remain high above the treetops. I followed them for a few minutes while they headed away from the building. As they were moving in an expanding counterclockwise patrol route, I knew they would stumble upon my trail eventually. I landed on the ground a dozen or so feet away from them and waited for the right time to strike.

"What's this, then?"

And that's my cue. I sent three stone spears into the green Naga's body: one in the pelvis, one in the stomach, and one through the throat. However, it didn't immediately die from the ambush and was able to warn the red snake-man before I could attack again, killing him with a stone spear through the center of his face.

"Red" quickly twisted around and pulled a short wooden bow off his back, nocked an arrow, loosed it in the span of a second. The arrow shot towards my face, presumably aiming for the pits on my nose.

I didn't bother to move out the way, trusting my aura to deal with it for me. The arrows dissolved the moment they entered my range.

The naga tsked. He pulled three arrows from the quiver on his hip and rapid fired them at me.

The first was dissolved easily enough, but my eyes widened when I saw the second and third arrows curve midflight, passing just outside of my aura's range. They tore through anything in their way: Plants, vines, even a lone tree was ripped in half as the arrow passed through its trunk.

I tracked the arrows as they made yet another sharp turn and shot at my back. *Getting hit by those might actually hurt.* I decided to use wind to redirect the arrows instead of letting my aura take care of it. I didn't want to risk getting injured this early in the game.

The wind knocked the arrows off course, forcing them into the ground where they buried themselves so deeply, I couldn't see them anymore.

Red nocked six arrows simultaneously and fired; two arrows curved around to the right, two curved to the left, while the last two arrows tore through my wind defense and bounced off my nose. Though it was dissolved a second later, I was still surprised it managed to touch me at all.

"I've got you now," Red said confidently as he nocked six more arrows.

"Yeah, about that." Hundreds of pounds of stone shot up and coiled around the naga, preventing him from releasing his arrows. "That's my line."

"You—" A rock shot out of the ground and smashed into his forehead. His head lolled against the stone bands for a moment while his body slumped.

I flicked my tongue a few times. Though not required, using my heat sensing skill was always easier this way. After half a dozen flicks, I didn't detect anyone nearby, so I moved past the dead green naga, allowing my aura to devour his body as I went, and approached Red.

Ding

∞∞∞∞∞∞∞∞

You've eaten the following race for the first time.

Naga: Tier 6

∞∞∞∞∞∞∞∞

I dismissed the pop-up as quickly as it came. I already had some idea of how powerful a naga was. After all, I'd had the opportunity to become one, once upon a time.

I studied Red's form from a distance of twelve feet and came to one conclusion—I should've picked naga all those years ago. Disregarding everything else, the naga had one clear advantage over my current form: arms. They had a pair of thickly muscled arms that ended in three-fingered hands. Red's hands also had short nails. I would hesitate to call them claws due to how dull they looked, but I wasn't going to discount them yet. Maybe keeping them short was a personal preference?

After circling around him a few times and inadvertently creating a small clearing, I found myself with a slight problem. How the hell was I supposed to create a puppet if I couldn't touch them?

I couldn't exactly experiment here, either. Once the Naga's body was gone, that's it. I'd have to hunt down another one and who knew if I could knock it out? Knowing my luck the way I did, something would happen and I'd end up killing it by accident.

I had to test my abilities on something, but what?

Boom!

The sounds of breaking tree branches accompanied by a heavy thud caused me to look away from the naga. I spotted an armored gecko crawling out of a crater in the ground about a hundred or so feet away, and a horde of spring bats attacking it.

Well, looks like I found myself some volunteers. I focused my magic on the stone bands and lifted them, and the naga, into the air. Then I carried the naga deeper into the forest. There was an inexhaustible number of test subjects just jumping at the chance to help me, so why deny them that chance?

The spring bats spotted me and threw a fit about my presence in "their" territory. They divebombed me with their tentacles spread wide, and their nasty looking nails flexed.

Chapter Thirteen

Yet another group of spring bats dissolved into nothing as I failed for the sixth time in a row to activate my puppet maker ability. *That was what, forty or fifty bats, and twenty geckos I'd already tried to turn into puppets?*

"Are ya daft, or just stupid? I dunno what you're attempting to do but give it a rest already."

I let out an annoyed sigh and swiveled to look at the immobilized naga. "The only reason you're still alive is that I keep failing. Keep it up, and I'll eat you just to get it over with."

"Bah, who cares? I was dead the moment I failed to stop ya," Red sneered. "Besides, I know my death will be avenged. No one can defeat his majesty."

"Fair enough," I allowed. I focused my magic on the plants around us, then flung some vines at Red's snout. They wrapped around his head nice and tight, then shrunk even further to ensure he couldn't speak.

No way was I about to let such a fine day be ruined by that kind of negativity.

I dragged Red around the forest for another two and a half hours before I became too frustrated to continue. Nothing was working. I'd tried suppressing my aura, pulling the bats close before my aura could touch them, pushing them away before my aura could grab them, and every other idea I could think of.

It was maddening.

"Well, looks like your time just ran out." Red rolled his eyes and gave me a "get on with it" look, so I did. I tried one last time to activate my puppet maker skill as I prepared to close the gap between us.

Ding!*Ding!*Ding!

I had time to glance at the pop-ups before the pain started. An earth-shattering, mind-breaking kind of pain that I couldn't describe if I'd spent my entire life obsessing over a thesaurus.

∞∞∞∞∞∞∞

Warning!! Incoming series of notifications!!

You have consumed the necessary 100 souls required to unlock the Dark Serpent evolution.

Calculating. . .

Warning! Corruption detected!

Attempting to rebuild profile.

Profile reconstruction complete.

∞∞∞∞∞∞∞

Then my hearing left me, the world going silent as the grave for a full ten seconds before my vision left me in a void of nothingness. I'm sure I passed out, but I had no way of knowing for how long.

However, upon waking up I found myself inside an evolutionary shell, which was weird because I didn't remember agreeing to evolve. I ripped my way out of the shell and collapsed onto my stomach. Residual pain and exhaustion had left me a quivering mess on the floor of a dark room.

I used what little strength I had to study my surroundings. Baskets of dried fruits, racks of meat, and smallish clay pots lay scattered around.

Was I in some kind of storage area? Had the jewel somehow managed to remain active the entire time?
Ding*Ding

∞∞∞∞∞∞∞

Your evolution is complete!

∞∞∞∞∞∞∞

Congratulations! You have done what only three others have ever managed to do: Become a Dark Serpent.

The Dark Serpent, otherwise known as the "Demon Serpent or the First Demon, is a creature of ancient power. This race is believed to be responsible for the corruption, and eventual fall, of the angels.

There have only been three Dark Serpents in history, and all of them were attacked and killed before they could control their power.

This race is the natural enemy of the gods because only this race possesses the ability to consume the vital essence that all gods need to maintain their power.

For attaining this evolution, you have been bestowed the title of "The Dark Serpent."

You are now the enemy of the gods, and none shall come to your aid.

However, with great risk comes great reward.

A new menu has been created for you.

Warning!

Some of your skills may have changed.

∞∞∞∞∞∞∞

Ding
Oh, no.

∞∞∞∞∞∞∞

You have been granted the Supreme Divinity Resistance skill and the Divine Consumer trait due to your evolution into a Dark Serpent.

∞∞∞∞∞∞∞∞∞

Ding!
No, please stop…

∞∞∞∞∞∞∞∞∞

Due to a combination of traits, a trait has evolved!
Divine Gluttonous Aura: Due to Aura of Gluttony +8 evolving into Aura of Gluttony +12, and factoring in your new race's dietary needs, the Aura of Gluttony trait, and the Divine Consumer trait have combined to create the Divine Gluttonous Aura trait.
Note: This is always active

∞∞∞∞∞∞∞∞∞

No, no, no, no, NO!

∞∞∞∞∞∞∞∞∞

You have been granted the Forever Growing trait due to becoming a Dark Serpent.

∞∞∞∞∞∞∞∞∞

Stop it, please!

∞∞∞∞∞∞∞∞∞

Name: Torga

Race: Gluttonous Dark Serpentine Dragon

Classification: Tier 7

Level: 86

Kenneth Arant

Experience: 942,810 / 1,000,000

Titles: Destroyer of Asgard, The Dark Serpent

Stats:

- Physical
    - Strength: 2,048
- Endurance: 2,048
    - Dexterity: 25
    - Speed: 11
- Mental:
    - Intelligence: 51
    - Wisdom: 36
    - Charisma: 19
- Resistances
    - Elements: 60%
    - Divinity: 80%
    - Mental: 20%
- Immunities
    - Mind Control

Skills: Major Stealth, Heat Detection, Supreme Gluttony, Supreme Growth, Greater Petrifying Gaze, Greater Acid Venom, Detect Concealment, Energy Breath, Fly, Magic Enhancement, Elemental Manipulation

Traits: Divine Gluttonous Aura +13, Growth +20, Strong Willed, Venomous, Aquatic, Winged, Forever Growing

∞∞∞∞∞∞∞∞

Why? I asked anyone who would listen. I didn't *want* this, I didn't *want* my gluttonous trait to grow stronger, I didn't *want* my menu to change, and I *certainly* didn't want the damn Forever Growing trait! I was fucking big enough as it was. Enough is *enough.* I struggled to move my body, but weakness permeated every fiber of my being. I stopped moving and just laid there, in the darkness of this room, and struggled to find a reason not to just give up and die. Wouldn't take long, I could already feel my upgraded hunger clawing away at my insides.

What difference does it make if I go on or not? It's not like anyone really cares about me or will miss me when I'm gone. "If I'm free to do whatever I want, then— I'll wait for your return, Torga."

I sighed. *What the hell am I doing? Since when was this me?* I made up my mind to try again. It took several attempts, but I managed to crawl forward a few inches. Those few inches turned into a few feet as my aura ate away at my surroundings, slowly refilling my empty reserves and giving me the energy I needed to move.

Though, I soon found myself with another problem: stairs… a lot of stairs.

I just had to be in the fucking basement, didn't I?

After reaching the top of the staircase, I found myself in the center of a big arena. The ceiling had a large opening that allowed the natural light of the twin suns to filter in. Before me was a sea of naga. Men and women of all shapes, sizes, and colors sat in chairs that lined the outer edges of the arena. Seeing as the arena was something like four hundred feet tall, the number of naga required to fill the seats of this place was staggering.

But they'd done it. There didn't appear to be an empty seat in the house. It reminded me of a football stadium from back home.

In the center of the arena, on a raised dais made of white bones, I saw a thin naga with pure white scales and purple lines crisscrossing his body. A large oval garnet sat in the center of his forehead.

I'm guessing that's Urosh. Did he get the idea for this place out of some evil overlord's handbook? I wondered after seeing the throne, the arena, and his appearance. It looked like something an edgy teenager would come up with.

"The intruder is here," Urosh said in a slow drawl. His words caused an uproar as the several thousand naga began chanting at the top of their lungs. **"Urosh, Urosh, Urosh!"**

Urosh lifted himself off of his "throne" and came down the three steps to the ground, where he began advancing on me. "You've kept me waiting, challenger. Who gave you permission to evolve before introducing yourself to me? Do you know the difficulties I had to endure in order to bring you here?"

"Look, I'm really not in the mood for banter, so how about we cut to the chase and just get to the part where I kill you and leave. Sound fair?"

Urosh continued to advance but didn't say anything.

"Yeah, I didn't think so." I canceled out the effects of my jewel and watched as first surprise, then anger came over Urosh's face when I rapidly left his weight class.

While I expanded, anything unlucky enough to be grabbed by my aura was instantly devoured. Hundreds of naga perished in the span of a few seconds, with more following when I quickly surpassed the arena's ability to hold me.

My tail burst through the rear wall, as my body continued to elongate.

Ding!

ထထထထထထထ

Strength: +380

Endurance: +380

ထထထထထထထ

Huh? I stared at the unexpected pop-up. I didn't understand what it meant. Was it some kind of warning or was it simply telling me of a change to my status? I didn't feel any different but maybe that was normal?

"I'm down here," Urosh drawled. His voice was so quiet I could barely hear him at my current size. I had to redo my sense enchantment in order to hear the rest of what he was saying.

"Have you come to surrender?" he asked. "It will be quick and relatively painless."

"No thanks."

"That's a shame." Urosh looked to either side of me and simply said, *"Kill him,"* in a voice much deeper than earlier.

I glanced around at the fleeing naga and wondered who he could've been talking to. Surely not the ones fleeing for their lives?

"Die!" A shrill scream tore through the air.

I looked in the direction of the voice and saw half a dozen naga forcing their way through the crowds to get into the arena. They backhanded, punched, threw, and otherwise beat anyone attempting to flee. The surprising part was the fact that it was working. Six naga were somehow forcing several *thousand* of their kinsmen to turn around and charge at me.

"Are you truly going to sacrifice them?" I asked Urosh over the sound of his subjects' screaming. He gave me a bored look and began moving in the direction of his dais. "Don't you feel anything for them? They're going to die, you know?" The first few naga slammed into my aura and were dissolved.

Ding

∞∞∞∞∞∞∞∞

Strength: +5

Endurance: +5

∞∞∞∞∞∞∞∞

"Don't say I didn't warn you."

A seemingly unending stream of naga ran into my aura bubble, killing themselves while trying to reach me. I'd foolishly thought after the first few, they'd catch the hint and would run away. If anything, they grew more zealous.

Ding,*Ding,*Ding,*Ding

For every naga that passed through my aura bubble, the number on the pop-up grew larger, soon exceeding two thousand for both "stats."

I knew I could've stopped them at any time. I could've conjured a hundred-foot-high wall, or a valley so deep and wide they couldn't cross. But honestly, why should I? If Urosh didn't care enough to call them off, and they were too stupid to stop on their own, they deserved to become food.

For three minutes I waited while the naga threw themselves to their deaths, and at the end of it all, was a pop-up.

ᏮᏮᏮᏮᏮᏮᏮᏮ

Strength: +3,428

Endurance: +3,428

Growth: +2

ᏮᏮᏮᏮᏮᏮᏮᏮ

"You killed my subjects," Urosh said, seemingly unconcerned with the events of the last few minutes.

"Don't worry, I'll kill you too—" My mouth slammed shut as Urosh waved a hand, and a stone pillar almost as large as I was slammed into my face. I felt a sharp pain in my mouth, followed by a warm liquid pooling at the back of my throat.

The bastard had made me bite off the tip of my tongue.

I landed hard on my back, then a second pillar hit me from the side hard enough to send me spinning through the air. I crashed through the wall of the arena and was met by a third pillar that knocked me higher into the air. Before I even began to fall, a fourth pillar came out of nowhere to send me flying away from the arena.

I crashed into the forest several hundred feet away from where I'd started. I tried to move, but the only thing to rise was the stomach fluids I puked up. *Okay—that hurt.* I groaned.

When I finally stopped puking, I looked up and saw Urosh crouched in front of me with a disappointed look on his face. "Pity, I hoped you would've lasted longer than this." He said in that same slow drawl.

"You know what? You're right. I should have taken this seriously from the beginning."

"You believe that would've made a difference?"

"Oh, I guarantee it. Allow me to demonstrate." I snapped off a beam of magic that hit Urosh in the chest. It only knocked him back a step, but I followed that up with a pillar of my own.

Driven by the sixty-foot-long pillar, Urosh flew three hundred feet to crash into the side of the mountain. He pushed the pillar to the side, and was immediately met by two more pillars of stone, followed by me launching myself at him.

I crashed into him with as much force as I could muster. However, instead of slamming him against the mountain like I'd planned, my aura allowed us to pass through the tough stone without interruption. We hit the ground on the other side of the mountain and rolled away from each other.

Urosh struggled to right himself on his own for a few moments, before finally giving in and sinking his fingers into the bark of a nearby tree, which he used to get up. "You'll pay for that," he hissed.

"Like I haven't heard that before," I groaned as I righted myself.

Urosh raised a hand above his head, and two things happened simultaneously: The sky darkened, and crimson light began pouring from his open palm. The light rose into the sky and began to saturate the atmosphere until it also turned crimson.

"Congratulations. Making me want to use this skill is something to take pride in of. Your ancestors should not be ashamed." The crimson light flashed, and a bolt of electricity tore through me. I bit back a scream, instead letting out a pain-filled grunt. I laid flat on my stomach and clenched my eyes shut.

I tried to muster my defenses by raising a barrier of stone around my head, but a second bolt hit me, this time directly on my tail. The bolt was powerful enough to leave me twitching for several seconds.

A third bolt hit me almost as soon as the second one finished. I tried to coil into a ball, but my body would not obey me.

A fourth bolt hit me a heartbeat later. This one left a line of searing pain across my back and I screamed.

The fifth and sixth bolts hit in rapid-fire succession, scorching my scales, and pushing me deeper into the ground. I don't know whether it was the pain or the fear that I might actually die that caused it, but my mind suddenly became crystal clear. I knew what I needed to do. The question was if I could do it without dying.

A seventh bolt hit me, and I felt my vulnerable insides being turned into extremely vulnerable outsides.

I angled by body towards the sky, coiled my tail beneath me, then launched myself high into the air. I spread my wings and flew directly into the storm clouds above. I sucked in a deep breath, and felt my aura pull in a large chunk of the surrounding clouds.

I hovered in place for a few more seconds, taking deep breaths and hoping my aura could steal as much as possible.

Ding

∞∞∞∞∞∞∞∞

You have unlocked the following evolutionary path: Gluttonous Draconic Naga

Would you like to evolve?

∞∞∞∞∞∞∞∞∞

"Yes!" I hissed.

∞∞∞∞∞∞∞∞∞

Your evolution is underway, and a shield has formed around you until it is complete. Time remaining until completion is 25 years, 11 months, 31 days, 23 hours. 59 minutes, 52 seconds.

∞∞∞∞∞∞∞∞∞

I felt my body crash to the earth shortly after my evolution began, and I immediately blacked out from the pain.

CHAPTER FOURTEEN

I CAME TO WITH A START. MY EYES WERE BURNING something awful, and I had no idea why. I twisted my body to the side, causing the shell around me to shatter like so much broken glass. I immediately began looking for Urosh. I doubted he had gotten far. He'd seemed pretty intent on killing me—

Ding,*Ding,*Ding

∞∞∞∞∞∞∞

Your evolution is complete!

∞∞∞∞∞∞∞

Oh, boy. I don't have time for this. Urosh could be lying in wait around any corner.

∞∞∞∞∞∞∞

Name: Torga

Race: Gluttonous Dark Draconic Naga

Classification: Tier 8

Level: 89

Experience: 476,912/ 4,000,000

Titles: Destroyer of Asgard, The Dark Serpent

Stats:

Kenneth Arant

- Physical
    - Strength: 5,861
    - Endurance: 5,861
    - Dexterity: 30
    - Speed: 13
- Mental:
    - Intelligence: 52
    - Wisdom: 37
    - Charisma: 20
- Resistances
    - Elements: 60%
    - Divinity: 80%
    - Mental: 20%
- Immunities
    - Mind Control

Skills: Major Stealth, Heat Detection, Supreme Gluttony, Supreme Growth, Greater Petrifying Gaze, Greater Acid Venom, Detect Concealment, Energy Breath, Fly, Magic Enhancement, Elemental Manipulation

Traits: Divine Gluttonous Aura +15, Growth +20, Strong Willed, Venomous, Aquatic, Winged, Forever Growing

∞∞∞∞∞∞∞∞∞

Congratulations!

You have successfully killed Urosh: The Royal Naga and taken his title from him.

+5,500,000 experience

Warning!
As you already possess the Naga form, you have been granted 50 bonus stat points to insert wherever you'd like.
Please climb to the next Royal Serpent territory.
Warning: The system will be locked for you until your journey is complete.

∞∞∞∞∞∞∞∞

"Wait... What?" I reread the pop-ups several times, then looked around for any sign of Urosh. Only instead of finding him, I found a destroyed wasteland where the forest used to be.
What happened to this place?
Ding

∞∞∞∞∞∞∞∞

With Urosh's death, this world has returned to the way it was before the King's Challenge began.
Xitara
An earth element world: This world has been ruined due to (@^$@%&). Because of this, it has been cut off from the greater Yggdrasil.
Warning! Now that your evolution is complete and following Urosh's death, this world has begun to collapse. Estimated time until collapse: 4 days, 7 hours, 12, minutes.

∞∞∞∞∞∞∞∞

"Okay, I know I'm repeating myself. What. The. Fuck. Is. Going. On? How did Urosh die?"

There was a long pause where nothing happened, then…***Ding***

∞∞∞∞∞∞∞∞

Urosh: Royal Naga

Cause of death: Extreme mana depletion due to contact with a parasite.

∞∞∞∞∞∞∞∞

"Parasite? What parasite could've—Wait, are you talking about me? Am I the parasite?" The pop-ups didn't respond. "Hello! Am I the parasite? Come on, you had no issue with insulting me a second ago, but now you're being bashful? Since when could you insult people anyway?" Despite my ranting, the pop-up didn't respond again.

I ranted for a few more minutes before I started looking for a way off this damn rock. However, as I lifted my torso off the ground for the first time, I felt something fall away from me.

I panicked and quickly looked down to see what horrible disfigurement I had to live with. Except, what I saw was two sets of thickly corded arms: One set extending out from my shoulders, which I was happy to have again. While the other set came out from my ribs. They ended in heavily scaled three-fingered hands hanging loosely by my side.

I—have arms? "Holy shit, I have arms!?" I twisted my torso back and forth several times and found myself giggling at the slapping sound the arms—MY arms— made as they hit my body. It was one of the stupidest things I'd ever done, and I wouldn't change it for the world. Sure, I would've felt obligated to kill myself if Ayla or Findral had seen me, but they weren't here… Right. They weren't here.

I pushed that line of thinking into the deepest pits of my mind. I couldn't afford to dwell on that, or on how I was completely and totally alone for the first time in over a decade. *Wasn't I supposed to be doing something right about now?*

I briefly wondered how I looked but couldn't find it in me to care at the moment. I still had my wings, I still had both eyes, and I had two shiny new sets of arms. I was practically golden.

I found myself before the branch a few hours later. I was large enough now that the branch, which I knew to have an average diameter of fifty feet, was smaller than the palm of my hand. In fact, I could probably use the branch as a climbing rope if I wanted to.

I reached out to touch it with my head—to activate the Bi-frost and zoom away to the next Royal Serpent.

But nothing happened.

That was when I recalled something I'd dismissed earlier. *"Please climb to the next Royal Serpent territory." That's what it said, right. But—surely it's not expecting me to actually climb the branch.* I followed the branch with my eyes as it went up, and up, and up… I sighed as I realized that was exactly what it wanted me to do. *Climbing rope, huh? You just had to fucking say it, didn't you?* I tentatively lifted one of my arms and wrapped my fingers around the pliable flesh of the branch. I gave it a few experimental tugs, then flexed the muscles in my arm and attempted to lift myself off the ground. The branch held strong, more than that even. It didn't sway or budge under my weight.

Which made sense now that I thought about it. It was used to holding up planets, and no matter how big I was, I was nowhere near that level. So, I began to climb in earnest. Left, right, left, right, left—this pattern saw me scaling the branch like I was the fat kid in bootcamp.

For close to an hour I climbed, and the higher I got, the more I noticed the falling temperature and thinning air.

Frost began to accumulate on my scales and permeate my body, making me sluggish and shortening the time between breaks.

Foot after foot and mile after mile, I wavered, but never fell. I took breaks as necessary by wrapping my tail around the branch a few dozen times to hold myself in place, giving my arms a much-needed rest.

Breathing became far more difficult once I'd made it into the upper atmosphere. As luck would have it, whoever designed this FUBAR of a challenge at least had the decency to create a ten-foot-deep bubble around the branch through which oxygen was present.

It was so thin I was constantly on the verge of passing out, but it was there.

Aside from the bubble of air around the branch, nothing out here supported life of any kind. Which meant no oxygen, no water, and most importantly for me, it meant there was nothing to eat.

Aside from maybe the branch itself... No, I don't know what would happen if I tried to eat Yggdrasil. Surely the next territory won't be that far away, right? Maybe if I hurry, I can make it there before food becomes an issue. I dumped my fifty bonus points into "speed" to help this along.

∞∞∞∞∞∞∞∞

Name: Torga

Race: Gluttonous Dark Draconic Naga

Classification: Tier 8

Level: 89

Experience: 476,912/ 4,000,000

Titles: Destroyer of Asgard, The Dark Serpent

Stats:

- Physical

    - Strength: 5,861

    - Endurance: 5,861

    - Dexterity: 30

    - Speed: 63

- Mental

    - Intelligence: 52

    - Wisdom: 37

    - Charisma: 20

- Resistances

    - Elements: 60%

    - Divinity: 80%

    - Mental: 20%

- Immunities

  - Mind Control

Skills: Major Stealth, Heat Detection, Supreme Gluttony, Supreme Growth, Greater Petrifying Gaze, Greater Acid Venom, Detect Concealment, Energy Breath, Fly, Magic Enhancement, Elemental Manipulation

∞∞∞∞∞∞∞∞

After confirming the points were inside the correct stat, I activated my magic enhancement skill, ramping up my speed even further beyond my natural limit.

With a strong thrust, I flung myself up the branch. Thanks to the ever-weakening pull of Xitara's gravitational field, I was able to fling myself greater and greater distances, though I always made sure to keep a portion of my tail wrapped around the branch to prevent slippage and subsequent death by the vacuum of space.

This technique did allow me to go much faster, but it also burned through my magic at an astounding rate.

However, after doing this for several hours, I'd again grown hungry. Almost debilitatingly so. I had to shut off my body enchantment before it killed me, which slowed down my progress to a snail's pace.

Hours continued to pass while I climbed. While my hunger grew ever more urgent, and my energy levels plummeted, I found myself hanging on for dear life. Unable to move my arms or my tail, I was forced to return to the idea of eating the branch. *Not like I'll ever be able to eat the whole thing, anyway*, I thought reassuringly. *Besides, my aura's been dissolving it a little at a time for the last few hours, and nothing's happened so far. I'll be fine if I just take a little bite, right?* I lowered my face to the branch and sunk my teeth into its tender bark.

Ding!

CHAPTER FIFTEEN

HOURS LATER, I CONTINUED TO PUSH MYSELF ever onwards, my arms carrying me the entire length of my body and then some with every leap. Occasionally I would stop to take another bite of Yggdrasil to refuel and perk myself back up.

I bit into the branch and the sheer amount of magic that flowed into me caused lights to flash before my eyes and my spine to tingle.

Ding

∞∞∞∞∞∞∞∞

Strength: +100

Endurance: +100

∞∞∞∞∞∞∞∞

I hissed at the simultaneous pleasure and pain I felt from that small mouthful. I wanted to take another, to eat until my body burst, but I couldn't. I leaped away from that spot and resumed my journey.

~ ~ ~

I'm not sure how many days passed before the flesh of Yggdrasil could no longer keep me awake. But I knew that I needed to rest now, or bad things would happen. I'd traveled as long as I was able. I'd earned this rest.

I coiled the entire length of my tail around the branch, then for good measure I wrapped my arms around it and laid my head down. I'd sleep for as long as I was able, then get moving again. I couldn't afford to stay out here forever.

I reached up and scratched at the itchy spot on my scalp where hair was growing.

~ ~ ~

Weeks, possibly months later, I was still feeling the same rush from eating the branch as I'd been feeling. However, recently my body felt like it was getting slightly heavier with each bite.

It was obviously due to the branch's magic having an odd effect on me. I wasn't in pain, nor was I feeling ill. In fact, it was just the opposite and I felt better than ever.

But as the increase in weight grew more noticeable, I started wondering if starving to death would've been the better option.

~ ~ ~

Lack of sleep soon became the bane of my existence. Every time I tried to fall asleep, my body was wracked with growing pains. After god only knows how long of eating nothing but the branch and drinking a combination of Yggdrasil's sap and artificial water I'd managed to pull from the rapidly shrinking amount of available oxygen, my body entered something of a second growth phase. My body was constantly growing longer, though thankfully I wasn't getting any thicker or thinner.

Forever Growing. I sighed.

After trying and failing to sleep, I gave up and pressed on. I'd try again when my body refused to move another inch.

༈ ༔ ༈

One morning, I noticed an odd sight above the tip of my tail. A tiny red sphere with the relative size of a grape hovered a few inches above it. No matter how I moved my tail, the ball never failed to move with it, and any and all attempts to forcefully move it away from its spot revealed that beneath its small size hid a weight I'd never encountered before. I'd thrown dragons that weighed less than the damn ball.

After half a dozen failed attempts to remove it, I decided to leave it alone and press on. Wasn't like I could do anything with it anyway. Aside from cutting my tail off, which I preferred not to do, I couldn't think of another way to remove it.

༈ ༔ ༈

Ever since the ball first formed several weeks ago, my body slowly acclimatized to the new weight. So much so, that I no longer even noticed it was there. Which was more than a little surprising, since it almost tripled in size and weight. And with that change, came a change in color as well, turning from a very dark red to a much lighter orange with yellow flakes.

After noticing the change, I started paying much closer attention to the ball and decided to inspect it after every meal. Though this slowed down my travel speed quite considerably, I believed it to be a fair trade-off for ensuring I actually made it to my next destination.

༈ ༔ ༈

For the first time in my life, I knew if I didn't hold on to my goal with every fiber of my being, my own mind would be my downfall. After an eternity of climbing, I'd started having hallucinations. I saw Ayla desperately calling out to me for help. I saw her dying over and over again in my mind because I wasn't there to protect her.

I saw Findral in her goblin form being beaten to death by a horde of angry goblins. Each night her deaths became more graphic, more defined. And again, I wasn't there to protect her in any of them.

My other friends also made appearances in my dreams: Siofs being executed, Holstig being mutilated, Hogunn being gutted, and after their deaths, came the elves...

I had nightmares that the slave trader I saved them from all those years ago managed to keep them. I dreamed of them dying and Fenris being sold off to some rich noble as little more than a mindless guard dog.

I dreamed I was truly alone in this vast world. An endless expanse of nothingness stretched out before me and with it came the knowledge that I'd failed everyone.

I shook the images away. *No, they're safe. I made sure of it before I came here. Is someone messing with my head again or have I been alone for so long that I've finally gone mad?* I wasn't sure how long I'd been traveling, after all. The branch didn't have day or night per se—only constant light on the side with the twin stars and a maw of nothingness on the other.

This far into space, nothing I could see looked anything like a planet anymore and even the twin stars were but glowing balls in the distance... *Wait a minute.* I stopped climbing and slowly turned my head until I could see the glowing orange ball above the tip of my tail.

You're losing it, Torga. Keep it together.

~ ~ ~

I really hate it when I'm right, I sighed.

I stared into the distance at the ball floating above my tail. It'd grown slowly, day after day getting bigger, until it was thicker than I was. Like the weight of a ring on a finger, I could always feel the ball's weight pushing down on my tail.

After losing all sense of time, I also found myself losing all motivation and just couldn't seem to push myself any further. I'd been traveling for so long I'd forgotten what it was like to enjoy my food. I'd forgotten what it was like to sit by a campfire and listen to the crickets' song… I'd forgotten what my friends looked like, what Ayla and Findral looked like. *I'm never going to make it, am I?* I wondered as I stared off into the dark reaches of space. I'd long since lost count of the "nights" I'd spent wondering at the fates of those I cared about. Would I ever see them again or was I destined to be stuck on this branch forever? Would I even recognize them when, or if, I saw them again?

~ ~ ~

I found myself floating aimlessly through space as I moved ever forward, pulling myself along the branch as more of something to do, rather than any true desire to go anywhere.

However, an upwards glance brought my apathy to an end. I could see it: the light at the end of the tunnel. "There it is... Holy shit... There it is!" I laughed. With a mighty yank, I propelled myself the length of my body and then some. The blue orb at the end of the branch was the most beautiful thing I'd ever seen.

~ ~ ~

Almost there. I panted as my body was pushed to its absolute limit, covering miles in mere seconds. I sustained this speed until the planet filled my vision and I broke through the atmosphere. The planet looked insanely large, but how would I know? I barely remembered what it was like to feel the dirt beneath my body. The planet was a mix of dark blue and light purple water, with little to no landmass visible from where I'd arrived.

Once I entered the atmosphere and felt the pull of gravity, I couldn't stop myself from sobbing. I activated the jewel mid fall and unfurled my wings a second before I would've slammed head-first into the surface of the water at terminal velocity.

My body shrunk rapidly: Over ten percent of my total body mass disappeared per second until I was only left with about ten percent. *Finally. I've finally made it.* I closed my eyes and inadvertently fell into a trance. The next thing I knew, I was being gently rocked by waves and staring up at the night sky.

Ding*Ding

ꝏꝏꝏꝏꝏ

You have arrived at your destination; Planet Beglore: Territory of Unger, The Primordial Leviathan

Goals:

Find and Slay Unger.

Survive.

Rewards:

Serpent Form

∞∞∞∞∞∞∞∞

Congratulations!

You have completed "The journey of 100,000,000 miles" in 57 years, 11 months. 27 days, 14 hours, 51 minutes, and 1 second. You have earned an increase in speed and the title of The Unwavering One for accomplishing this feat.

The system has become available to you again.

∞∞∞∞∞∞∞∞

I blankly stared at the window for several minutes before my mind kicked into gear and I could comprehend what I was seeing. *Fifty-seven years? I spent fifty-seven YEARS climbing that stupid, motherfucking, BRANCH!?*
Ding*Ding

∞∞∞∞∞∞∞∞

Due to acquiring the title known as The Unwavering One a trait has evolved. The Strong Willed trait has evolved into the Indomitable trait.

Indomitable: Your will is the stuff of legends.

Illusions no longer affect you, and pain will not stop you.

∞∞∞∞∞∞∞∞

You have unlocked a hidden evolution!

Due to eating massive quantities of Yggdrasil's flesh, your body has mutated into a variant of the normal species.

Dark Draconic Naga —> Dark Star Naga

A Naga whose body became so large, and so full of divine energy, they began to grow their own star.

You are the first of your kind. As such, you have received bonuses to your stats.

You have been granted the Gravity Manipulator skill as a sign of your new race.

∞∞∞∞∞∞∞∞

Name: Torga

Race: Gluttonous Dark Star Naga

Classification: Tier 8

Level: 89

Experience: 476,912/ 4,000,000

Titles: Destroyer of Asgard, The Dark Serpent, The Unwavering One

Stats:

- Physical
    - Strength: 73,912
    - Endurance: 73,912
    - Dexterity: 1,030
    - Speed: 1,163
- Mental
    - Intelligence: 54
    - Wisdom: 38
    - Charisma: 20
- Resistances

- Elements: 60%
- Divinity: 80%
- Mental: 20%

- Immunities
  - Mind Control
  - Illusions

Skills: Major Stealth, Heat Detection, Supreme Gluttony, Supreme Growth, Greater Petrifying Gaze, Greater Acid Venom, Detect Concealment, Energy Breath, Fly, Magic Enhancement, Elemental Manipulation, Gravity Manipulation

Traits: Divine Gluttonous Aura +25, Growth +50, Venomous, Aquatic, Winged, Forever Growing, Indomitable

∞∞∞∞∞∞∞∞∞

I dismissed the pop-ups with a sigh and closed my eyes. I was actually looking forward to sleep for once.

Chapter Sixteen

I woke up the next morning to a sight I'd only dreamed about: a multicolored school of fish swimming above my head, as the light from the twin stars was filtered through the surface of the water, turning it in a living sapphire.

Unfortunately, this sight would not last another night if my aura continued to devour the ocean at its current pace. When I'd first landed yesterday, I was able to easily submerge my entire body. However, after only a single night of sleeping, the water level had dropped some four-hundred feet.

I sat up, the motion causing several millions of gallons of water to be displaced, and surveyed my surroundings: Nothing but ocean and clear violet sky as far as the eye could see. However, something in the water caught my attention. It was my reflection.

I brushed my obscenely long hair to the side and studied my face first. My eyes were as red as ever, though they glowed so brightly I was having trouble seeing my own pupils. They were sunken into a face with high cheek bones and a wide forehead, from which a pair of thick horns extended and curled around to the back of my head, and a slightly crooked nose. I had visible ears, which was weird but not unexpected. I'd known they were there ages ago; I just couldn't see what they looked like. Turns out, they looked like human ears—I think. I was having trouble remembering what humans looked like for some reason.

My scales were the same color they always were: dark green with a gray line that ran from my jaw to the tip of my tail. Though, what was truly interesting about my naga form was the "armor" my scales had evolved into. They were thick as plate mail on my chest, shoulders, forearms, and back. Thin gaps existed in between the various plates to allow ease of movement. Every few feet along my tail you could see a mass of armor plating as well.

Though I was sitting on the ocean floor, my shoulders were approximately two or three thousand feet high and yet my hands were digging into the sand behind me. I could barely see the ball at this distance, and that's only because it produced its own light, creating a beacon effect on the horizon.

I shivered at the realization that I was this big at only ten percent of my full size. I curled up and went back to sleep. I wasn't ready to deal with this crap yet.

Ding

∞∞∞∞∞∞∞∞

You've eaten the following race for the first time

Water Titan Boa: Tier 3

∞∞∞∞∞∞∞∞

Hmm? I looked away from the pop-up and found a group of blue snakes swimming around my head. They must've already lost a couple of their number because they were doing well to avoid entering my aura. *I envy you, little ones.*

I used my arms to push myself out of the water and stood up. I stretched my body and performed a few light stretches to loosen up before I set out for the day—Or, that was the plan until I saw a mass of shadows that twisted and turned as it came over the horizon. It appeared to be several miles wide and was so long I couldn't see its end. *Well, that sucks.*

The mass came within a hundred feet of me and two shadows split off and sped in my direction. They split apart and curved around to my backside before exploding out of the water.

The shadows revealed themselves to be two of the largest creatures I'd ever seen. They were Leviathans, and the head of each was as high as my own, though they were much thicker than I was.

The giant shadow exploded out of the water a few seconds later, revealing that it was composed of hundreds, possibly thousands of Leviathans equal in size to the first two.

And they were all aiming for little old me.

"I'm guessing you're Unger?" I asked the swarm.

They chuckled simultaneously, which was about the creepiest thing imaginable.

The swarm split apart to reveal a pure white serpent at the center of them all. Its scales were the color of fresh snow, its eyes were milky white as if it'd long since lost the light in them, and It. Was. BIG! Its body was easily several thousand feet in diameter. I couldn't see how long it was from where I was standing, but I assumed it was proportional, and to top it all off, its whiskers were as thick as the other Leviathans.

"Surprised?" it asked with a musical lilt to its voice.

"You're..." I struggled to find the right thing to say.

"Beautiful? Gorgeous? How about perfect beyond measure?"

"I was gonna say fat enough to be registered as your own country, but hey, to each their own." Unger's eyes narrowed and her lips pulled back to reveal obscenely large teeth. **"You're a rude one, aren't you?"**

"Me, rude? Never." Suddenly, one of her whiskers slammed into my side and sent me crashing into the waves. I quickly pushed myself back up and answered with a haymaker to the face of the first thing I saw, which happened to be one of the Leviathans. Its head burst like an overly ripe fruit, then I turned back to Unger—only to see empty air.

"Where'd she go?" I asked the swarm. They hissed simultaneously, and I took back what I said earlier. *That* was the creepiest thing ever.

I ducked under the jaws of another serpent, then came back with a swing that hit the Leviathan just beneath its mouth. My fist passed through the serpent like it wasn't there, cleaving it in two, and giving me enough time to reorient myself. *Fine, you want to hide from me? We'll see how long you can hide once I start tearing this place apart.*

"Soo… dramatic!" Unger's voice came from behind my left ear. Before I could turn around, I was suddenly flying through the air. I crashed into the water and was immediately set upon by the swarm.

Unfortunately for them, my aura didn't care how many of them there were. They were food, and my aura would treat them as such.

"Surprised?" Her voice came from behind my left ear. ***"Good. You should be."***

"Is this the moment when you start bragging about your power or does that come later?"

"Now, why would I do that? Do you think I'm stupid or something?"

"Honestly? The thought had crossed my mind."

"Is that so?" Unger laughed. **"Well, I hate to disappoint you, but I'm far too old to fall for such paltry taunting."**

"Old? Please, old isn't what I'd use to describe you." I slapped a serpent out of the air when it tried to grab my head, then I went back to letting my aura devour anything stupid enough to come near me. "Now, FUBAR, that's more your speed."

"I'm guessing that's an insult of some kind? Did no one teach you to respect your elders?"

"Yep," I said, as I grabbed two serpents out of the air and slammed their heads together. My aura dissolved them so quickly I ended up clapping instead. "Then again, my elders also had the sense to die before they became so old, they breathed dust instead of oxygen."

"That's quite enough of that," she hissed angrily.

Unger wrapped her whiskers around my waist and began to squeeze. **"Be a good lad and die for me... Won't you?"** she asked in an overly sweet tone.

I was momentarily surprised my aura hadn't torn through her whiskers but rationalized she was too powerful for it to work. I fake struggled for a bit, then sighed. "Alright, you win. I'll die for you."

"Really?"

"Of course not. What kind of person do you take me for?" I asked as I released the jewel's enchantment and quickly began to grow larger. "It'll take a few seconds for me to return to full size; would you mind waiting a moment?" Her whiskers tightened around my mid-section even further. "Eh, didn't think so." I flexed my arms and pushed the whiskers ever so slightly apart, then I shoved them off of me.

Two arms grabbed each whisker, then I yanked. The whiskers tore but didn't completely separate from Unger's face. She yelped in pain and pulled her head out of my reach.

Water exploded in every direction as the swarm attacked as one. They slammed into my body and pushed me away from Unger, while she ducked beneath the waves.

I'm getting tired of this crap. I pulled back my right arms and threw out a haymaker my old boxing couch would've been proud of. My fists knocked into several Leviathans, stopping their forward momentum, and turning them into a shield against the swarm's charge as they blocked me from view. The swarm fought against me the entire time, eventually pushing me back several hundred feet as I struggled to remain standing.

Even at the rate my aura dissolved them, they were being replaced too quickly for me to keep this up for very long. *Let's try this.* I reached inside myself and pulled out my new skill: Gravity manipulation should be similar to elemental manipulation, so I tried to activate it the same way.

My left arms swung towards the sky and a wave of force pushed its way out of my fists. The center of the swarm was caught in an invisible wave of gravity and thrown back the way they'd come.

I pulled my arms in to my chest, then shoved them out to my sides, pushing the left and right swarms away in a tidal wave of gravitational energy. *Works better than I expected it to*, I smirked.

"You're too confident for someone about to die," Unger said from behind me.

I turned around and had to look up, and up… and up. "You're even bigger than I thought."

"I am the largest serpent on Yggdrasil. Or at least, I was until someone took my title from me."

"Hmm, that's a shame. But ultimately not my problem."

"You're right. The dead have no worries." Unger lifted her massive head into the air; it was far larger than I was, and she seemed to still have most of her body beneath the waves.

Unger pulled her body back then sprung at me. I met her charge with a gravity-infused double punch. I managed to deflect her strike to the side, then I dug my fingers into her hide and pushed her onto the ocean floor. While holding her there, I opened my mouth and launched four blasts of condensed mana into her neck.

Unger roared in pain and ordered her swarm to attack. I tried to hold on, but I was forced to let go as the swarm slammed into me.

I grit my teeth and braced my tail against the floor of the ocean. "Fuck. Off!" I yelled. Gravity exploded out of me in a wave that sent the swarm sliding off to either side and giving me the time I needed to attack again.

I opened my mouth and charged a large ball of condensed mana. Before I could fire it, Unger's whisker struck my side and knocked me into the water.

I pushed myself out of the water and glared at her.

"You think you're the only one who can use magic!?" Unger hissed. Her body began to glow and suddenly the swarm dissolved into bright white lights and fixed itself to her body, forming a clear "shell" of magic around her.

I stood up and fired three weak mana balls at her body. They simply bounced off the shell.

"Well... That's just not fair."

Unger raised her head high into the sky, then shot towards me with that massive mouth of hers wide open.

Thinking quickly, I twisted my tail around and slammed the ball into the ocean floor, then braced my body against it. I held out my arms and caught Unger's mouth before she could close it on me.

Not my best idea considering I didn't even slow her down, but it probably saved my life. As it was, she carried me along the surface of the water until the ball got caught on an underwater mountain and forced me under the water. She passed overhead for several seconds before she realized I wasn't in front of her anymore, then she dove after me.

"Lunchtime!" she hissed.

I grunted as she slammed into me, struggling to hold her mouth in place and keep those wicked-looking teeth where they could do the least amount of damage. Then a memory came unbidden to me of the last time I'd fought a Leviathan.

I'd forgotten about her until now, but it couldn't hurt to try. I planted my tail into the ground, then braced myself. I pried her mouth open, which she was only too eager to help with, as that was the only way she could eat me.

I waited until I had a clear shot, then fired a beam of highly concentrated magic down her throat.

Unger's white eyes widened slightly a moment before the magic ripped through the back of her neck and punched through her magic shell.

I held her mouth open for a few more seconds to ensure she was dead, then I tossed her now lifeless head to the side.

I fell onto my back, my chest heaving as I sucked in huge mouthfuls of air and stared into the midafternoon sky.

"I'm so hungry," I moaned.

Ding*Ding

∞∞∞∞∞∞∞∞

Congratulations!
You have successfully killed **"Primordial Leviathan Unger"**
You have been granted the ability to shift between your current form and that of a purely serpent form.

Please proceed to the next Royal Serpent territory.

∞∞∞∞∞∞∞∞

"Later," I sighed.

∞∞∞∞∞∞∞∞

Warning!!!
Due to Unger's death, the core of this planet has become unstable.

Total planetary collapse in 90 days, 20 hours, 37 minutes, and 15 seconds

∞∞∞∞∞∞∞∞

I swiped away the pop-up. "Ninety days. That's plenty of time to eat my fill." I tore into the corpse with renewed energy.

Interlude: Thor's Anger & Amaar's Game

"Gods damn it!" Thor raged. He grabbed a lamp from a nearby table and hurled it across the room and into the opposite wall. His mother and brother winced at the sound but didn't otherwise react.

"Breaking our furniture won't change the past, Thor." Frigga said in a calm voice.

"I know!" He paused for a moment, then let out a deep breath. "I know... I... I failed to protect her."

"Jeez, you're acting like she died. So, she has a scar, what's the big deal?" Loki, his half-brother asked. Loki was a head shorter than Thor, with slicked back black hair and bright green eyes.

"That's not the point. If Findral hadn't been there, Ayla would have died to that damn assassin." Even while saying so, his mind went back to the previous night when he heard the scream and the sounds of battle coming from inside her room.

He almost broke down the door in his haste to enter and what was the first thing he saw? Why, it was Findral standing over the would-be assassin in her "true" form; Her ebony skin had turned blood red, her hair appeared to be made of living flame, and a slender onyx-black tail ending in a dangerous looking point swayed just above the man's left eye.

Occasionally, a wave of fire would encircle one of her limbs or her torso, then travel down her body and burn the man.

"Thor?" His mother interrupted.

"Yes? What is it?"

"Have they made any progress in determining his allegiance?"

"No, they have not," he replied.

"Well then, what are you still doing here?" she asked.

"What do you mean?"

"It was your bride-to-be that was attacked, correct?"

"Yes. What's your point?"

She rolled her eyes at the question. "Why haven't you asked for my permission to interrogate him yourself? I'd think you'd be itching for a chance to question him, or was I mistaken?"

"I... May I? And Dad won't mind?" he asked.

"I'll handle your father. Just make sure you ask Fira to heal him, so he doesn't die before you get what you need," she replied with a tight smile.

Thor's mouth briefly hung open, then it snapped shut and he smiled grimly. "Thank you, Mom." He bowed low, then left the room with Loki on his heels.

As he made his way down to the dungeon a cruel smile appeared on his lips. "Time to stop the goody-goody act. For a while, at least."

"Oh, this is going to be so much fun," Loki drawled.

Thor wound his way through Gungnir and arrived at the brig where a guard stopped him.

"Sorry sir, but the king has stated that no one is allowed to see the prisoner."

"I've been given orders to interrogate the prisoner for information on his allegiances," Thor stated matter-of-factly.

"I'll need you to wait here while I confirm this information—" The guard began but halted after seeing the look on Thor's and Loki's faces. "Uh. Go on in." the guard stammered, then stepped out of their way.

"Find lady Fira and bring her here," Thor ordered.

"Right away, sir!" The guard saluted, then ran off to obey his command.

Thor waited a few seconds for him to leave, then grabbed the key off of the nearby wall, unlocked the solid iron door, and stepped into the cell. Once inside, he took off his leather vest, armbands, pauldrons, and the white shirt he wore beneath. All the while, he stared into the would-be assassin's eye.

Meanwhile, Loki stepped off to the side and somehow magicked a leather bedroll out of nowhere. He sat it on the lone table in the room and unfurled it, revealing a wide assortment of "questioning utensils."

"I do so hope you're more durable than you look." Thor held out a hand. Without looking. Loki placed a wicked looking dagger into it, then went back to fiddling with his toys.

"You may just die before Fira even gets here," Thor finished with a cruel smile.

A while later, a middle-aged blonde woman rushed into the cell and came to a stop at Thor's side. "What have ya done now, ya foolish boy!? And you, why'd you let him take it this far?" she yelled at them. She dropped to her knees heedless of the blood now staining her white dress.

"Sorry, I—Uh—made a bit of a mess," Thor said lamely.

"A bit of a mess!?" the woman yelled. "Yer went far past 'A bit' of a mess!"

Which was true. The would-be assassin's body was mangled almost beyond recognition. His arms and legs were bent in ungodly painful ways and a few bones were poking through the skin in multiple places, the skin on his face had been peeled off in various sized strips, and his right ear had been cut off.

"You need to get that temper in check, boy!" she ranted, as she frantically worked to save the man's life, if only so he could be interrogated further.

Thor watched her work in silence for ten minutes, before he re-dressed and said, "I'm sorry, Fira. But that little shit tried to take what's mine," Thor coldly said as he finished fastening his armor.

The woman sighed and looked over her shoulder at him. "Did ya get whatcha need, boy?" she asked.

"Unfortunately, not," Loki said. "The poor bastard's more stubborn than he looks."

"Then go find yer girl and leave him to me. I'll see what I can do to keep him alive, so you can try again tomorrow," she finished.

"Thanks," Thor said gratefully, then he left her to work.

Thor and Loki walked in silence for several minutes, each contemplating the things they'd done inside that room.

"Why a snake?" Thor asked suddenly.

"What?"

"The staff you gave Ayla has a serpent's head on the end of it. You didn't know about Torga until he showed up, so why a serpent?"

Loki shrugged. "I've always liked snakes, you know that. Truth be told, I believed I'd have one of my own by now, but the gods had other plans. Speaking of, has she named it yet? You know a staff is only as powerful as the name given to it."

"Jormungandr. I think she's taken to calling it Jormungandr."

Loki suddenly stopped walking, which prompted Thor to stop as well. "Where did she come up with that name?"

Thor shrugged. "Dunno. She said it just felt right."

"Yes, well, I've just remembered I've got business to attend to. Have a good day, brother. And tell the missus I approve of the name!"

"Yeah, you too," Thor said in confusion as he watched his brother disappear around a corner at the end of the hall. *You're weird as ever, Loki.*

～ ∴ ～

Talerius, Mortal God of Law and Earth rushed down the centermost street of the Golden City, home and birthplace of the mortal gods.

As he was on his way to an emergency meeting called by his patron, Salaroo, Mortal God of Magic, he could not take in the sights of the city as he normally did. Even after eight hundred years of living in the Golden City, the sight of various races and powers moving to and from the local bars, inns, stores, and homes still gave him a feeling of pride.

He, Talerius, son of a cabbage farmer, smallest of his siblings, and lawyer to the King of Zakora had actually become a god! Granted, he was a mortal god, and not a powerful one for that matter, being only slightly more powerful than a tier 6 monster. But even so, He. Was. Proud!

It'd taken him nearly one hundred and five years of dedicated service to both his king and his god, before he caught the attention of Salaroo and become his champion upon his death.

Talerius, of course, was reincarnated and served as the champion of Salaroo for almost five hundred years. Talerius wore many hats during this time; he was a soldier, a lawyer, a general, and even a king for a few decades. But none of that compared to his ascendance to god-hood and Salaroo bestowing upon him the title of Earth God. And, because of his actions during his time as champion, he was given the title of God of Law.

After making his way to the street's end, Talerius climbed the golden steps to the door of his faction leader's home. It, like most of the buildings in the Golden City, was carved from one extremely large golden block. The building was several hundred feet tall and just as wide; it was carved into the shape of a stately manor with pillars lining the front entrance and forty-foot-tall double doors carved from obsidian.

The building was heavily warded to only allow faction members inside, and even then, only if they were invited.

Opulent as ever, Talerius thought as he grasped the golden ball situated to the left of the door and used it to knock.

He knocked three times, then folded his arms across his chest to wait. A few minutes later the door opened to reveal a young man in a butler's uniform. "Hello, Orlus. Is the master home?" Talerius asked politely.

The light-skinned youth slightly nodded his head, then stepped to the side and beckoned Talerius in. "He's waiting in the dining room, sir. You're the last to arrive," Orlus said neutrally.

Talerius grimaced. "How mad is he?"

Orlus shrugged. "It's not my place to assume the master's state of mind," he said.

Talerius thought he saw a slight smirk flash across the boy's face, but it was gone as fast as it arrived.

"I'll just go join them then, shall I?" Talerius asked nervously.

"Of course, sir." Orlus nodded his head, then closed the door behind Talerius and led him across the large entryway, under a flight of stairs, and to some obsidian double doors.

Orlus opened the doors and stated, "Master, Sir Talerius has arrived."

"Oh, good! Send him in!" a nasally voice replied.

Orlus nodded and stepped aside to allow Talerius to enter, then shut the doors behind him.

Talerius glanced around the room at his twenty compatriots sitting at the grand marble table before finally settling on the man sitting in the master's position.

The man was extremely short, just barely reaching three feet in height. His trimmed mustache and beard combo and extravagant silk outfit gave him an air of nobility, in spite of his childlike body.

Talerius bowed low and said, "Greetings, Master. I apologize for being late, but I—"

"Never mind that, Talerius," Salaroo interrupted. "We have much to discuss and little time to talk. So please, have a seat."

Talerius acquiesced. He pulled the only free chair out and sat down.

"Now," Salaroo began, "As some of you may have noticed, many of our older members have gone missing."

"Missing?" a goddess asked.

"Yes, missing," Salaroo agreed.

"Perhaps they've simply decided to go on vacation? I hear the Life spring is nice this time of the millennia," a god suggested.

Salaroo shook his head and grimaced. "If only that were the case." He sighed. "I have received numerous reports from our allies saying that their gods are disappearing, as well."

"So... It's not just us?" Talerius asked mildly.

"No, it certainly isn't."

Before anyone else could speak, the double doors were thrown open as a human-sized dark object slammed into the table, knocking over glasses and spilling wine onto the pure white tablecloth.

"Who dares—" Salaroo began before he noticed what had slammed into the table: It was a black skeleton in a butler uniform.

"Orlus?" Salaroo gasped.

"Well, that was boring," a voice said from beyond the doors.

"Amaar!" Salaroo growled as he and the other gods stood to their feet and turned to face the intruder.

The intruder was a skeleton with bones the color of freshly fallen snow and eyes like the void. He was wearing a charcoal tuxedo along with a dark blue tie and a pair of obsidian-plated skull cufflinks. **"Oh, sorry, was this yours?"** Amaar asked as he grabbed Orlus' leg and shook it for emphasis.

"You killed him!" a goddess gasped.

"Killed him?" Amaar asked with a tilt of his head. **"Yes, I suppose I did,"** he agreed.

"Why!?" Salaroo demanded, loudly.

"Why not?" Amaar asked; his abyssal black eyes seemed to suck some of the light out of the room as he stared down Salaroo.

"My family gave you these lives so you could monitor and run Yggdrasil while we relaxed. But you haven't done that, have you?" Amaar stated matter-of-factly. Suddenly, a pitch-black cane appeared in his hand and he propped himself up with it. **"You lot—you haven't been doing your duties. No, instead you've been slacking off and playing power games with your 'siblings,' while Yggdrasil has been spiraling out of control."**

"That's not—" a god began.

"Did I ask for your opinion?" Amaar interrupted and looked the man in the eye.

The god grit his teeth, but remained silent.

"I didn't think I had, but it's nice to know I'm not going senile in my old age." Amaar "smiled," then continued.

"Of course, I'm not laying all of the blame at your feet. All of your 'siblings' will also be punished," Amaar said calmly, still smiling.

A young god stood abruptly and marched up to the skeletal man.

"This is bullshit!" the god yelled. "We've done everything the ancients have asked of us and more, and yet you dare accuse us of being lazy!? Who the hell are you to make such a claim?" he finished with a growl.

"Me?" Amaar asked while pointing at himself.

"Yes, you!" the god yelled.

"Galdos, sit down!" Salaroo demanded but was waved off.

Amaar bent at his waist to look around Galdos. **"No, it's alright Salaroo,"** Amaar said. **"After all, it's a good question."**

Amaar waved his free hand through the air, and a black top hat with a white brim appeared in it. Then he bowed at the waist.

"Amaar is the name and Death is my game!" Amaar said cheerfully.

"What's that supposed to mean?" Galdos asked.

"It means," Amaar said, after standing up straight and pointing the end of his cane at the god's chest, **"That you're my bitch."**

The god's eyes widened in surprise as Amaar's cane lightly tapped his chest. Galdos disappeared in a flash of light while a loud boom thundered in the distance.

Every god in the room turned to the wall behind Salaroo and saw that a portion of it was missing. What wasn't missing was splattered with silver blood. Everyone in the room slowly turned their heads back to face Amaar and saw him propping his chin onto the head of the cane.

"Anyone else need a refresher on just 'Who' I am?" Amaar asked with a grin.

The group almost simultaneously shook their heads in silence.

"Good. I do so hate to repeat myself." Amaar returned to his full height and placed the hat atop his head. **"Anyway, I have some good news to accompany the bad."**

"S—Such as?" Salaroo asked after a few moments of silence.

"We, my siblings and I that is, are prepared to give a full pardon to anyone capable of completing a... minor task for us."

"What will you have us do?" Talerius grimaced.

Amaar looked to a nearby goddess and smiled as he walked over to her.

She flinched as he placed his hand on her shoulder and leaned down to whisper in her ear. The goddess shakily nodded her head.

"Good, then you can assist me for a moment." He grabbed the top of her head and forced her to look into the air.

"This," he began as the goddess' eyes began to glow, and a truly massive serpent appeared in the air above the table.

"Is Torga. He's a Dark Star Naga of not inconsiderable power," Amaar finished with a chuckle.

"So?" a god asked.

"So he is the newest contender for the title of Serpent King." Amaar smirked as the gods gasped.

"He must be truly powerful if he can challenge Orochi!" Salaroo said.

"He is," Amaar easily agreed. **"Which is why you're going to kill him."**

Chatter erupted as the gods all began to talk amongst themselves. "Quiet!" Salaroo demanded in a booming voice without a trace of his normally nasally voice to be found. The room immediately became silent as the chatter died in their throats. Salaroo took a deep breath and said, "You're sending us to our graves. You know that, right?"

Amaar shook his head and waved a finger at Salaroo.

"Not at all," Amaar chuckled. **"I'm giving you a choice. You can either die here and now, by my hand or you can face Torga and possibly live. Either way is fine with me,"** he said cheerfully.

"Either way is a death sentence," Talerius said.

"Not necessarily," Amaar replied. **"Despite Torga's strength, he is but one creature. Meanwhile, every mortal god on Yggdrasil is being given this choice."**

The gods were silent for several minutes as they all began to think over this "deal." Eventually, they nodded their heads in agreement and stood up.

"Have fun!" Amaar smiled at the gods as they flashed away.

CHAPTER SEVENTEEN

89 DAYS LATER

*D*AMN, *I'LL NEVER FINISH IT AT THIS RATE.* A LITTLE OVER half of Unger's body remained and that had long since begun to decay under the heat of the twin stars. Though I didn't mind a little decay in my food, the sheer size of Unger had given even me some pause. Her body was coiled into a tight ball beneath the planet's surface, but it still had a radius of at least five thousand miles.

Despite my voracious appetite, I couldn't possibly eat so much in a mere three months.

I think this is the first time since my arrival that I've been unable to finish what I started. If only I had more time. I sighed.

As I'd eaten, the planet began to decay and die, as the pop-up said it would. The ecosystem died, the atmosphere began to break down, and gravity slowly lost its hold as I ate away at Unger's body. In fact, the gravity had become nearly ten times weaker than when I'd first arrived. Water would float through the sky as if it were air, and the sky had become almost completely transparent as the atmosphere dissipated, leaving me with an amazing view of the stars—and a constant reminder of the imminent death of a once beautiful planet.

Suppose I start making my way back to the branch. I don't want to get too distracted and let this place become my grave, after all... I ripped off a mountain-sized chunk of Unger's body for the "road" and left the planet behind. Now that I could manipulate gravity in order to fly instead of using my wings, it was time to see just how fast my body could go.

Next planet, here I come! I launched myself into the air and tore off towards the branch.

～ ～ ～

I was flying at a moderate pace and periodically looking up to check my position relative to the twin stars or swapping between my Naga form and my serpent form, which was just my Naga form without the arms. It had been a little over a year since I defeated Unger and nine months since I'd fled the collapsing planet.

In that time, I'd grown— a lot. I could no longer see the tip of my tail unless I turned back on myself and flew for a while.

I'd had to work my way through more than a few bouts of depression as I tried to rationalize my current size. I was far too large to even have a chance of interacting with humans, elves—or almost anything else, for that matter. The sheer length and mass of my body would undoubtedly cause problems for any planet I happened to land on.

I sighed and ripped another chunk from the branch to nibble on while I flew. But, what else could I do? It's not like I could live in space for the rest of my life. Living off nothing but Yggdrasil and the ambient magic in the "air" would surely drive me even madder than I already was. *Never mind the fact that I promised Ayla I would return. Which I can't very well do if I'm the size of the FUCKING PLANET, NOW CAN I?* I internally screamed.

However, my size was not the only thing weighing on my mind. Ever since I'd eaten Unger, my metabolism had kicked into overdrive and was burning through food almost as fast as I could eat it.

Seriously, I sighed again. *Why couldn't I have gained some other trait besides Gluttony? If it had to be one of the sins, why that one? Why not wrath, greed, or sloth? Hell, at this point, I would have taken lust over gluttony. I mean... Surely it wouldn't have been as bad—right?*

My train of thought ground to a halt as I saw something out of the corner of my eye. I stopped flying to look at it. A sea-green dwarf planet was slowly rotating and two moons chased it. One moon was pale blue and the other was light red. They were moving east to west.

Just as I was about to continue towards the planet, I noticed something that caused me to pause again. The branch wasn't going to the planet. Instead, it split into two smaller branches and connected with the moons.

That's new.

I watched the moons for a while longer, then proceeded onward. Though I was much more cautious in my approach this time, I still arrived at the split in only a few hours. *Now, which one do I go for first—*

"Hello." A voice from my right surprised me.

I briefly entertained the thought of just hitting it with a mana beam, but upon turning my head and seeing an old snake with snow-white scales, the head of a cobra, and the body of a scaled muscular man casually lying on the branch with his eyes closed, I decided to hold off for at least a few minutes.

"Hello?" I asked.

The old snake opened one eye and slightly inclined his head to look up at me.

"You're a big one, aren't you?"

"That's an understatement if I've ever heard one," I chuckled.

"Eh? You say somethin?" the old snake asked.

I shook my head. "Nothing important."

The old snake watched me for a few more seconds then shrugged and laid his head down. "Suit yourself," he said with a yawn.

"So, who are you?" Torga asked after a few moments of watching the old snake-man sleep.

"Hmm?" he asked.

"Who are you?" I repeated.

"Hmm, I'm Naunet, the royal snake-man."

I blinked in surprise. "You're the snake-man king?"

The old snake waved flippantly. "Pleasure to meet you, and all that jazz."

I watched the old snake for a few more minutes, then said, "You know... Usually, this is where we'd fight, right?"

The old snake sighed, then sat up and looked at me. "Now, why would we do that?" He trailed off as his eyes grew wide and he looked at something over my head.

My curiosity got the better of me and I turned my head in the same direction he was looking, but only saw the ball floating on the horizon. Over the past year, it'd grown exponentially, and I could now see it shining brightly even from this end of my body. It glowed a deep orange and its intense light was turning the horizon a similar color.

"How... How do you have that?" Naunet asked, his pupils briefly contracting as he stared at the ball. They returned to their normal slits when we locked eyes. "Come with me. I'd like to make you an offer."

"What could you have that I'd want? I'm supposed to kill you," I interrupted.

Naunet grimaced. "Would you believe me if I said I'd let you kill me?"

"Not a chance in hell."

"Suppose that's the most I can expect at the moment." Naunet sighed. "Fine. I can train you to fight."

I narrowed my eyes at him. "I can fight. Your friends Unger and Urosh can attest to that."

"They're not my friends. If anything, I'm glad they're dead. And alright, then you shouldn't have a problem proving it."

"Gladly—"

~ ~ ~

My eyes snapped open and I sat up—and immediately had to grab hold of the branch before I fell off.

"Morning."

I looked over my shoulder and saw Naunet floating next to my head with a cocky grin on his face.

"You—You knocked me out?"

"Something like that."

I narrowed my eyes at him, again. "Alright, you've made your point. But if I go with you, you understand that I will still kill you when the time comes, right?"

Naunet rolled his eyes and nodded. "Of course, I do. Hell, were it in my power to do so, I would help you kill me."

"Wait, you want to die?"

Naunet shrugged. "I'm as much a prisoner here as Lord Orochi, so death will be a sweet release for me."

"You have nothing to live for?" I asked curiously.

Naunet glanced at the other moon then slowly shook his head. "Not anymore."

I followed Naunet's gaze to the other moon, then nodded my acceptance. "Alright, then. Just out of curiosity, what do I get if I agree to this—offer?"

Naunet shrugged, "The only thing I have to trade with is knowledge. I was a fairly well-known brawler in my youth," he admitted.

"Could you teach me to control my skills?"

Naunet blinked, then grinned. "I can teach you a lot more than that if you do what I ask."

I nodded. "Let's get this over with then, shall we?"

Naunet nodded, then slowly lifted off the branch and began following it back to the closest moon while I followed closely behind.

CHAPTER EIGHTEEN

I FOLLOWED BEHIND NAUNET UNTIL JUST BEFORE entering the moon's atmosphere. Naunet held out his arm and asked me to stop. "Before you can approach any further let's do something about that size of yours."

"Like what?"

"I realize that you may not like what I'm about to say, but you're simply too large. If you were to land at your current size, it would crumble under your weight."

"Oh, come on! I'm not that heavy," I protested.

"Were this a normal planet you would be correct. However, both of the moons here are hollow on the inside. The shell simply cannot take such a large creature landing on it."

I stared at Naunet in surprise, then shrugged. "If you say so. How small are we talking?"

"Much, much smaller than you are now." He paused and cupped his chin. "I couldn't say for certain, of course, but I would have to guess that anything below a few hundred feet should allow you to remain under the maximum weight capacity," he finished, while looking pointedly at my tail.

"Well, I can shrink myself, but that size eludes me. Believe me, if I could, I would stay at that size," I admitted.

"Why? If you possess the ability to shrink yourself, then shouldn't you be able to become any size you choose?" Naunet replied with a shake of his head.

I thought about the answer to his question seriously for a few moments, then carefully said, "I don't possess the ability to shrink myself. An item I carry does that for me."

Naunet's eyes widened and he gave me a look of simultaneous amusement and disgust. He mumbled something under his breath and exhaled a sigh. "I guess we're starting from scratch then," he finally said. "Before we get into that, however, what kind of training have you had?"

"In what field?" I asked.

"Take your pick." Naunet replied with an annoyed sigh.

"Well, I learned several martial arts forms decades ago, but I'm out of practice with most of them. I can handle basic weapons with some degree of competency, and a friend taught me how to manipulate the elements around me and I taught myself how to fire off a beam of magical energy."

"And? What else?"

"That's it."

Naunet's eyes snapped up to meet mine. "That's it?"

"That's it," I agreed.

Naunet's right eye twitched in annoyance. "How have you survived this long without killing yourself from magic overdose?" he asked tiredly.

"Magic overdose?" I asked.

"Wait—let me guess. No one explained that to you either?"

"First I've heard of it."

"Okay, let's do it this way," Naunet began. "Let's pretend you're a child and we'll start with the utmost basics. Okay? Okay, great. Let's start with that." He floated up to my eye level and folded his legs under him. "Magical overdose occurs when a living creature becomes so saturated with magical energy, their body can no longer filter it out and they die."

"But don't they need magic to live?"

"Yes, usually. However, just because something is good for you, doesn't mean it can't kill you in higher doses. Take water, for example. Most creatures need it to live but if we were to drink too much water at one time, we could die. Same applies to magical energies. Your body needs it to support itself, but if you take in too much at one time, it'll poison you."

"What constitutes 'Taking in' magic?"

"What do you mean? Anytime you use magic you're taking it in. Magic spells by their very nature cause magic to flow through you and into the spell."

"That's not true. I know for a fact that druids manipulate the ambient mana in their surroundings to use magic. No true 'spell work' required."

"Interesting. I was unaware of that." Naunet paused to think it over, then he nodded his head. "Yes, I suppose that would certainly help prevent the magic poisoning. And probably also explains why you were never taught the basics."

"Why do you say that?"

He shook his head. "Never mind. We've wasted enough time standing around talking when you could have been practicing."

"Okay. I'm ready whenever you are. But—do you have any idea how long this'll take? I need to get something to eat soon."

Naunet shrugged. "Everyone's different. Some are born with the innate ability to control their magic, while some require many years of dedicated training to gain even the slightest hint of control. Basically, what I'm trying to say is this. You'll be here anywhere from thirty seconds after we begin to the moment you die of old age," he finished with a smile.

"Oh, well then—We should probably get started." I blandly replied. "By the way, how do you know so much about magic? I thought you were a martial artist or something?"

"That's a story for another time. Suffice it to say back in my day, you had to be at least passable in multiple disciplines in order to make it in this world. Nowadays, you kids have no idea what it takes to live outside of the civilized world," he finished cryptically.

~ ~ ~

And so, a month passed without anything too interesting happening. Naunet shot me some strange looks the first time he saw me take a bite out of Yggdrasil, but he didn't say anything about it.

I floated in place with my eyes closed. I'd been following Naunet's instructions to the letter and happily managed to shrink myself by a few hundred feet. Of course, Naunet wasn't impressed, but I'd learned pretty quickly that he wasn't impressed by much of anything.

I wanted—no needed—to be small again, and no matter what Naunet said about several hundred feet being the minimum, I wouldn't be satisfied until I was below one hundred feet long again.

While the actual technique to shrink myself wasn't too difficult, it required tremendous amounts of concentration to pull off for any length of time. I was actually surprised I hadn't done it completely by accident. It was basically my beam trick, but in reverse. Instead of compressing magic into my mouth and shooting it, I covered my body in magical energy and began drawing it towards my forehead, thus pulling my body into a more compact form.

Then came the tricky part: While I was doing all of that, I also had to focus on reducing my weight via gravity manipulation—a feat Naunet claimed was something any child should've been able to do before they left the nest.

That was the one thing that never failed to grate on my nerves. Naunet, though he was one of the nicest people I'd met in a long time, was one of the most insufferable know-it-alls I'd ever had the displeasure of meeting. He was always talking about his past and explaining everything as if I were either a small child or dumb, though lately he tended to favor option two.

I breathed out a frustrated sigh and refocused on the task at hand. I didn't have time to be thinking about this stuff. I had to maintain focus or I'd—

"How's it coming?" Naunet asked.

Pop

My eyes snapped open in surprise and I lost focus. The next thing I knew, I was suddenly back to normal. "Damn it!"

~ ~ ~

Once again, I was floating in place with my eyes closed. It'd been a little over a year since I began trying to shrink myself and I was actually making good progress. But I was still far too large to stop.

"You should've been done with this exercise ages ago," Naunet complained.

Pop

"Godamnit, will you shut up? Every time I start making progress you open your mouth and I'm back to square one." Of course, once I successfully shrunk to a certain size then I could quickly and easily return to it, but that wasn't the point.

Naunet was just doing it to annoy me.

"My bad," he laughed. He leaned against the branch and closed his eyes, presumably to go to sleep again. "Say, would you mind if I ask you some questions?"

I narrowed my eyes at him. "If you agree to answer my questions, then I'll answer yours."

Naunet thought it over for a moment, then shrugged. "Sure, I'll agree to that."

"Then I'll go first," I said, before Naunet could say otherwise. "How old are you?"

"I don't know," he admitted. "Time moves in odd ways here. Though, unlike most of the other royals you'll meet, I came equipped with my own prison." He finished, gesturing to the ground beneath us.

"So, you're senile. Got it."

"I wouldn't say that." He laughed. "Do you know how old you are?"

I wanted to blurt out "of course," but—That wasn't true anymore. I had no idea how old I was or how long I'd been on the path of kings. "Touché," I sighed.

"My turn. Are you a naturally born serpent or a reincarnation?"

"Reincarnation. I used to be human."

"Figures. No natural serpent is stupid enough to challenge Orochi."

"I have something I want to accomplish," I said. "How'd you become a Royal Serpent?"

"You kill enough people, you'll earn yourself some titles you don't want too. Now, if they'd only asked me before giving me the title, I would have informed them exactly what I thought of their proposal and where they could shove it," he said with a twisted grin.

I found myself thinking about Asgard in that moment, and the citizens I'd let fall to their deaths.

"Anyway," he shook his head. "What planet are you originally from?"

"Originally? As in, before I was reincarnated or after?"

"Before."

"I'm from a planet called Earth. It's a—"

"Oh? Which one?"

Any thought of future questions was blown away and I stared at him in stunned silence...

"What did you just say?"

"Which Earth are you from?" he repeated, slower this time.

I just stared at him.

"What? What did I say?

"You—How—What do you mean 'which Earth?' You know about Earth?"

"Okay, that's two questions, so I'll be asking two questions iin return. But yes, I do know about Earth. I know about all five of them, as a matter of fact."

"How? How do you know about Earth?"

"That's three questions and, well, I've been there—Well, to one of them anyway."

"You reincarnated?" I blurted out.

"No." Naunet replied in confusion. "Wait a minute, you are aware that Earth exists on Yggdrasil, yes? Four of them are somewhere near the very top of the tree, while the last is somewhere in the center. Why they all have the same name, I have no idea. Then again, humans always did have a weird naming sense. I once met a man who named his sword "Big Bertha." Can you imagine—"

I didn't hear what else he said. My mind went blank and my vision blurred. When I snapped out of it, Naunet was laying on the branch with his arm over his eyes.

"Oi! Hey Naunet, wake up!"

"Hmm?" He grumbled for a minute then opened his eyes. "What?"

"You said Earth exists here, right?"

"Yes?"

"Is it my Earth or just something using the same name?"

"How the hell am I supposed to know? Like I said, humans aren't the most creative bunch when it comes to naming things." Naunet rubbed the sleep from his eyes and sat up. "Though, I do remember that it was mostly water with, uh—a white moon and a yellow star?"

"What're the names of the surrounding planets?" I asked as calmly as I could.

"Don't remember. This trip was ages ago, Torga."

"What do you remember?" I hissed.

Naunet sighed. "I remember there being eight or nine planets in the cluster I visited, and that particular Earth was weird because it was solely dominated by large reptiles—Hey, put me down!" Naunet barked in surprise as I yanked him into the air and yelled,

"Yes! I can actually go home!"

"Put-Me-Down!" Naunet hissed.

"Oh." I released my grip and allowed him to fall to the branch. "Sorry, I'm just so excited!"

"Yeah, yeah, well, don't get too excited. It's highly possible that Earth isn't yours and even if it was, it might no longer be there."

That took some of the wind out of my sails, but I couldn't stop smiling. "Even so, it's a chance."

Naunet sighed. "How about you focus on getting this exercise down, then you can worry about going home. Sound fair?"

"Oh, I'm going to master it. Just you wait."

∼ ∼̇ ∼

"Well, would you look at that! You finally managed it, did you?" Naunet asked sarcastically.

I grimaced and directed a sharp glare at him. "Shut. Up," I hissed. I was sitting on the branch in my Naga form, while desperately fighting to maintain my current size. After three years, I'd finally managed to shrink my body to around one hundred and thirty feet in length and about eight to ten feet around. Every attempt to get smaller than this resulted in failure, for whatever reason, so I'd simply stopped trying.

"How do you feel?" Naunet asked after a few minutes of silence.

I stared at my arms. I felt like if I so much as twitched, I'd lose focus and lose my tenuous grasp on my size. "Like I'm wearing clothes ten sizes too small."

"Don't worry, that feeling will pass as you get used to maintaining your current size and soon you won't even notice you're doing it," he said while nodding his head.

"I hope so."

"Can you move?"

"I—I think so."

"Good, then we can finally begin your training!" Naunet said with a bright smile.

"Wait—" ***Pop*** "You mean this wasn't the training!?" I yelled.

"Of course, it wasn't. I told you at the start." A sinister smile spread across his face. "This was only the beginning."

Chapter Nineteen

W E WERE JUST ABOUT TO BREAK THROUGH the atmosphere when suddenly Naunet glanced over his shoulder at me, an irritating smile on his face. "You're very durable, aren't you?" he calmly asked.

"Yes?"

"Excellent! Then this should be a good learning opportunity for you," he replied as we broke through the outer atmosphere and clean air flooded my lungs.

"What will—" I screamed in surprise as gravity grabbed hold and an overwhelming force sent me hurtling towards the ground.

"Don't forget to maintain your size!" Naunet yelled at my back.

Before I could even think to reply, I slammed into the unforgiving ground at high speed. I groaned in pain and tried to lift my head, but even that proved impossible as the sheer weight of my own body prevented me from moving.

"Wow, I'm impressed you managed to maintain your size throughout that fall," Naunet cheerfully said as he landed beside my head.

"W—What h—happened?" I mumbled while struggling to keep my eyes open.

"Everything feeling incredibly heavy?"

I groaned my agreement.

"Well, you've just experienced the power of a god. Congratulations." Naunet sat cross-legged in front of me and propped his head on one hand. "What you're feeling right now is a result of this planet's trait."

"T—Trait?"

"Yep. The goddess that created this moon made it so I'd never be able to move freely. Unfortunately for her, I was never one to live up to the expectations of others."

"How?"

"How do I move so easily?"

I groaned my agreement and Naunet laughed.

"Practice mostly."

"Hmm?"

"You should have an easier time of it than I did since you can manipulate gravity, and all that jazz." Naunet smirked at me.

I felt like an idiot for forgetting I could do that. In my defense, though, manipulating gravity wasn't second nature to me yet. I closed my eyes and focused on pushing the dominating force of gravity away from my body. It took a minute, but I managed to push myself into a standing position.

I rounded on Naunet. "Why didn't you warn me?"

"It was funnier this way." Naunet shrugged.

"Has anyone ever told you that you're a dick?"

The smile on Naunet's face dimmed a little. "Not in a long time."

I wanted to say more, but the look on his face told me it was probably a bad idea.

"Can you move yet?" Naunet asked after a few moments of silence.

"Oh, yeah, I can move."

"Good. Because we have work to do. Starting with that aura of yours."

"If you can help me rein it in, I'm all ears."

~ ~ ~

"Stop trying to hit me and hit me!" Naunet hissed as he swiped his left hand through the air and knocked away a ball of condensed mana as if it were nothing more than a child's toy. The ball flew into the distance and collided with a mountain range a few miles away. The explosion reduced the top of the mountain to slag and produced a shockwave that flattened every tree for miles. But the only reaction Naunet showed me was a slight thinning of his eyes and a wave of his left hand. "I've told you once, I've told you a thousand times, Torga. Your problem lies not with your power, but with your speed. Even the most powerful skill is useless if you can't hit anything with it."

I narrowed my eyes in frustration and shook my arms to loosen them up. I held them out wide and conjured two blood-red balls of energy the size of watermelons. "Then let's try these."

The two balls orbited around each other as they raced towards a waiting Naunet. The sheer magical power behind them was causing the ground to erode wherever they passed.

Naunet shook his head. He waited for the moment they were about to hit him and spun, his palms guiding the balls as they passed by, and redirected them back at me. Or more specifically, at the ground beneath my feet.

After the explosion was over and I could see again, I pried myself out of the crater I'd been blown into and moved over to a disapproving Naunet. "You let your aura loose again. Fix it."

"Oh, sorry." I focused for a moment, then hauled my aura back inside my body. A simple technique to perform, but a pain in the ass to use. Just like the technique I used to shrink myself, I had to focus on keeping the aura contained at all times or it would burst out and start devouring everything again. I ended up having to sleep outside until Naunet could enchant the guest bedroom to mirror my technique, though he refused to tell me just *how* he pulled that off.

"You're still holding yourself back," he accused. "Even after all these years, you still refuse to use your magic to its fullest potential," he growled in frustration as he turned and moved away.

"Believe me, it's not on purpose," I mumbled. I turned to see the massive five-hundred-foot wide crater my magic caused. I continued to watch until it slowly melted away and the naturally green meadow returned to its previous appearance, devoid of any and all blemishes. The beautiful scenery filled my eyes before I turned and followed after Naunet.

After catching up to the only person I'd been able to talk with for the last seven years, I couldn't help but ask, "What do you think is causing my block?"

Naunet glanced at me and sighed. "I don't know. You should be much stronger than this." At my look of amusement, he snorted and continued. "Yes, I'm aware of just how powerful you are physically, but magically?" He shook his head. "You're barely as powerful as a newborn dragon."

"Oh no. I'm only as powerful as a tier eight beast. Whatever shall I do?"

Naunet smacked me upside the head. "Alright smartass, that's enough of that."

"Seriously though. What's wrong with me?"

"I honestly don't know. Physically you're fine. Hell, you're better than fine! Physically, you're one of the most powerful beings I've ever seen, and I'm including gods in that assessment."

I waited a few seconds for him to continue, but he remained silent. "I'm sensing a *but* in there somewhere."

"But magically, you're suffering from something, and I can't figure out what it is. Something is eating away at your magic energy faster than you can draw it out, resulting in this little 'problem' you've got." He finished speaking just in time for his home to appear on the horizon: A tree of truly gargantuan proportions with silver colored leaves and black bark stood as a testament to Naunet's time here. Supposedly planted by his wife when he was first crowned king, the tree was meant to be a symbol of her promise to always remain by his side. But she was killed by an overzealous serpent looking to make a name for himself just ten years after he'd been crowned king. Naunet still hadn't said what happened to that serpent, but the cold fury in his eyes as he told this story probably meant he escaped from whatever fate Naunet had planned for him.

"Maybe I've just reached a plateau?" I suggested.

"While that's certainly possible, it's also rather unlikely. You've still got a lot of growing to do. I can feel it in my bones."

"If you say so."

Naunet waved me off as we entered the tree through a large hole at the base and split up. While Naunet headed for the study to do some research, I went to the guest bedroom to sleep for the night.

CHAPTER TWENTY

"Torga! We've got a problem!" a voice cut through my dream and caused my eyes to snap open.

"What is it? What's happened?" I called back as I climbed out of bed and headed for the door. I pushed it open and moved into the hallway, where I found Naunet staring out of a window at the sky.

"We have visitors," Naunet whispered.

"Visitors? Anyone you were expecting?"

Naunet turned and looked me dead in the eye. "No one you'd want to meet."

"Who is it?"

"Gods, two of them." He pushed past me and entered the study.

"What!? Why would gods be coming here?"

"My guess? They're here looking for you."

I followed along behind him and, as always, was slightly awestruck at the sight that greeted me: The tree Naunet called home was well over three thousand feet tall and had a radius of about a thousand feet.

The study occupied the entire center of the tree: From the very bottom of the trunk to the very top, it was completely covered in shelves Naunet had painstakingly carved into the walls as the tree grew. Each shelf had between ten to twenty tomes ranging from ordinary paperback novels to ancient stone tablets that would've been more at home in a museum.

I shook my head and walked over to Naunet's desk. It was large and carved plainly, without any opulent trimmings or decorations and, like most furniture in Naunet's home, it was carved from the tree. Naunet was sitting in a chair scouring a large leather-bound tome.

"Please, tell me you found a solution to my problem?"

"I think I just might have... But we lack the time to fix it before the gods are knocking on my door."

I leaned on the desk and looked at the page Naunet seemed to be staring at. "Magic corrosion?"

"Mm. I racked my brain for anything that could have possibly pierced your scales and infected you with some kind of magic eating bug or virus. However, after going through my old notes and observations of you, I remembered that damn artifact you used to use as a way to shrink yourself."

"You think it's corroding me?"

Naunet shook his head and exhaled a sigh. "No, I think you're corroding **it**. I don't believe the stone was ever designed to hold such concentrated magic for as long as it has, and your magic, or possibly your aura, is dissolving it from the inside out."

"But—if it's the one being corroded then why is my magic being held back?"

"I'm not a hundred percent certain, but I believe the dissolved stone is leaking back into your body and forming 'blocks' that are keeping you from bringing your full power to bear. The stone was designed to contain extreme levels of energy, so blocking your mana pathways isn't out of the question—" Suddenly, the entire tree shook and the booming sound of thunder nearly rendered me deaf.

"Serpent Naunet, we know you are harboring a fugitive and request you turn him over to our custody," an obnoxiously high-pitched voice yelled.

"You have two minutes to comply or we will come in after him!" another voice of a much deeper tone finished.

"Arrogant little shits, aren't they?"

"Don't even think about it. They're gods; they have the right to be arrogant."

"One minute forty-five seconds!"

"How long would it take you to fix me?"

"Well, first I'd have to find a way to get through your scales, then I'd—"

I used mana to enhance the sharpness of my nails, then stabbed them into my neck. I pulled my bloody fingers out, then motioned for him to get on with it.

Naunet sprang into action, grabbing a knife off the desk and jamming it into the open wound on my neck to keep it open as long as possible. Then he pointed one finger at the wound and started whispering under his breath.

"One minute fifteen seconds!"

I sunk my teeth into my arm to keep from screaming as something deep inside my neck began to wiggle and force itself through my muscle tissue.

"Forty-five seconds!"

"Almost there." Naunet whispered. A wide smile spread across Naunet's lips as he jammed his index and middle fingers into my neck and pulled out a red stone about the size of a grape. "Got it!"

I hissed through gritted teeth, then moved towards the door.

"Where are you going?"

I ignored him and left the study.

"You can't go out there! You'll die!" Naunet yelled while chasing me.

"Can't help it... I'm hungry," I hissed. I could feel the wound closing as I moved but it still hurt like hell.

"Hungry!? Then go eat some of the planet. At least it won't kill you!"

"Relax. You said it yourself. I'm stronger than they are."

"I said you were physically stronger than most gods. And I don't know if you're aware of this or not, but gods—not really known for fistfights. They're usually more of the 'blast you and be done with it' kind of people."

"Good thing I have you to help me then, isn't it?"

There was silence as I headed down the stairs. "Fine. You want me to help you with this? Then afterwards it's time to call in that favor you owe me."

I stopped walking and turned to look at him. The look in his eyes told me all I needed to know about just how serious he was.

"Fifteen seconds!"

"Deal." I nodded.

I ducked out of the tree with Naunet following close behind. My eyes narrowed slightly at the sight of the "gods," the first I'd ever seen outside of the astral form Niabus always used.

The first was a young girl, approximately nine or ten years of age. Her hair was the color of blood and hung down her back in a wave. Her eyes were the same color as her hair and her skin was pale like a corpse's. Her outfit consisted of shining silver-white plate armor that covered everything but her head and hands. She had no visible weapons on her person.

"Hi." The little girl waved and spoke in a surprisingly deep voice.

"I told you he would be here, Carlas!" the obnoxious voice cheered.

He was a tall thin man who looked to be in his thirties. His hair was bright blue and was shaved into a military-style buzzcut. His eyes were dark green, and his skin appeared to be made of solid gold. His outfit consisted of dark robes, a tall metal staff, and a large kite shield strapped to his back.

"You certainly did, Arkos. When we return home, I'll be sure to tell Mom to bake you some cookies as a reward."

"Yay! Cookies!" The tall man cheered again and clapped as if he were a small child.

"Are all gods this weird?" I muttered.

"Unfortunately, most of the gods I've met have been—erm, eccentric as well."

"That's disappointing." I eyed the two gods up and down. "Guess I'll take the big one."

"What? Why do I have to fight the little one?"

"She's closer to your size," I replied with a smirk.

Naunet opened his mouth to argue, but the sound of approaching footsteps caused us both to return to the task at hand. We turned back and saw the little girl walking towards us—alone.

"No need to bicker, boys. I'll take you both," she told them, a wide smile on her lips. As she drew closer and closer to them, a small forked tongue flashed out of her mouth and ran around her lips, revealing extremely sharp teeth.

Definitely not human. I stepped up to face the little brat. I towered over her by almost ten feet and the fist I raised into the air was as big as her torso. My fist caused a sonic boom as it collided with Carlas' face.

I had just enough time to allow a small smirk of pride to flash across my face for getting the first hit off on a god, before I was suddenly staring at the stars while floating miles above the ground.

We're in so much trouble. I slammed painfully into the ground and carved out a long trench in the unforgiving soil.

Slowly, painfully, I climbed to my feet and looked down at the arm I'd used to punch a god in the face. Everything below the elbow was gone and dark red blood was staining the grass red.

"Torga! Run!" a voice yelled.

I swiveled in the direction of the voice and saw Naunet's broken, bleeding body lying on the ground two hundred feet away. He was desperately crawling past a large golden portal that was floating in the air behind him. Through the portal, I could see the gods watching me.

The little girl casually stepped through the portal.

Oh, hell no! I pointed my palm at Naunet and used my gravity manipulation to suck him towards me. He covered the distance in the blink of an eye, and I caught him by the arm. I threw him over my shoulder, then launched myself into the skies and fled as fast as I could.

However, before I could even get twenty feet off the ground, something grabbed my tail and stopped me cold. I slammed into the dirt hard enough to send Naunet rolling away from me as my earlier momentum continued to carry him forward and away from them.

"Sorry, snake-boy, but I'm afraid I can't let you escape."

I was flipped onto my back and a metal boot was pushed into my throat. My eyes widened as she pressed down on my windpipe and cut off my ability to breath. I grabbed her foot and tried to throw her off, but it was like I was a kid trying to throw an SUV off of my chest.

"After all, if I let you get away, what kind of precedent would that set for the other people I'm hunting? I'd have to let them go as well or I'd be seen as 'unfair.' You don't think I'm an unfair person, do you?" she asked with a wide smile on her face.

When I couldn't answer her, she stomped down on my throat several times and punctuated each stomp with, "Do you!? Do you!? Do you!?" She kicked my ribs and sent me spiraling away. "Answer me damn it!" she hysterically yelled after I'd bounced off the ground.

"Carlas!" the man whined. "Can we go now? I'm hungry."

The little goddess patted her messed up hair down and slowly allowed a smile to spread across her lips. "Of course. Let me finish up here, then we can go."

She walked over, bent at the waist to look me in the eye.

I spat blood in her eyes.

She pulled a napkin out of her back pocket and wiped her face with it. "Don't worry your pretty little head. I'm a God of Time and Justice, so trust me, you won't feel any pain and it'll be over quick. I promise." She reached out her pale, ungloved hand and grabbed my face.

A Snake's Path

The last thing I saw before my vision went black was the demented grin on the little bitch's face.

CHAPTER TWENTY-ONE

THE FIRST, AND WELL, THE ONLY THING I SAW when I opened my eyes was a vast white emptiness around me. I lifted my head off the cool floor and slowly stood up. *I'm back here again, huh?* Looking down at my hands, they, like the rest of my body, were made of an inky blackness that seemed to draw in light. Though, occasionally, bits of emerald green light would flash across my body like a bolt of lightning.

"It's been a while, mortal," a gong-like voice said from my left.

"Niabus—What's it been, fifty years? Or was it sixty?" I asked as I turned to the golden being.

"I'm not quite sure. Time becomes rather meaningless once you've been put in my position."

"And what position is that? Gatekeeper of hell?"

"Unfortunately, not," the being laughed.

"Then, why are you here?"

"Well, I'm not here. Not really, anyway. The form you see before you is just what remains of my magic after I gave you those little 'gifts.'"

"So, you've been... what? Just freeloading here ever since?"

The being tilted its head to the right and folded its arms across its chest. **"You're much braver than the last time we talked. Finally grown a spine, have you?"**

"No thanks to you," I snorted. "I've had to face death more times than I care to remember. Facing you down doesn't seem like such an incredible thing anymore."

The being unfolded one arm and lazily pointed at him. **"You know, part of the reason you died was believing you were invincible. If you'd been smart, or even the least bit cautious, this wouldn't have happened. But I can't say I'm surprised; I did program you to think that way."**

"You—What?"

"Let me be frank with you, Torga. Consider it a parting gift if you'd like: You were never meant to meet with your wife again. You were meant to fail. The fact that you lived this long is just a testament to your stubbornness and luck, nothing more."

I felt the strength leave my legs and I stumbled back. "What are you talking about? No, you told me if I evolved, that if I did everything in my power to grow stronger, I could see her again. You promised me that!" I yelled.

Niabus shrugged. **"I cannot recall ever promising such a thing. But did you honestly believe it would be so easy? That she would just be waiting for you with open arms? You're a monster and a damned good one at that. You've slaughtered countless people in your quest to see her again. But—did you never stop and ask yourself if I could have been lying?"**

"Of course, but what else was I supposed to believe?"

The being let out a deep sigh. **"Be that as it may, I suppose congratulations are in order. You've fulfilled your destiny."**

"Destiny? What fucking destiny are you talking about? I. Died. How is me dying without seeing Sarah again a 'completion of my destiny?'"

"Your destiny wasn't to meet Sarah again. It was to die here, now, in this very spot."

I stared at him for several seconds. ***"Why?"*** I hissed.

The being shrugged. **"I made a deal."**

"What kind of deal?" I asked weakly.

"The kind where I get what I want, and in exchange, someone else gets what they want. But you want specifics, don't you?" As the being said so, a tremor rocked the ground, causing me to lose my balance and fall over.

"What's happening!?"

"You asked 'Why' you had to die here and 'What' was the deal I made," Niabus said, ignoring my question entirely. **"Well, they are one and the same. Long before I had the pleasure of meeting you, my sister Forna and I were mortals—"**

I opened my mouth to speak, but he silenced me with a gesture. **"We don't have time for interruptions, so please, be silent. I am—was the Dragon King and she was a Royal Phoenix. Upon our ascension to godhood we kind of... drifted apart. I led my dragon followers farther down Yggdrasil than any being before or since and she—"** He took a deep, ragged breath. **"She met *him,"*** he hissed.

"She never told me just *what* that bastard did to her, but it fundamentally changed her. She became cold, cruel, and full of hate. But she stayed with him. The fact that I, a God of Destruction, did not notice when my own sister was being slowly destroyed from the inside out—it almost broke me to see her reduced

to *that*." He shook his head. "So, I killed the bastard. Scattered his body to the four corners of Yggdrasil. But the damage was done. She no longer trusted anyone, and I couldn't blame her.

"The man she loved entrapped her within her own mind, while treating her body like his personal toy. And I was so focused on myself that I completely ignored her cries for help.

"I was locked within a temple on the very planet my dragons had claimed was their home world as she and her pantheon destroyed all the work I'd done over the years. Her way of paying me back for leaving her trapped within her own mind while her body was destroyed, I suppose." He took another pause, then continued. "I scoured my personal library for eons for something—anything that could help her move past her hatred. I eventually found it in the Tribunal, an organization dedicated to upholding the Hero system and ruled by the gods of Fate, Life, Death, and Rebirth.

"An accord was made. In return for my help, they would convince the heads of their respective departments to give her another chance at life. A chance to be happy."

I felt my eyes involuntarily widen.

"Yes," Niabus laughed, "I suppose that wish would sound quite familiar to you, wouldn't it? Seeing as that was your wish as well. You have no idea how much I had to restrain myself when you told me your dream. How excited I was to find someone so like myself, and yet, so very different.

"I knew you would do whatever it took to find your wife, so I simply pointed you in the right direction and off you went. Of course, I had to step in a few times to make sure you would survive some of those earlier encounters, but that's a paltry sacrifice in the grand scheme of things."

The ground was again rocked by intense tremors as a large black object began to rise out of the ground a few tens of feet away from us. "How does my death help you then?"

"It doesn't, but it wasn't my idea to have you die, you understand. If it were up to me, I would've left you alone and let you do whatever you wanted. But my associates wanted this conversation to happen, so here we are," Niabus chuckled.

"The time has come."

"For what?"

"For you to move on. Don't you want to go home?"

"You said I could never go home."

"Yes, I lied about a lot of things. Can we get this over with, already? I've had enough of this place to last me a lifetime. Or two, in your case." Suddenly, against my will, I was violently dragged towards the circle.

Just before I was pulled inside, I lifted my arms and pressed them against it in an attempt to keep myself away from it. Though the circle continued to try and pull me inside, I was just barely able to keep a hold of its edges and keep from falling in.

"You're as stubborn as ever, aren't you?"

"What is this!?" I hollered.

"Don't you remember? This is how you were brought to Yggdrasil in the first place. A little more violent this time, perhaps, but the premise is the

same. You go through that portal and you're home. You'll still be dead, but at least you'll be able to see your family again."

Something clicked in my mind. I glared over my shoulder at him, "You're lying. I go through this portal and I'll cease to exist, won't I? This was all just some sick fucking game to you, *wasn't it!?"* I hissed.

"A game you would have gladly played had it been *your* wife at stake."

"You know what?" I laughed. "You're absolutely right, I would have." I extended my arms, pushing my body further away from the portal. "I would have done everything you've done and more." The white space around the circle began to crack. "You say this is my destiny?" Another crack. "I say you're *wrong.*" I shoved with my arms and stood on the edge of the portal. My body began to twist and expand, then I was suddenly in my true form: My body extended far beyond the horizon, my wings cast a shadow over the entirety of the white space, and my eyes were locked onto Niabus. "I decide my fate. No one, not you, not the gods, and not some 'Tribunal' will *ever* tell me otherwise."

My hunger exploded out of me in a brackish aura that dissolved the portal, a wide-eyed Niabus, and the white space itself…

～ ～ ～

I opened my eyes and glared at the little god still holding my face.

Ding

ထ ထ ထ ထ ထ ထ

For defying the fates and rejecting your destiny, you have been granted a new title and trait.

Free:
Sometimes being free isn't all that it's cracked up to be. You are now free from the machinations of fate and are free to decide your own path.
Good luck Torga. If we ever meet in person, I'll buy you a beer.
Signed, Shai: God of Fate
P.S. Here's one for the road.
Would you like to evolve?

∞∞∞∞∞∞∞∞

Yes.

A transparent white shell formed around my body so fast the goddess barely had time to pull her hand out of the way before it was sealed shut.

"Oh ho. He had an evolution hidden up his sleeve." The little goddess laughed.

∞∞∞∞∞∞∞∞

You will evolve in... ??????
WARNING: Yggdrasil magic detected!
Commencing absorption of excess Yggdrasil magic
Magic absorbed!
Remaining time until evolution completion is.... 10 seconds

∞∞∞∞∞∞∞∞

The influx of power flowing through my veins caused me to scream in pain. I felt my body break endlessly only to be rebuilt again. I felt the wings on my shoulders rip apart and begin shifting and moving as if the individual strands had minds of their own.

After an eternity of pain, my eyes opened, and I was staring down at the little goddess.

Ding

∞∞∞∞∞∞∞∞

Name: Torga

Race: Gluttonous Dark Naga Hydra

Classification: Tier 9

Level: 94

Experience: 2,971,652/ 12,000,000

Titles: Destroyer of Asgard, The Dark Serpent, The Unwavering One, Royal Serpent, Free

Stats:

- Physical
    - Strength: 899,752
    - Endurance: 899,752
    - Dexterity: 1,051
    - Speed: 1,201
- Mental
    - Intelligence: 60
    - Wisdom: 45
    - Charisma: 21
- Resistances
    - Elements: 60%
    - Divinity: 80%

- Mental: 20%
- Immunities
  - Mind Control
  - Illusions

Skills: Major Stealth, Heat Detection, Absolute Gluttony, Absolute Growth, Greater Petrifying Gaze, Superior Acid Venom, Detect Concealment, Energy Breath, Fly, Magic Enhancement, Elemental Manipulation, Gravity Manipulation

Traits: Divine Gluttonous Aura +40, Growth +70, Venomous, Aquatic, Forever Growing, Indomitable, Supreme Regeneration

∞∞∞∞∞∞∞∞

"Alright, you stupid little bitch, it's time for Round Two!" nine voices said in unison.

"Umm..." The little girl gave me a funny look. "I'm a guy."

"Oh... Then I don't feel nearly as bad about doing this." I wrapped a gravity field around my fist and slammed it into his face. Unlike before, this time my arm wasn't destroyed by simply connecting with his face. Instead, I felt all the bones inside my remaining arm turn to dust a moment after the god was knocked off his feet.

I followed the punch by opening my mouth and firing a beam of condensed mana into his face at point blank range, though I was pleasantly surprised to see nine other beams flowing over my head, striking the god and pushing him deeper into the ground. This also created something of a smokescreen, which I used to steal Naunet and make a break for it.

I was under no illusion that I'd done anything more than piss the god off with that move.

"What the hell happened to you?" Naunet asked from his position, dangling over my shoulder as I flew through the air.

I glanced over my shoulder at the spot where my wings used to be: Nine thirty-foot-long eyeless serpents of varying shades of green were flicking their tongues at the horizon. They appeared to be ninety percent mouth, as the entirety of their heads were split in half by a giant maw full of dagger-like teeth.

"It's a long story," I sighed.

"I imagine so. You know what? Never mind, it can wait."

"We need to get out of here."

"Correction, you need to get out of here. I need to head back and hold them off for as long as I can."

"What? No, I can't let you do that."

"I'm not asking you; I'm telling you. Besides, of the two of us, only you have something you're meant to be doing."

There was a pregnant pause as neither of us wanted to give in.

"You aren't meant to die here, Torga. You have a wife to find, a daughter to marry off, and friends waiting for your return… I have none of those things. Besides, I haven't fully paid up yet."

"And I haven't found your wife's murderer yet either."

"No need. I know where he is," Naunet said.

"What, where?"

"Look to your right."

I did so and saw the overly large planet Naunet's moon orbited.

"When you get to that planet, find the serpent known as Rajah and tear his head off for me, won't you?"

"If he's that close, then why the hell haven't you killed him already?"

"Because I'm forbidden to leave my moon. Trust me, if I could've killed him when I first noticed him inside the Bi-frost on the way here, I would have. As it is, I'm going to have to get you to do it."

I let out a sigh. "I don't like this."

"You don't have a choice. Just put me down and go on with your life. The gods' pride won't allow them to let me live, so I'm betting they'll come after me first. Besides—" He held out a small red stone for me to inspect: It was the one he'd pulled out of my neck. "I still have a few tricks up my sleeve."

~ ~ ~

One of my serpent heads was staring in the direction of Naunet's moon and had the job of alerting me if I was being followed.

While it was different from seeing through my own eyes, in that I couldn't actually *see* what they saw, I somehow still knew.

Each head swayed back and forth as they looked at anything that caught their eye—er, tongue. Currently, most of them were transfixed on my rapidly regenerating arm. I flexed the muscles in my broken right arm and had to grit my teeth to avoid yelping at the pain.

My arm was still mostly destroyed, but at the rate it was healing it would be back to normal before I arrived planet side. My left arm, on the other hand—I glanced down at the stump where my lower left arm used to be and sighed. Sure, I had a spare left arm, but I was still sore about losing it.

Boom!

I stopped flying and turned to look at the moon. A wave of mana was in the process of glassing the surface and creating a crater large enough I could see it from space.

I hope you find your wife again in your next life...

~ ~ ~

I broke through the final atmospheric layer and saw something I hadn't seen in decades—a city. It was a large urban metropolis with towering gray-metal skyscrapers and a colossal golden statue of a Serpentine Dragon with a halo of jewels encircling its head. The statue towered over the city surrounding it. Its head was tilted slightly down, giving it the appearance of a permanent scowl as it stared at the city below.

I shook my head at the garishness and landed away from the city in a blood-red canyon. As soon as I touched down, the ground beneath me began to melt away. *No, I need to control it... I am the master of my hunger, not the other way around.* I drew my aura into my chest and locked it down tight.

I need to find Rajah and kill him before those damnable gods show up. I had faith that Naunet held them off as long as he could, but I also realized that the explosion wouldn't kill them. Wound them, maybe, but they were too powerful to die from such a trick.

I started flying in the direction of the city and the large golden statue of what I could only assume to be my target.

I landed just outside of the canyon, within sight of the city's imposing walls. I'd made it through the canyon without issue and even managed to catch a few grizzly bear-sized black rabbits with antlers to hold me until I could finally relax and take time to eat again.

The problem was, they did nothing to sate my hunger. Despite eating several of the creatures, I still felt empty. At least the simple act of hunting was useful for keeping my mind off of Naunet's death and my impending doom.

However, about an hour or so into my little jaunt over the canyon, my stomach started to cramp, and I developed a migraine. To make matters even worse, I noticeably began to lose muscle mass. Because my body could no longer devour its surroundings to fill the void that was my stomach, it'd begun eating *itself* in an attempt to keep me alive.

Eventually, I'd have to loosen the reins on my aura or else I'd end up starving to death. However, if I did that, I'd be back to square one and I could potentially cause the planet irreversible damage.

Of course, I didn't actually care if the planet was obliterated, or its people killed. But I couldn't breathe in the vacuum of space, and it was in my best interest to avoid destroying my only source of oxygen until I was ready to leave.

I began scanning the road leading to the city for signs of life and found a group of people walking towards me. *Suppose I could try asking for directions. Who knows, they may be able to lead me directly to Rajah and I can cut this trip short.*

INTERLUDE: THE HUNTERS

THE LITTLE GOD WAS STARING THROUGH narrowed eyes at the being sprawled on the ground before him. "Where. did. he. go?" he growled. Each word was punctuated by an intense burst of divinity being forced into the body of the serpent through the hand holding Naunet down.

"Give it up, Carlas." Naunet groaned as his body began to rapidly age. "You know you can't kill me. I'm protected."

The little god growled in indignation but didn't disagree. "And how I wish it wasn't true. Nevertheless, you do not meet the criteria," he said while removing his hand and stepping away. "Unlike you mortals, we gods must hold ourselves to a higher standard. The law is everything and no matter how much I may wish otherwise, you haven't *technically* broken any laws in my presence. So, you may live—for now."

Naunet began to laugh, quietly at first, but it soon built into a loud cackle as the serpent sat up. "You couldn't kill me if you tried and you know it," the serpent said as any remaining wounds rapidly healed and vanished as if they were never there. "The only beings in this universe that could kill me are the original nine and Torga. Xitas saw to that personally."

Carlas grabbed the serpent by its throat and slammed his head into the ground.

"Let's get one thing straight here, you little worm. I can, and will, kill you if you cross the line. So, watch your damn mouth," he harshly whispered.

He let go of the serpent's throat and stepped away. He walked over to Arkos and motioned for the much larger god to follow him while using his other hand to brush his hair out of his face.

"Let's go, Arkos. We've got a worm to catch."

"Have a pleasant day, gentlemen. And—don't mind the noises you may hear," Naunet chuckled after them.

~ ~ ~

Carlas and Arkos had been flying along the branch, while following Torga at a safe distance, waiting for the moment he would stop to sleep or eat, so they could avoid spending any unnecessary energy. However, their plan was thrown off the rails when they sensed a familiar energy racing towards them.

"Arkos... We have an unwelcome visitor," Carlas muttered as he came to a stop.

Arkos, following Carlas' lead, slowed to a stop and floated just behind the much smaller god.

"Who is it!? Who's coming!?" Arkos asked excitedly.

"I'm hurt, Arkos. I thought that you, of all people, would recognize your own brother," a raspy voice said from behind the two.

Carlas slowly turned to face the new arrival and groaned in annoyance when his fears were confirmed.

The man standing before him was one of the three "major" gods of the Calarian pantheon. He was currently slightly taller than twelve feet and was wider than most horses were long. His long, obsidian-colored hair was pulled into a bun on top of his head, and his thick, curly beard hung down to his navel.

However, even though he was clad from neck to toe in silver armor, you could tell something was... off. His arms and legs didn't quite fit his body and the overly large head certainly didn't help to even things out.

But what could be done about the appearance of a dwarf? Even if it were an ascended dwarf.

"Lord Fieren... How nice to see you," Carlas said in a faux-polite voice.

"Hello, dead-thing. Have you been properly watching out for my brother?" Fieren asked in a voice that clearly showed what he thought of the "dead-thing" standing before him.

Carlas grimaced at the casual insult. He ground his teeth together and plastered a cheery, but just as fake smile on his face. "Of course, I have, my lord. Arkos is in perfect health." Carlas' statement was reinforced by Arkos nodding over his head.

"Hmm... Good," Fieren muttered while stroking his beard.

"I mean no disrespect, my lord. But... What brings you here?"

Fieren's pale blue eyes briefly glanced over to Arkos, then returned to meeting Carlas'. He stopped stroking his beard and reached into a small leather pouch tied to his dull-white belt. After rummaging around inside the pouch for a few seconds he pulled out a sealed envelope and held it out for Arkos to take.

"A letter from Mother. She asked that I get this to you personally, Arkos," was his simple response.

Ahh, yes. The momma's boy rears his ugly head, Carlas thought while suppressing the smirk that threatened to show on his face.

Fieren was rather notorious within the pantheon for his unhealthy obsession with his and Arkos' shared mother. No one knew for sure why Fieren felt the way he did, though most assumed it came from the lack of love he received from her as a child.

Both of them, Fieren and Arkos, were born from the union of a mortal man and their goddess mother, making them originally demi-gods. This, of course, led to them being *much* more powerful than their fellow gods once they ascended to godhood. But as with nearly all demi-gods, the divine parent usually left them to fend for themselves in the world of mortals.

It was rumored that being abandoned is what led to Fieren's obsession, and his distaste for Carlas, as he was one of the few mortals to be chosen by Mother to be her champion. While most in the pantheon begrudgingly accepted this, Fieren never could stand the thought of a "dead-thing" sullying his mother's image, so he'd been actively trying to interfere in Carlas' assignments, even if it meant dragging Arkos down with him.

"Thanks, Fieren!" Arkos cheered as he gratefully accepted the letter.

"Hmph," Fieren grunted as he vanished in a flash of light.

Carlas stared at the letter in Arkos' hands cautiously as he used his magic sight to thoroughly inspect every corner of it. *I don't see any enchantments on it, aside from a sealing spell with Mother's magic signature. Though I wouldn't put it past Fieren to booby-trap the letter with something that could break through Arkos' defenses.* Carlas began muttering to himself a prayer to mother for protection. It wouldn't do anything since she couldn't actually hear him from inside the time dilation, but it certainly made him feel better.

Boom!

Carlas turned in the direction of the sound and saw a wave of fire glassing the planet.

~ ~ ~

Naunet appeared in a flash of silver light. He stood in the center of the frozen wasteland known as the Neutral Zone. The nine pillars, dubbed the Pillars of Orochi by the "lesser" royals, began to shake as the snow-covered ground thawed, revealing a frozen lake beneath the snow.

Naunet knelt down and placed the palm of his right hand on the ice. He closed his eyes and breathed deeply. *It's almost time. The pieces are falling into place, and soon you will be free. We will take our revenge on the ones responsible for imprisoning us. Of that, you have my word, brother.* Power pulsed from Naunet's palm, causing the ice to crack beneath his fingertips.

He took another deep breath, then released a second burst of power from his palm, cracking the ice even further.

The Neutral Zone began to shake as the pillars started to glow with a faint violet light. Soon after, the first of the nine pillars cracked down the center and shattered into a billion purple particles that slowly rotated in place, forming a three-foot high hurricane of magic that sunk into the ground. The second pillar came next, followed by the third, fourth, fifth, and so on.

As the last of the pillars sunk into the ground, an intense violet light lit up the frozen lake.

"So, the seal is finally weakening?" a hissing voice echoed across the land. It was an oily, venomous sound that would've made even the bravest hero pause.

"Yes, it took some digging, but I've learned that the god responsible for sealing you away has met his end."

"Good!" The voice laughed. **"And what of our followers? Have they come to greet their king?"**

"They've—No, sire. Most of them have turned their backs on us. Though we do still have some allies in the Golden City."

"I see. Then it seems I must remind them who it is they serve, and why my name instilled respect and fear into the hearts of my enemies. Hurry up and free me, Naunet. I've kept them waiting long enough."

"Yes, my lord. Soon the pieces will be in place, and your replacement will—"

"Replacement?" Orochi hissed.

"Sorry, sire." Naunet hurriedly apologized. "Not replacement, no one could possibly replace you. But it will be enough to fool the enchantment on your prison and those idiotic gods that monitor it."

"Hmm—Yes, perhaps you are correct," Orochi softly hissed. **"Forgive me, Naunet. This place has made me... irritable."**

"No apologies necessary, Sire," Naunet replied, a chill racing down his spine.

Chapter Twenty-Two

"Hey, wait up damn it!" A young man who appeared no older than fifteen with shaggy brown hair and a scruffy face yelled to the group of adventurers.

"Go home, Steven," the tall blond woman at the front of the group replied without looking.

"What? B—but you said I could join you. You promised me that last night, Kiera!" Steven hollered as he caught up to them.

"Did you really promise the boy that?" a towering man at the back of the group asked.

"No—"

"That's a lie! You swore you would help me get revenge for my brother!"

"No, I didn't!" Kiera yelled in his face, then continued in a softer tone. "I told you *we* would get revenge for all those Rajah has imprisoned here and forced to serve as his slaves. *We*, not you." She turned on her heel and motioned for the others to follow her. "Go home Steven and leave this to the professionals."

Her traveling companions had mixed reactions to her refusal of the young man, but they all followed along after a few murmured words of encouragement to him.

"Was that really necessary, Lady Kiera?" an older woman of elvish descent asked. Her head was completely shaved and she wore a yellow robe with the symbol of the elven goddess of life; Ysvarna, emblazoned on her chest.

"Aye, that seemed a bit harsh even for you, " said the towering man, who stood well over thirteen feet tall and as wide as three men standing abreast. He had a leather shawl draped over his bare chest and a pair of loose cotton breaches as his only protection from the elements. Not that a cyclops needed much protection.

"Better his feelings get hurt than his life be taken," said the fourth and final member of the party, a yellow-scaled dragon-man. He was wearing a thick layer of chainmail over his entire body with only his face exposed.

Kiera, the leader of the group, an Amazonian woman with resplendent blonde hair and bedecked in loose-fitting yellow robes, rolled her eyes at the dragon-man's apparent agreement.

It was no secret that he'd been attempting to mate with her for decades, and part of his latest attempt at getting into her pants was to be as agreeable as possible. As if she were attracted to that. While she hadn't known Agronok, the cyclops, and Sheena, the elf, for very long, at least they *seemed* to have noble intentions.

Q-Shan, on the other hand, she'd known since long before she was brought to this cesspool of a planet. As the first warrior of an Amazonian tribe, Kiera was the strongest warrior in the tribe and was in charge of training the younger generations.

The problems only arose when they sent her out to find a group of men to father the next generation. As first warrior, she was exempt from this, as she needed to be combat ready at all times—a fact Q-Shan blithely ignored after he and several other dragon-men were offered the job, and unfortunately for Kiera, he'd been after her ever since.

After several hours of traveling in near silence with only Q-Shan and Sheena attempting to hold a conversation, the group began to notice a strange sensation in the air: like an oppressive force was bearing down on their shoulders and attempting to drive them into the ground.

"What on Yggdrasil is that?" Q-Shan asked anxiously.

Kiera glared at him out of the corner of her eye but didn't rebuke him since she felt it too.

"I don't know, but we should remain cautious moving forward. This could be another of Rajah's tricks." After saying so, she slipped her hands into the ebony-colored gauntlets at her waist and tightened them to the point they wouldn't slip off. After making sure they were fastened to her satisfaction, she slammed her palms together, which caused spikes to jump out of the many small holes dotting the back of the gauntlets and lock into place.

The other members of the group all readied their own weapons within seconds of Kiera. Q-Shan drew a claymore from his back. It was easily as long as Kiera was tall and almost as wide, with a plain ebony hilt on the end.

Agronok was far too large to wield ordinary weapons, even those made by the dragon clan, who were known for their ridiculously oversized weapons. He instead opted to use his natural weapons... Teeth, horns, and sheer overwhelming might to beat his enemies into submission.

And Sheena, as an elven priestess, began whispering prayers to her goddess to grant her allies "buffs" and to weaken her enemies.

However, once she started asking her goddess to affect their guest personally, a large shadow suddenly appeared behind her and an eyeless serpent with a mouth large enough to swallow even Agronok whole coiled tightly around her body.

"Don't take this personally," the monster said in a dreadfully terrifying voice that seemed to echo multiple times before coming to an end.

The adventurers spun on their heels and instinctively charged the monster, but the sight of Sheena being hoisted into the air by the odd-looking serpent gave them pause. Better to find out what it wanted and possibly convince it to let her go, than piss it off by attacking and guarantee her death. After all, it had spoken, so it had to be intelligent enough to bargain with, right?

Kiera raised her hands with the palms facing the monster.

"Hey, easy now. You don't want to do this," she said while taking a few small steps towards the towering creature. It had short black hair, and stern-looking eyes that were deep red. Having nine eyeless serpents tracking her every movement was creepy, to say the least, but she didn't want to insult the creature by staring.

"Who here knows of a serpent that goes by the name Rajah?" the naga asked in that eerie voice of his.

The sudden question put the group on edge and caused Sheena's eyes to widen even further than they already were. Unable to control her anxieties, she began to struggle against the serpent's hold.

The naga glanced at her and said, "If you answer my question, I have no problem with letting you go. But you need to stop struggling before you get hurt."

Sheena began to fight even harder as panic set in, and her higher thought processes were overridden by fear. Before Kiera could tell Sheena to calm down, Sheena began screaming in pain as the snake tightened around her.

"I said. Stop. Struggling." The naga said in a tone which brokered no argument.

It was a combination of the sight of their companion in pain, the naga's voice, and the overwhelming pressure they'd been feeling for the past few minutes that ultimately led to the group's first mistake.

"Let the lass go!" Agronok roared as he swung his meaty fist over Kiera's head and slammed it into the naga's cheek.

The naga's head was turned slightly to one side and he loosened his grip enough that Sheena slid out and collapsed to the ground. Except, the moment she touched the ground, before Kiera's eyes, Sheena's body, clothes, and jewelry seemingly evaporated into bright blue particles of light and flowed into the naga.

"I apologize for your friend. I didn't mean for that to happen," the naga mumbled.

"What did ye do!?" Agronok yelled as, in a fit of rage, he began swinging.

Each hit slightly turned the naga's head from side to side. However, that was the only reaction they received, as not even the look of apathy on his face changed to reflect the damage he should be feeling.

An adult cyclops like Agronok was capable of bending steel beams with his bare hands. As such, no matter how large the naga was, there was simply no way he wasn't feeling Agronok's punches—right? Kiera wondered.

Suddenly, as if in answer to her unasked question, the naga moved around a still swinging Agronok. "You should have just listened to me," the naga sighed as he moved out of the way of a punch. "You would have lived longer." As the naga moved past a suddenly unmoving Agronok, he pulled the shawl from the cyclops' shoulders and wrapped it around himself just before Agronok pitched forward and dissolved into blue dust.

After seeing the imposing cyclops reduced to nothing more than dust in the wake of the naga, Kiera's mind was flooded with fear, and her fight or flight response kicked in. She ran with all the might her legs could generate and in a flash of lightning, she left Q-Shan alone with the monster that would come to haunt her dreams.

~ ∴ ~

Gotta get away, Gotta run, I gotta leave! These thoughts repeated in her head over and over again as the events that had just transpired played on a loop inside her mind's eye.

The monster appearing, Sheena evaporating into the pale blue lights, Agronok falling to dust, and the look of betrayal on Q-Shan's face as he realized what she was about to do. *I'm sorry!* Was all her fear clouded mind could manage as she fled and left him to his fate.

As the walls of a large city filled her empty eyes, she snapped back to reality. She slid almost to a complete stop just outside the city's gate, prompting the line of people trying to get in to turn to her in surprise.

"Jeez, what's her problem?"

"Oi lady, watch where you're going!"

"Is she okay?"

The crowd began murmuring as they watched her pant with wild eyes, disheveled hair, and robes tattered from racing through the forest, though she didn't even notice the last thing in her haste to get inside the city walls.

"Help—Please." She muttered as she fell to her knees.

Luckily one of the guardsmen at the gate recognized her and came running to her aid. "Lady Kiera, what is it? What's wrong?" the guardsman asked while removing his gray-metal helmet to reveal a weathered face filled with frown lines, short gray hair, and a thick mustache.

"Monster—" Was all she could manage to say as the adrenaline began to wear off and inky blackness clouded her vision.

"Monster?" the guardsman asked.

"Serpent—" she whispered, then her head fell forward and she passed out.

~ ~ ~

Dorian, the guardsman, lifted her into his arms and carried her through the gates in spite of the protests from those waiting to get in.

"Hey, what about us!?"

"We were here first!"

"That's not fair!"

One burst of outrage led to another as a cacophony of voices soon began to rail against the guardsmen at the gate.

"Silence!" Dorian roared. Their voices died in their throats as the glare of the captain's anger pressed down on them. "The next person to open their mouth is barred from the city for a week," Dorian informed the men standing at the gate as he walked through it.

"What—"

"We'll die—"

"Those two, no entry for a week. Anyone found letting them in will have me to deal with, am I clear?"

"Sir!" the guardsmen yelled.

Once inside, Dorian made his way to the gate barracks and started barking out orders to the men under his command.

"Kiera returned without the others. I want a full regiment sent to investigate!"

"But sir, we don't have the manpower to–"

Dorian rounded on his lieutenant. "Those adventurers, shabby as they may be, are our best shot at killing Rajah and getting off this godforsaken world! I don't care if I have to borrow men from the other captains, we will find them!" Then, in a much quieter voice, he asked, "Do I make myself clear, lieutenant?"

The shorter man swallowed thickly and nodded. "Crystal, sir."

"Then get on it. And tell the healer I'm taking her up to the holding cells until we can get this sorted out."

"Sir!" The lieutenant gave him a one-armed salute and left to follow his orders.

The barracks, much like the city it protected, was almost solely created by Earth magic millennia ago, back when the serpent lord Rajah first decided to start abducting people from the wider verse and imprisoning them on this planet. A young prodigious thaumaturge was one of the first hundred abducted.

Whether it was by design or accident, no one is sure, this mage would become the hero they needed more than anything, as he alone used his knowledge to form the walls that protect them to this day. He spent the remainder of his life creating this city as a bastion for those Rajah had doomed to walk this planet.

However, not every battle was won so easily. The city had been lost to Rajah's serpents more times than they cared to remember, and each time it'd been changed by the loss. The statue in the center of the city was a prime example of this change. Rajah had his serpents build the statue out of nearly indestructible materials and enchanted to withstand damage even further.

All of this was done to remind the people within its walls just who it was they served, and what would befall them if they disobeyed.

~ ~ ~

The next morning Kiera sat up on the small cot she'd been placed on. Her blanket fell off and revealed her bare chest—which made Dorian uncomfortable in a number of ways.

He cleared his throat and promptly turned his back on the nearly naked woman. He'd taken to personally watching over her ever since the healer informed him of the status of her health. She was physically fine, aside from being exhausted. The doctor did notice some skin discoloration near her chest and warned him of the potential meanings it could have: poison, curses, and certain magic-related skills that were known to disrupt the delicate balance between exoteric and interior magical pathways.

While those were not intrinsically fatal, Dorian was informed that whatever caused her condition would have killed her, had she been exposed to it any longer.

This simple fact worried Dorian far more than he'd like to admit. Not for any romantic reason or even for something as trifling as "friendship." No, Dorian was worried for himself and the lives of his people, rather than the health and wellbeing of some backwoods adventurer. "Lady Kiera," he began. His words drew her out of her mental stupor and into the present. "Please, get dressed and accompany me for a while... We need to have a talk."

"Hmm," Kiera hummed. She threw the blanket off of her legs and stood from the bed. The only covering she still had was a pair of loose breeches the doctor borrowed from one of the soldiers in the barracks. However, modesty didn't appear to be a concern for Kiera at the moment.

When Dorian heard the rustling of fabric stop, he turned to see Kiera wearing a simple green tunic, also borrowed from the same soldier. "Ah, good. If you'll follow me, please."

Kiera robotically followed him out of the room and down three flights of stairs to an open courtyard. While normally being used for one-on-one combat drills, the courtyard was currently devoid of people, save for one man wearing snow-white robes and a small silver circlet atop his head.

The "King," as most people liked to call him due to his choice of attire, actually wasn't even of noble blood. He was a lion beast-man, with orange-bronze fur, a thick black mane, glowing silver eyes, and the heavily muscled body of a warrior.

"Tyr? What are you doing here?" Kiera asked with only the slightest hint of emotion in her voice.

Tyr glowered at her tone and a low growl seemed to vibrate his entire body. "I'm here to clean up your mess, of course!"

Kiera shrank back from his outburst, but her Amazonian pride began to bristle at the insult. "You'll die."

Tyr's eyes widened at her rather frank choice of words and he snorted in amusement. "I've yet to find the monster capable of killing me," Tyr replied in a serious tone.

Most people would have mistaken Tyr's words as a sign of pride or hubris. But Kiera knew better. In the fifteen years since she'd met him, Tyr had never lost a fight.

It was rumored that he was the one originally meant to kill Rajah and free the people from his tyranny. But as a Titan—a rare form of magical warrior that utilized small metal trinkets to enhance their bodies far beyond the limits of a normal warrior—he was simply a bad match for the lightning magic their enemy preferred. Because of this, and the lack of support he received from the human-controlled city, he was relegated to being a guardian and only saw battle when the city was under direct attack.

Before Kiera could open her mouth and say something to further escalate the situation, Dorian interjected with his proposal. "Which is why I have decided to send three cavalry units with you when you leave."

"Can they keep up?" was Tyr's immediate reply.

"Of course. They are some of the finest soldiers in my army."

Kiera rolled her eyes and turned to leave.

"Lady Kiera, a word—please?" Dorian said before she could take more than a few steps.

Kiera stopped walking. "I'm formally requesting that you accompany Tyr to deal with this... creature. After your rather sudden appearance yesterday, I sent a regiment of soldiers along the road to find your party."

Kiera looked over her shoulder and stared at him with a hopeful expression. "And?"

Dorian sighed and shook his head. "We've yet to hear back from any of them. A group of mages conjured crow golems to scour the road, but all they found were scattered bits of armor and a few loose swords. I don't know how, but an entire regiment of trained soldiers seemingly disappeared into thin air."

Kiera's eyes went dim and she continued walking away. "I refuse to go after that thing. You should alert the families of those you sent out that their husbands and wives won't be coming home."

After saying her piece, Kiera left the courtyard and headed into the barracks to hunt down her equipment.

CHAPTER TWENTY-THREE

I WATCHED THE BLONDE WOMAN FLEE, LEAVING behind the dragon-man and what remained of her friends.

I honestly hadn't meant for any of that to happen. I'd only wanted to ask where Rajah could be found, not slaughter them. But I couldn't let the elf girl put any debuffs on me. The slightest distraction could've made me lose control of my aura and hurt someone and I had my aura completely under my control until the stupid cyclops punched me and caused me to lose focus. By the time I'd shoved my aura back down, it was too late. The elf girl was already gone.

'S—Stay back, monster!" the dragon-man yelled. He had his oversized sword held high above his head, ready to chop me down if I came too close.

I doubted it would work, but hey, you never know.

"I mean you no harm," I said placatingly.

"No harm? You killed my friends!"

"Yes, but those were accidents. Besides, your friend attacked me first."

"Lies! Hurting Sheena is what provoked him. Do not try to rewrite the past, serpent!"

"Right, okay, yes. I squeezed too hard. That's my bad. But I did warn her to stop struggling before she got hurt. If she'd only listened to me, this could've been avoided."

The dragon-man pointed the tip of his blade at me. "Do not besmirch the lives of the dead," he growled. "My friends are dead because of you. Nothing you say can change that."

"No, you're right." I narrowed my eyes. Directing my attention at his feet, I increased gravity's hold on him by a factor of two. He fell to his knees, sinking his blade into the soft soil and using it as a brace to keep himself from falling. "It's my fault they're dead, and it's my burden to carry. But do not take my guilt as permission to point your weapon at me. Do so again, and you'll be reunited with them before you can blink." I released my hold on him and allowed him to stand. "Understand?"

"Ku—Yes."

"Good." I turned from him and looked at the golden statue of Rajah. "What can you tell me about Rajah?"

"Surely, you already know?" he asked. "There's no way someone of your power hasn't already met our resident god-king?"

"And why's that?" I asked curiously.

"Well—I mean—" He waved his hand at me. "That."

"That?" I laughed. "Because I'm powerful, because I'm a man, because I'm a snake, what is 'That?'"

"The last one."

"Right, well, I haven't had the pleasure. If I had, we wouldn't be having this conversation, would we?"

"It could be a trick," he insisted. "You could be working for Rajah, and this could be happening because you want to find out what we know and report back to him!"

I noticed him gripping the handle of his sword tighter and sighed, "Throw your blade aside."

His fist tightened further. "Why, gonna kill me too?"

"That's entirely up to you. Though the odds of that happening increase the longer you hold that sword like you're about to take my head off."

He stared defiantly into my eyes. "I'm thinking about it."

"Yes, I can tell. But you will die."

"I'd rather die fighting with a sword in my hand, than on my knees like a dog."

"Jesus, did you rip that straight out of an action movie? That was badass."

He batted his eyes a few times, presumably in confusion. "You really think so?"

"No, it was stupid. You're speaking to a being strong enough to kill you literally without effort, and your plan is to—tell me your plan? What kind of ass-backwards bullshit is that?"

"W—What're you—"

"Seriously, Kid. You didn't think this through at all, did you?" I stepped forward and snatched the blade from his hand. He tried to fight back, to hold on, but it was like playing tug of war with a newborn. I held the blade out of his reach and lightly pushed him away.

"What do you plan to do now, huh?" I asked hotly. "I have your weapon now. Not only that, but you let me take it from you while you stood there and watched."

"I tried to hold on, but you're too strong."

"Who gives a crap how strong I am? Hit me, kick me, turn the blade around and stab me with it, for god's sake. But don't just stand there and let me take your weapon from you." I tossed the blade down at his feet. "Just like your friends back there, you can always do something different." I waggled my stump of an arm at him. "Believe me, that's a lesson I was painfully reminded of not too long ago." I turned from him and began moving towards the city.

"Did Rajah do that to you?"

"Hell no. I made the mistake of clocking a god with a left cross."

"Wait—" I heard the sound of his footsteps jogging to catch up with me. "You punched a god? Like, an actual deity—from one of the pantheons?"

"Unfortunately."

"Which one?"

"Carlas something. Why're you following me?"

"Oh, right. I can show you where Rajah is."

I abruptly stopped moving, which caused him to run into my back. I twisted around and looked at him. "So, you do know where Rajah is?"

"Of, course. Everyone does. Rajah sent out a challenge for anyone stupid enough to take him on. It even came with a map."

"If it's such common knowledge, then why didn't your friends just tell me and be done with it?"

"How the hell were we supposed to know you were serious? You show up out of nowhere and took one of us hostage. You're lucky we didn't just jump you."

"No, you're the lucky one," I chuckled.

"Whatever. Point is, taking people hostage doesn't usually make them want to have a friendly conversation with you."

"I didn't take her hostage; I was trying to stop her from doing—whatever the hell she was doing. If anything, my trying to stop her delayed her death."

"What do you mean?"

I glanced down at him, then told him to move over to a nearby tree. He looked confused for a few seconds, then thought better of questioning me and did as I asked. Once I was sure he was out of my aura's range, I released it. My aura covered all one-hundred and thirty feet of my body in an instant: destroying the land around me and causing me to sink into the ground. I quickly shoved it back into its cage where it couldn't hurt anyone.

"What the hell, man!?" the dragon-man yelled. He scrambled back to his feet and took several generous steps back.

"My hold on that is tenuous at best," I informed him. "It's not something I control, it's something I suppress: nothing more or less. Had your friend successfully used her magic on me, there's every chance I would've lost control over it and you all would've died."

"Most of us died anyway," he reminded me.

"Yes, and one of them dumped you faster than a bull throws its rider."

"W—What does that even mean!?"

"Doesn't matter." I sighed. "Point is, you were left behind, most likely as a diversion so the blonde could get away. Am I wrong?"

"Hrk—" He looked away.

I scratched the back of my head. "Where can I find Rajah?"

"There, in that mountain." He pointed at a medium-sized mountain a few miles away. "That's where Rajah told us we could find him."

"Thanks." I moved towards the mountain. However, after a few minutes I could hear footsteps coming up behind me. "What're you doing?" I sighed. I was doing that a lot lately.

"Like you said, I was ditched," he said in a much more cheerful tone than I expected.

"You don't seem all too torn up about it."

"Eh, fuck her. I tried for years to make her like me. After this, I just don't care anymore. So…"

There was a pause as I stared him down.

"Can I come with you?" he asked in a quiet voice.

"Can you come with—Kid, I don't even know your name."

"Q-Shan, Q-Shan Astigeus. How about you?"

"Torga, just—Torga. Don't you think you need to get back to the city? What if people come looking for you?"

"They won't. The only one they cared about was Kiera and she ran for it. And knowing her, she'll forget about us by morning. So, don't worry about it."

"If you say so," I tentatively allowed. I grabbed him by his arm then leaped into the air and began flying towards the mountain.

A few minutes later we were standing at its base. Q-Shan didn't seem too excited about the prospect of flying, which I found particularly amusing since he was a dragon-man. "This is where I can find Rajah, right?" I asked while surveying the area.

There was a cave set into the side of the mountain. The mouth of said cave was about twenty feet tall and forty feet wide. Q-Shan had informed me that this was a conscious decision on Rajah's part because Rajah wanted entire armies to come after him at once, and the oversized entrance reflected that.

Q-Shan's head bobbed up and down. "This is the place alright.

"Good, then you wouldn't mind waiting for me here, would you—What're you doing?"

Q-Shan was rifling through his bag and would periodically take out a curious looking stone, only to throw it back into the bag with a disgusted look on his face. "I'm trying to decide which jewel would be the best fit for the job."

"Job? What job?"

He looked up at me with a look of confusion on his face. "I'm coming with you."

"No—You're not."

"But you said—"

"That you could come with me, yes, but not to face Rajah. I'm not going to be able to protect you and kill Rajah."

"You won't have to protect me!"

"I know." The ground beneath Q-Shan rose and he was quickly imprisoned within a cage of bedrock. "Wait here." I smirked as Q-Shan tried in vain to break or bend the solid stone bars.

"You can't just leave me here!"

I shrugged and moved past him into the dense canopy of trees.

Right away the cave showed signs of being lived in. The tunnels appeared to have been carved with some kind of crude tool. The walls and ceiling, though large near the opening of the cave, shrunk rapidly until I could barely move.

This led me to believe two things: The first was that whatever creature this Rajah was, he was significantly smaller than I was. Whether that was because Rajah was naturally smaller or he made himself smaller through a technique similar to my own, I didn't know.

I also believed Rajah's claim of wanting an army to attack him was hogwash. Unless he planned to make a kill room and funnel people into an area he knew they couldn't maneuver in... *Actually, that's not a bad idea.*

One of my serpents picked up a scent and hissed loudly. *"What's that smell?"* So far I'd only walked a few hundred feet into the mountain, but already the atmosphere had taken a drastic turn for the worse. An obnoxious odor was sending my snake into a frenzy, his tail was sticking to the floor due to a dark gel-like substance covering it, and probably the most troubling thing was the sense of wrongness I felt.

With every fiber of my being, I knew I shouldn't be here. Nearly every step was followed by a tingling in my spine and butterflies in my stomach.

Am I—nervous? I couldn't remember the last time I was nervous.

A flash of yellow light nearly blinded me after being in the dark for so long. I instinctively held up my right arms to shield my eyes from the painful light.

A sharp pain exploded in one arm as a large set of jaws bit down and immediately tore a chunk off. Dark-gray bone and pink muscle tissue were exposed to the dank air. I backhanded my attacker's head with the damaged arm.

The attacker, a forty-foot-long serpentine dragon with gray scales and a single large horn on its snout, had the top part of its head reduced to little more than paste, and the momentum of the blow caused it to spin into the wall.

I waited for it to fall to the ground before moving to inspect it. As I drew closer to the body, two of my serpents opened their mouths and allowed magical energy to seep out. This caused two things: The cave suddenly got much hotter and it filled with an orange/red light.

It would have been nice to know you could do that BEFORE I got attacked. I sighed. I would have complained more, but since I was already talking to myself, I decided to do something decidedly less crazy and inspect a dead body.

The body, now that I'd gotten a good look at it, made me worry about the possibility of my catching whatever disease it was riddled with. Its scales were paper thin and were just barely hanging onto its skeleton by sheer force of will. Its eyes, or the one I found lying on the floor anyway, was milky white and lacked a defining pupil. Its teeth were rotten to the point of being completely black, and, from what I could see, its body was infested with maggots.

Not a pretty sight by any stretch of the imagination. *How was this thing still alive?*

A raspy hiss coming from my right caused me to rise to my full height and the serpents to shine their light in that direction.

Well, that certainly answers that question.

The creature I saw creeping towards me was another serpentine dragon and, just like the prior one, it didn't look great. The bottom half of its jaw was missing, as were large portions of its scales. Actually, now that I thought about it, it looked like it'd been skinned.

I seriously doubted the creature could still be alive with such grievous injuries, which led me to only one conclusion: It wasn't.

"Undead serpents," I muttered. I glanced at the rapidly closing wound on my arm. *Theoretically, my regeneration should protect me if it's virus based. But I can only hope it's not magic based, or I'm well and truly fucked.* Though it was true that I'd had very little experience with the undead, what little experience I did taught me a valuable lesson and convinced me of one truth: Never. Underestimate. The undead.

From what I'd learned during my adventuring days, undead can be divided into two types: The Undeath and the Monstrous.

The Undeath, more commonly referred to as just "the undead," are undead beings brought to life by highly infectious spells, viruses, or other unnatural elements. They are, for all intents and purposes, just mobile corpses with little to no higher thought processes and can be killed fairly easily by a semi-athletic human, so long as they target the brain.

The Monstrous are an entirely different bag of worms. The only positive to this type is that most of them couldn't pass on the curse themselves and needed their creator to do it for them. They are created when the soul of a creature is destroyed, and foul magic is used to sustain them. Vampires, ghouls, and yes, even my puppets are considered Monstrous undead.

It was this last fact that led me to conclude this welcoming party was of the latter variety. Especially once the second one stretched its lower jaw wide and began to create a magical ball of yellow energy, and the first serpent lifted its destroyed head off the ground and gurgled.

This is about to get interesting. With my back to the first serpent and the second serpent blocking my path, I tensed and readied myself for the inevitable.

The second serpent fired a lightning bolt out of its mouth and struck my left pectoral. However, due to my elemental resistances, I barely noticed the impact as I began to move. My aura flared to life as I ducked under a leaping bite from the first serpent and tackled it into the wall, pinning it there with my right arms. I was momentarily surprised to see my aura fail to dissolve the undead, but I didn't have time to dwell on it. I used my remaining left arm to pummel its face into the cave wall.

The lone hit cracked the serpent's head wide open and shattered the cave wall behind it. I turned in time to see three of my serpent heads snatch a leaping undead out of the air and slam it into the ground. Then two other heads blasted it with condensed mana.

The sound of scales on stone prompted my serpent heads to shine their lights around the cave. I spotted two divergent pathways; each one sounded occupied at the moment. I stepped in between the two pathways and waited for the undead to show themselves.

A lone undead slithered out of the left tunnel, and my serpent heads struck, easily ripping the undead serpent apart and throwing the pieces as far away from my body as they could in this narrow space.

However, before I could even think to celebrate, the walls of the cave began to violently shake as tens of undead serpents poured out of each opening and attacked.

Though the undead serpent horde attempted to dog-pile me, my serpent heads kept them off of me without me having to direct them. It was a reminder that I didn't really know what my other heads could do, though I had good test subjects to experiment on.

I waded into the horde, trusting that my serpent heads would protect me from any nasty surprises.

For the first time since I'd gained them, all nine heads attacked in unison. While I focused on shoving my way through the undead and crushing their bones into a fine powder, the serpent heads were free to attack completely independently from one another.

Five of the heads used magical forces—Lightning, Fire, Ice, and Wind—to form a nearly impenetrable wall of magic that tore apart anything stupid enough to try and get through. Meanwhile, the other four heads worked in concert with me to crush the undead lucky enough to make it through the wall, creating a three-pronged assault.

Any undead fortunate enough to remain in one piece after this was quickly devoured and helped suppress my insatiable appetite. So far I'd managed to keep it just beneath the surface, but with my current situation worsening by the second, I wanted to err on the side of caution and get it under control before it had a chance to become a problem.

Once the swarm was crushed, I picked a direction and pressed even deeper into the cave.

Occasionally another horde of undead serpents would spew out of a hole in the wall and attack me, but for the most part it was a relatively boring walk through a disgusting cave.

Without warning, one of my heads curved around my chest and spewed a line of fire out of its mouth. An undead let out a sound I could've gone my entire life without hearing as it fell apart, its rotten tendons and bones not possessing the strength it needed to keep itself together.

All nine heads pressed off the wall across from me, shoving me aside in time for an electrically charged serpent to bust through the wall and miss me by only a few inches. Before the undead serpent could turn its head, a stone hand shot out of the opposite wall and crushed it flat.

I pulled back my right arms and shoved a minor gravity well down the tunnel, multiplying the weight of everything in its path by a factor a five. Three of my heads sprang forward, headbutting four serpents and crushing them against another wall. With the four serpents still pinned to the wall, another head opened its mouth and fired a beam of compressed energy into the head of the leftmost undead, before quickly dragging it ninety degrees to the right. The heads of the other three undead were instantly vaporized, and their bodies were dropped to the ground.

Wave after wave of undead came spewing out of the walls, ceilings, and floors of the next three caves, and I was quickly overwhelmed. I was forced to retreat, stumbling over my own tail in the process.

Okay, that's it. Time to see what this magic can really do. I created a gravity well inside my own mouth. The black vortex of energy began to swirl faster and wilder the wider I opened my mouth. Within five seconds of activating my magic, I witnessed its effect first hand. The walls, ceiling, and floor of the tunnel began to stretch towards the vortex as if they were made of rubber, the undead serpents were crushed under an invisible force and sucked in, and the very mountain itself began to moan and groan as if it were alive.

As the seconds passed and more and more of the mountain was compromised or outright destroyed under the invisible force exerted by the vortex, the void I always felt inside my stomach was being filled and my hunger pains were beginning to fade away.

"Enough!!" a shrill voice screamed.

Almost by sheer reflex, I snapped my mouth shut and "turned off" the vortex. Three serpent heads turned in the direction of the voice and began to hiss quietly.

"I've had it with you!!" the voice continued as the sound of footsteps echoed throughout what remained of the cave system. The inside of what used to be a rather large mountain had been hollowed out under the force of the vortex. The walls, ceilings, and most of the floor had all been eaten away until an almost perfect spherical hole was all that remained.

As I listened to the footsteps growing ever closer, I couldn't help but notice a beam of sunlight filtering in through the severely compromised roof, and it was because of this light, that I got my first glance at Rajah.

A severely decayed lizard-man walked into the light in a suit of resplendent golden armor.

"A dragon-man?"

"Dragon-man? Do I look like a fucking 'dragon-man to you!?" the lizard-man screamed. **"I am Rajah, the god of this world and you!"** He pointed a decaying finger at me. **"You destroyed bodies I've been carefully maintaining for over a thousand years!"**

Rajah began to shamble towards me.

"Do you have any idea how difficult it is to maintain a constantly rotting body!?"

"No, but I'm sure you're going to tell me."

"VERY!"

I would say I told you so, but I doubt he's actually listening.

The shambling picked up speed and the lizard-man's voice somehow grew even more shrill. **"Why are you here!? Tell me! Explain it to me!"** As the lizard-man came within a few feet of me, I crossed my arms over my chest and narrowed my eyes at the annoying creature.

"Explain in five words or less why the fuck you thought you could just walk in here, destroy my stuff, kill my servants, and RUIN MY HOME!!" He spat in my face.

Eight of my nine serpent heads bit down on the lizard-man and practically ripped him in half. However, the lizard-man didn't even flinch, which all but confirmed that I was correct in assuming that this was just another puppet and the real Rajah was still loose on the planet, somewhere.

"This means war, you ignorant cur! I am the king of this world and here, I'm not just a king, I. AM. GOD!"

I smashed his body into the ground, then two serpent heads came forwards and disintegrated him with two gouts of flame.

CHAPTER TWENTY-FOUR

I STEPPED OUT OF THE CAVE AND INTO THE LIGHT OF day. I took several deep breaths, letting the fresh air of the outside world cleanse my nostrils of the rot that clung to my scales.

I twisted my head from side to side until I felt a satisfying *crack*.

Now that my stomach no longer ached as much, and I'd had the opportunity to work out some of the stress I'd accumulated since I'd—died? I wasn't actually sure what happened, but I pushed it to the back of my mind like oh so many other things I didn't want to think about. It was just something I didn't understand and probably never would. Strangely enough, I didn't think I cared.

As I finished stretching and loosening the tension in my body, one of my heads noticed a snake staring at him with its head tilted to one side. It was barely over six feet long, and it had ruby red eyes and brown/gold scales.

"Can I help you?" I asked.

The "little" snake slowly blinked at me, then nodded its head.

"Greetings your majesty. I just wanted to be the first to congratulate you on your new title," it hissed, but not in an angry way.

Now it was my turn be confused. "Which one?"

"Pardon?" the snake replied.

"Which title do you mean?" I clarified.

The snake blinked at me and hesitated, as if it were thinking of what to say.

"The Royal Serpent title?"

A stray thought entered my mind and buzzed around like an annoying gnat. "You called me "Your majesty." Does that mean I am now the king of this place?"

The snake nodded its head in confirmation.

I smiled. "Good. Because I'm going to need your assistance in tracking down a particularly annoying maggot." I scooped up the snake and flew off into the sky, only to re-land outside the cage I'd built for Q-Shan, who was right where I'd left him.

"I can't believe you actually left me here—"

Without giving him a chance to finish, I dissolved the bars with a thought and grabbed him by the arm. "Better clench up. We've gotta go."

I coiled my tail beneath me, then leaped into the air and departed for the city.

~ ∻ ~

I sighed as I spotted the statue looming over the horizon. I shook my head to clear it of any distractions, then looked over my shoulder at the small brown and gold serpent following me.

I'd offered to let Q-Shan come with me to storm the city in order to find Rajah, but he'd declined. Said he had people to warn, and a girl to see.

"I know he's in there," I told the serpent. "Until I find and end Rajah for good, no one is allowed in or out."

The serpent nodded its head in understanding, then left me alone on the road to the city's gate. A few seconds after the small serpent departed, I felt the forms of several thousand snakes moving towards the city in unison. And while most of these serpents were small—barely reaching ten feet in length—a few were rather obviously not, as I heard the sound of a tree being pushed over. "I could get used to being king," I muttered as I departed for the city.

~ ~ ~

A cold chill raced down his spine and an overwhelming sense of dread settled in as he looked over the walls of the city. It started only three or four minutes prior, when thousands upon thousands of snakes began to surround his beloved city. Then came the monsters. Serpentine dragons of all sizes and classifications darkened the skies, and the sightless Earth Leviathans tore themselves free from the ground and began using their long tongue tentacles to feel for weak points along the base of the wall.

"Sir!" one of his lieutenants yelled.

Dorian barely spared the man a glance before turning back to watch the continuous nightmare unfold before him.

"Sir, what are your orders!?" the lieutenant repeated as panic began to set in. The assembled troops began chatting nervously.

Dorian ignored them in favor of staring at the Earth Leviathans. They were now staring at the top of the wall. This caused another cold chill to race down his spine as flashes of previous encounters with the eyeless horrors raced through his mind.

"Quiet," Dorian said as he continued to observe the situation.

Even though his words were barely above a whisper, they cut through the voices of his soldiers like an axe and caused years of training and discipline to kick in. The gathered soldiers quieted down almost immediately and awaited his next order. A few minutes passed before Dorian turned to the first speaker, the lieutenant, and whispered, "The magic barrier above the wall will keep out the dragons, so they are currently a non-issue."

A soldier opened his mouth to interrupt, but a harsh glare from Dorian caused the man to remain silent.

"However, as we lack any such defense against the Leviathans, I'd greatly appreciate it if you could avoid drawing their attention by screaming like frightened children. Understand?"

A chorus of near silent Yesses answered him.

"Good." He nodded, then turned to the lieutenant.

"Take the first, second, and fourth squadrons and scour the city for the civilians. I want any that can make it to the fort to go there, and all others inside the wall as *quickly* and as *quietly* as possible."

The lieutenant nodded his head and left to follow his orders.

Dorian sighed and ran his gauntleted hand over his face to wipe beads of sweat from his brow. There were only three options available to him at the moment and none of them was preferable.

Option one: Wait for the mages inside the city to come up with a spell that could remove the threat from the air and use the airships to escape. However, there were multiple issues with this plan. The first was that as with all members of the dragon family, serpentine dragons are resistant to snagic. Some legends even go so far as to say they're completely immune. This made relying on the magic of mages an extremely dangerous gamble and one Dorian wasn't sure he was ready to make. And besides, even if they could escape via that route, they lacked the airships necessary to transport all of the civilians at once, so some would have to be left behind.

Option two: Round up all of his men inside the city and push through the gates.

This option was even worse than the first due to the sheer number of monsters they'd have to fight and because there was simply no way for them to protect the civilians while fighting. Sure, some casualties are expected in battle. But Dorian knew that if he tried this option, even if he survived, very few others would be so lucky.

Option three: Bunker down and just worry about surviving.

Unfortunately for them all, this was their only real option at this point. Their lack of manpower, combined with the number of civilians they needed to evacuate, meant attempting to flee in any capacity would doubtlessly end with their deaths.

At least by fortifying their position here, behind the impenetrable walls of his beloved city and with their current stockpiles they could yet live—for a few more weeks, at least.

"Captain Dorian, sir!" a voice yelled.

Dorian sighed and turned in the direction of the voice. He saw a young man wearing the standard army uniform, consisting of a gray tunic, brown breeches, and leather boots that came up to his shin, running towards him.

"Quiet down, soldier!" Dorian hissed as the man opened his mouth to yell again.

Though the man clearly wanted to say something, he saluted and stood in attention until Dorian gave him the go-ahead to speak.

"Sir, there's, uh—something you need to see at the gate."

Dorian raised an eyebrow in question at the man, then turned to one of the higher-ranking officers standing nearby. He ordered the man to continue surveying the wall while he went to see what all the fuss was about. After receiving a salute from the lieutenant commander, Dorian followed the young man off the wall and into the city proper.

Upon arriving at the base of the gate and climbing four flights of stairs to the "lookout point," as dubbed by the soldiers, they reached a rectangular section of the wall with an open view of the outside world. It was so wide open, in fact, that a fully grown wyvern could enter and exit the city from this area... Well, if not for the magical shield stopping such a thing from happening.

Inside, Dorian saw several high-ranking officers—Lady Kiera, King Tyr, and a priest of the church—staring at something outside the gate.

"What're you all doing here?" he asked the group as he made his way over to join them. "Don't you know we are in a state of emergency?"

His words trailed off as he caught sight of the thing, or rather, the creature that had the group's undivided attention. Though he lacked the eyesight of some of his younger peers, he could still make out several divining characteristics of the *thing*. It was incredibly tall and covered in dark green and gray scales and, from what he could see, it had nine overly long serpents hanging over its shoulders.

However, all of that paled in comparison to the simple fact that it was surrounded on all sides by creatures no normal man could even dream of defeating and it did so almost casually.

"Ah, good. You must be the leader of this city. I've been waiting for you to arrive," the creature announced as it stared straight at Dorian.

"What is it that you want, creature?"

"I want entrance into the city, of course," it replied as if it were obvious.

"If you plan to attack then be forewarned. We will fight until the last man to defend our home."

The creature stared at Dorian with what appeared to be amusement on its face. "You seem to be a good man and I'd hate to have to kill you. So, take this advice in the spirit that it was given." The serpent moved forward. "I mean neither you nor the inhabitants of your city any harm. However, I believe a creature I've been hunting for some time now is within those walls and I will do whatever is necessary to drag it out of hiding. Even if it means tearing this wall down to do it. So, please, open the gate and let me in."

Upon hearing this declaration Tyr turned from his place at the rail and stormed down the stairs.

"Don't do it—"Dorian heard Kiera whimper.

"Lady Kiera, you know this creature?" He asked.

"Don't let it in!" she repeated, but much louder this time.

As Dorian placed his hands on her shoulder and turned her to face him, he saw the madness within her eyes as she stared at the creature.

"Priest, please tend to Lady Kiera. She is not well."

The priest, an old human male with graying hair, dark skin, and faded blue eyes solemnly nodded his head and gently guided Kiera over to a chair near the far wall.

Dorian turned back to the creature just in time to see the gate open slightly and Tyr walk out in full battle regalia.

"What the hell is he doing!?" Dorian cursed as he turned from the rail and raced after Tyr.

~ ~ ~

I watched as a large lion-man marched towards me with a scowl on his face. While tall and extremely muscular, the lion-man was vastly smaller than I was at my smallest size. So then, why were his steps causing the ground to cave in?

As he drew closer, his skin began to take on a metallic sheen, his claws grew thinner and sharper, and his muscles bulged under his robe.

There's always one, I sighed as the lion closed in and pulled back his right arm.

The punch came much faster than I predicted and slammed into my face with all the force of a building falling on my head. The blow almost managed to knock me over, but I regained my balance and faced the lion.

I threw a backhand at his head, intending to take it clean off and be done with it, but as my hand flew through the air, the lion raised his left arm to block. A loud clanging sound echoed across the field as the lion's arm was torn clear from his body. In response, the lion spun with the blow and kicked me in the stomach hard enough to push me back. Before I could recover from the surprise of actually being pushed back, metal shards flew from the ground and rapidly rebuilt the lion's arm.

Despite the blows and my curiosity about his strength, I wasn't interested in actually fighting. I was here for Rajah, nothing more. That all changed when I saw the lion-man's eyes flash a sickly red color and I realized who it was I was fighting.

"Hello Rajah, you sneaky little shit. How've you been?"

Tyr stared at Torga in confusion, then his face twisted into an insane grin that showed off his teeth. **"I've been better,"** Tyr admitted. **"But after I kill you, I'll be doing MUCH better."** He laughed manically. His smile grew so wide it split his face. **"After all, I've been waiting to kill you since you so rudely intruded on MY PLANET!"**

"Keep waiting." I took a blow with my left arm, then twisted to the side and allowed two of my serpents to headbutt Rajah. His body was bent in half and sent flying. Rajah bounced off the ground, leaving large trenches wherever he landed, until he finally slammed into the base of the city's front gate. The gate bent in the middle as if it were made of cardboard instead of metal and Tyr vanished inside the city.

"Looks like peace talks have failed," I said. "Enter the city and prevent anyone from leaving." As the serpents moved to obey, I added as an afterthought, "And don't kill anyone that doesn't attack you. I don't know how many of these people are truly innocent, but until I am sure, they are not to be harmed."

"Oh, how noble of you!" an insane voice laughed from just behind the gate.

"It never ends," I sighed while turning to face the voice. What I actually saw, however, was several hundred humans, a bisected lion-man with his guts hanging out, the leader I was talking to earlier, and Q-Shan all staring at me with blood red eyes and wicked grins on their faces. "You know what? Fuck it. Kill 'em all and let Amaar sort them out."

The serpents and the "citizens" charged at each other, while the now fully healed lion-man, leader man, and Q-Shan charged me.

Surprising, Q-Shan was the fastest of the three, so I took him out of the fight immediately. "Sorry, Kid. But you really need to sit this one out." I pulled my head out of the way of a particularly vicious slash, then clapped him across the back. Q-Shan was knocked into the air, where one of my serpent heads caught him and coiled around him to both protect him, and to keep him out of the fight. "When this is over, no sword for a week," Q-Shan screamed at me as if he'd lost his mind.

A heavy blow knocked me aside and was immediately followed by the lion-man raking his claws across my chest. At the same time, Leader man drew his longsword and spun beneath my arms, leaving thin cuts on my side and waist.

I stared at the rapidly healing wounds, then frowned at the two adversaries. I wasn't sure what Rajah had done to them, but if they were capable of leaving even small wounds on my body then I couldn't afford to play with them.

I turned my body slightly to the side and raised my fists in a classic boxing stance. My other eight serpent heads fanned out behind me and let out simultaneous hisses at the two men. "Don't disappoint me now."

They looked at each other, then charged. Leader man swung his sword in a heavy downward slash intending to finish the battle quickly. But one of my serpent heads bit down on the flat of the blade, while another wrapped around Leader man's body and threw him into the air.

Meanwhile, the lion-man had once again leaped at me with his claws leading the charge. I tucked my chin into my chest, pivoted left and down, and sent a double-fisted right cross into his side. Before he could be blasted aside, two serpent heads rounded on him and bit into his legs. They swung him high into the air, then slammed him into the ground headfirst.

I twisted to see Leader man kicking the head holding onto his sword. The serpent head was forced to let go, then Leader man swung his blade in a downward arc, which bisected the head. His victory was cut short when another head bit him on the leg and lifted him into the air, before violently and savagely slamming Leader man into the ground. This gave the injured serpent head time to regrow and rejoin the fight.

The lion-man hit me from the left, then quickly cut across to my right and unleashed a bone-breaking haymaker into my side. The blow had me reeling. I stumbled and winced in pain. The blow wasn't a bad thing, however, as it taught me something.

The lion-man was getting stronger with every exchange.

I had to exchange a few more blows with him before I noticed what was happening: Every time I hit him, he would pull in metal from the ground. This made him stronger, tougher, and much, much heavier than he had any right to be.

I leaned back to avoid a particularly nasty swipe of lion-man's claws, then grabbed his arms and yanked them apart. For the second time in this fight, I was surprised. His arms weren't ripped off like I intended; they were merely dislocated.

The lion-man planted his feet on my chest and pushed off, kicking me in the chin as he flipped out of my grip.

The heads were closing in on Leader man. Every swipe, every slash, and every stab was returned with an attack of their own. Slowly but surely, they were overwhelming him, and the only thing that allowed him to continue fighting for as long as he did was whatever Rajah had done to him. And even that was slowly beginning to fail him. I glanced down at his right leg and noticed why. The bite wound from earlier was leaking a clear fluid and had already rotted to the point of exposing his bones.

Apparently, they carried my acid venom too.

Suddenly, a head swung around behind Leader man and knocked his legs out from under him, then another head bit into his shoulder and lifted him high into the air before it and another head ripped his arms off. A third head grabbed his leg and slammed him into the ground where he lay unmoving.

I blocked yet another kick to my head with my aching left arm, then grabbed it with my right and pulled the lion-man in close. This knocked him off balance and allowed me to finally wrap my hand around his throat and lift him into the air where he could not escape.

The lion-man struggled, kicked, punched, and screamed, but it was cut short when I sunk my teeth into the side of his neck and ripped out a generous helping of his throat. I held him off the ground while his heart pumped my acid venom throughout his body and sent arterial blood spray flying into the air.

However, a scant few seconds later, I began to feel the lion-man's weight increasing at a rapid pace.

"What's—wrong, bastard?" the lion man gurgled. **"Am I getting too heavy for you?"**

I grit my teeth against the weight. "Are you trying to destroy your body as well as mine?"

"Fool!" the lion-man yelled. **"Haven't you figured it out yet? Look around you!"**

I did so. More and more civilians continued to pour out of the city walls and attack my snakes. Their eyes glowed uniformly red as they hit with surprising power, killing serpentine dragons and Earth Leviathans alike.

"Every living creature on this planet *IS* my body!" he shouted as his weight began to stretch his body into grotesque proportions. The weight of the lion-man's body had long since passed what could be considered "healthy."

"Oh—" I looked over my shoulder at a still thrashing Q-Shan. "Thanks for the heads up," I muttered. My grip around the lion-man's throat tightened until the metal beneath my fingers screeched. "Is there a way to save them?" I asked, already knowing the answer but wanting it said out loud.

"T—They were dead the moment my spores infected them. You can't save them, 'hero,'" he mocked.

"I'm no hero." I reversed gravity in a fifty-foot radius around me. The lion-man's eyes widened as his weight became at first negligible, then it started pulling him into the sky. "A hero would've found a way to save these people. I'm a monster, just like you." I let go of the lion-man's throat, then quickly flipped gravity once again and amplified it. His body fell through the planet like he was shot out of a cannon. The ground shook, and a literal *wave* of stone and magma crashed into the wall, destroying it and the city in the process.

CHAPTER TWENTY-FIVE

*H*OW DO *I* ALWAYS GET MYSELF INTO THESE *situations?*

I raised my arms in an X in front of me in time to block a bolt of lightning striking the dead center of my body. It was immediately followed by a large explosion as the body within the lightning slammed my arms and folded in on itself. After hitting the ground, the broken body rose to its feet and healed faster than I ever thought possible.

"Really wish you'd stop doing that," I sighed.

A slim fist waved away the dust and debris still floating in the air from the intense speed of the lighting strike. A human woman of about thirty years of age snapped her neck back into place, then grinned up at me. She was tall for a human and stood somewhere around six-five. Her long, flowing blonde hair seemed to vibrate from the electrical current that surrounded her, and a deep golden-colored robe was draped over her shoulders with seemingly only a cloth belt holding it together.

However, what stood out the most about the woman was her crimson eyes, which seemed to radiate a sense of wrongness.

She lifted one leg and leaped off the ground. Her lithe body spun at such speeds that the air around her began to distort from friction and she threw her leg at my face.

I tilted my head back as the foot passed less than an inch in front of my face. One of my serpent heads opened its mouth and fired a beam of energy at the woman's waist. The only thing it succeeded in doing was making a hole in the wall a hundred feet behind her.

Damn.

Suddenly the woman was standing in front of me again. She slammed her fist into my chest before I could react. However, her magic was consumed the second she came within ten feet of me, causing her bare hand to smack into my body. She screamed in pain as her hand was violently broken upon impact. The woman growled and her body began to spark once again as she prepared herself for another attack.

I swatted her lightning enhanced fist away from my body and slapped her across the face. The blow sent her flying into the canyon wall over a hundred feet away and buried her up to her waist in solid stone.

"You're coming with me whether you like it or not, Rajah. Just be glad I want you alive for the moment or else I'd have expedited the process."

Rajah pulled her body from the rubble and glared at me with eyes that ran red with blood. **"Ohhhh, well sorry for wasting your time! Let's just go then, SHALL WE?"** Rajah's body glowed yellow as she ramped up her magic and was suddenly gone.

I was hit three times before I could react, each blow was hard enough to break stone. However, all the hits served to do was break the limb she was hitting me with.

Such was my durability now, the blows felt more akin to being smacked by a plastic bat than an actual strike meant to do damage. I turned my head to the left and saw a large trail of dust leading into a wall. As I moved, the air around me picked up and a gentle breeze blew the dust away.

"You know, parrying your attacks were so *you* wouldn't get hurt. Not the other way around." I bent down and lifted Rajah's broken body by the throat; All four limbs were a deep purple color and were bent in odd angles. Even so, Rajah attempted to bite my hand as he was lifted into the air. Eventually, Rajah gave up and his eyes dimmed.

"Fine, you win this round, but I WILL have my revenge!"

I lightly flicked Rajah on the nose, causing it to turn black. His eyes immediately returned to their normal color, and he started whining from the pain of having his nose broken.

"None of that shit. You're not some two-bit demon-lord, so stop acting like one. You lost, I won, get over it and yourself." I bent my knees and was preparing to fly when a sudden thought occurred to me. "Oh, and no trying to abandon your body and escape. I'm destroying this planet from orbit whether you're with me or not."

"WHAT!? WHY!?"

"Because, hunting your bacteria-ridden ass all over this planet for the last two days has A. Pissed me off, and B. Made me *very* hungry. So please, do keep reminding me *why* I'm pissed off and hungry. I'm sure it'll work out great for you."

"No thank you. I'd prefer to live a little while longer."

"Excellent, now shut up." I lifted into the air, slowly at first, and then I began to pick up speed once I was above the canyon walls. Within a few minutes, I was at the branch and climbing rapidly. Once I broke through the upper atmospheric layer, I turned away from the branch and drifted closer to the planet, while trying to remain close enough to the branch that I could still breathe.

One of my serpent heads coiled around the Rajah's body. Rajah's eyes widened, but he didn't make a sound as the head carried him as far from me as it deemed safe. *Don't try to escape. I may not be able to digest food like the main body, but I guarantee you won't like it if I try,* I heard the head whisper.

"You can talk!?"

Are you supposed to be talking?

Rajah shook his head and looked away from the *very sharp* teeth that lined the snake's mouth.

My body rapidly expanded and grew until I was looking down on the planet. It was still bigger than I was, but I was almost as tall. My tail swung around and coiled around the planet, while my eight other serpent heads stretched out as far as the eye could see. They reached out in either direction and observed what I was about to try from every angle they could get.

The first to go was the atmosphere of the planet. My aura sucked it away and devoured it in only a scant few minutes.

Without the atmosphere, the planet began turning a deep black color, starting from the areas closest to the branch and rapidly expanding outwards as a wave of blue energy flowed into my mouth. I greedily drank in every last bit of the blue energy like a man dying of thirst. This process took several days, during which I was in something of a trance, completely unaware of my surroundings, save for the constant supervision of my serpent heads.

And then the planet *itself* was devoured: I created a gravity well stronger than any before and focused on pulling everything in my sight towards my body. Everything was crushed, stretched, and ripped under the insane gravitational pull until it was reduced to little more than dust then it was sucked into my aura. What was originally a beautiful planet with a radius of over ten thousand miles was destroyed and devoured in less than two weeks.

I shrunk until I was at my smallest size—around a hundred and thirty feet—then approached Rajah.

"Has anyone ever told you that you are a right bastard?" he asked.

"Says the guy who enslaved tens of thousands of people. I may not be the best man around, but at least when I kill something, it stays dead."

"You have no idea what you're talking about! I gave them *purpose*. Don't you see that? Before I came along, they were living out their miserable lives in some backwater planet on the edge of Yggdrasil. Sickness, war, starvation, these things propagated like maggots among the population for *millennia*! I. Helped. Them!"

"No, you helped yourself. You stole them from their world, their friends, their families, and for what? To give them the "honor" of being your spare bodies? I'm sure they really appreciated that, didn't they?"

"That came later! I very rarely had to change out my body before you came along and even then, I *wanted* something close to my original body. No, I gave them something to fight against—a monster in the dark to ally with their fellow mortals against. And you know what? Probably for the first time in the

history of their people, there *was* no war, no sickness, and no starvation. The strong protected the weak, the rich fed the poor, and *no god* could torment them. There was peace."

"I can't tell if you see the irony in that statement and have chosen to ignore it, or if you're just full of shit. Actually, now that I think about it, you're probably just so insane it makes sense to you."

"Am I insane? AM I!?"

"Yeah, you kinda are."

"And what does that say about you, "the snake that challenged god"? Are you insane?"

"Most definitely. You'd have to be to think a mortal could win against a god."

"Then why do it if you know it's insane?"

"Simple. I don't care if it's insane. A god took something from me a long time ago and now—now, I'm going to make sure they all regret allowing it to happen."

"And you have the gall to call me insane," Rajah scoffed.

"Yes. Now, shut up before I eat you."

"You just ate a planet! How the hell could you still be hungry? What, do you have some kind of parasite or some shit?"

"You're still talking."

"You can't expect me to keep quiet after you forced me to watch *that!*"

"Sure, I can. Watch." I created a gravity well inside my mouth, then sucked Rajah inside.

Ding!*Ding*Ding*Ding*Ding

∞∞∞∞∞∞∞∞

Congratulations!

Due to the absurdity of devouring a planet, you have earned "The Devourer of Worlds" title.

(Error) Y—You you you, have reached max level—level.

You have unlocked the following evolutionary path

Tier 10 ascension

This evolution is automatic and has already been applied.

Name: Torga

Race: Gluttonous Dark Naga Hydra

Classification: Tier 10

Level: 100(?)

Experience: N/A

Titles: Destroyer of Asgard, The Dark Serpent, The Unwavering One, Royal Serpent, Free, The Devourer of Worlds

Stats:

- Physical
    - Strength: 8,482,629
    - Endurance: 8,482,629
    - Dexterity: 1,051
    - Speed: 1,201
- Mental
    - Intelligence: 60
    - Wisdom: 45

- Charisma: 21
- Resistances
  - Elements: 60%
  - Divinity: 80%
  - Mental: 20%
- Immunities
  - Mind Control
  - Illusions

Skills: Major Stealth, Heat Detection, Absolute Gluttony, Absolute Growth, Greater Petrifying Gaze, Superior Acid Venom, Detect Concealment, Energy Breath, Fly, Magic Enhancement, Elemental Manipulation, Gravity Manipulation, Size Control

Traits: Divine Gluttonous Aura +40, Growth +70, Venomous, Aquatic, Forever Growing, Indomitable, Supreme Regeneration

∞∞∞∞∞∞∞∞

I dismissed the popups and began following the branch to my next destination.

Ding

∞∞∞∞∞∞∞∞

Due to the rules of the King's Challenge being broken, translocating to the Neutral Zone in 10 seconds.

∞∞∞∞∞∞∞∞

"Wait, what!?"

∼ ∼ ∼

I arrived in the Neutral Zone approximately eleven seconds after reading the pop-up. I looked around at the frozen wasteland and immediately noticed a problem. The pillars were missing.

I don't like this. Something's wrong. I slowly spun in place, taking in my surroundings and trying to find anything out of the ordinary, anything I could use to confirm my suspicions.

The sight of Naunet standing off to the side with a completely unreadable look on his face cemented the "trap" theory in my head. I plastered a fake smile on my face and approached him. I had no way of knowing if Naunet was involved in some way, but the last I'd seen him, he was supposedly going to sacrifice himself to delay the gods. Since I hadn't seen them since the explosion, I'd assumed it worked. But what if he sold me out after all?

It would certainly hurt to find out that Naunet had betrayed me. But, at the end of the day, I'd known from the beginning that one of us would need to die in order for the other to live. I honestly couldn't blame Naunet for looking out for himself. After all, it's what I was best at.

"Naunet, you're looking good for a dead guy. What's your secret? " I asked.

"You don't sound happy to see me, Torga. I'm hurt."

"Oh, no, I am happy to see you again. You're one of the few friends I've made in this life."

"Likewise," Naunet responded with an awkward smile on his face.

"So—what happens now?" I asked, never once taking my eyes off of him. "I suppose we can't just go our separate ways here and be done with it?"

Naunet's magic came to life, a transparent dome appeared around him, and he bowed his head. "I'm not against you, Torga. I meant what I said about you being my friend. Those years with you were some of the best I've had in a long time. But, I'm with them now." Naunet pointed up.

"Them?" my gaze inched upwards until I was staring at a moon—a moon that was getting closer by the second.

"Is that your moon?" I asked incredulously.

"Yes."

"Are you throwing your moon at me?"

"Yes."

"You know this will destroy it as well, right?"

"That's the idea."

"Oh, well in that case," I laughed, "bring it on."

Chapter Twenty-Six

THE MOON CRASHED INTO THE SURFACE AND crushed Torga beneath its mass. Naunet, on the other hand, was teleported away just before it made contact. He reappeared on the branch and was quickly surrounded by eleven people. Five were serpents of varying sizes and the rest were gods.

The first serpent was Amatzin, the basilisk, said to be older than any "mortal" god. While he wasn't the largest of the serpents and was technically blind, even Naunet feared both his venom and his control over the element of earth. His pale white scales, eyes, and spines were littered with scars from battles long since forgotten by all but the oldest god.

Next was Shabaka, the Sun Wyrm. He was the largest fire wyrm to ever exist. He'd grown much too powerful, and his flames too potent, to live on a planet like the rest of them. So, he spent his days within the depths of a young star at the center of the system. After spending who knows how many millennia inside a star, his scales had turned a deep crimson, his beady eyes had turned pitch black, and his body constantly gave off enough heat to melt granite.

Then came Dragar, the Titan Serpent, whose defenses were said to be unbreachable by even the most powerful weapon. His onyx-colored scales and violet eyes were a stark contrast to the almost transparent Amatzin.

The fourth serpent was Sereath, the Lamia Queen. Her exposed chest, long black hair, and kind blue eyes sent shivers down Naunet's spine—not of fear, but excitement. How long had he dreamed of holding her to his chest? How long had he dreamed of once again feeling her supple skin against his scales?

And the last was Rajah. He was back in his true body, thanks to last minute interference from Carlas. His golden scales were in the same state of grotesque rot as always.

"While I understand your surprise and excitement over seeing her again, need I remind you that we are currently pressed for time—" Carlas, one of the only two gods to appear in their physical form, was interrupted when a cataclysmic **boom** sent waves of kinetic energy racing along the branch and almost caused some of the weaker beings to lose their footing.

"If you throw one more moon at me, friendship or not, I'm going to get really cross with you." Though Torga had dirt and debris all over his body, he didn't have any visible wounds. And the absolutely furious expression on his face said he was already beyond angry.

"Hello Carlas, Arkos, fancy meeting you here. Who're your friends?" While Torga's words were normal enough, his tone was anything but. The venom and murderous rage in his voice sent cold chills down everyone's spine.

"Do not fail Mother. You know what awaits you if you do," Carlas said. He grabbed Arkos by the arm and the two vanished in a flash of golden light.

"You all know the plan. Go!" a violet-colored god ordered.

Sereath removed the barrier around Naunet, allowing him to dash at Torga with Dragar and Shabaka following closely behind. Amatzin used his magic to create three humongous boulders and threw them at Torga's back, and Sereath reluctantly began to remove the rot from Rajah's body. While the serpents faced Torga, the gods began chanting in a strange language.

Torga did a one-two combo on the boulders. His right fists broke through the first two, then his left shattered the last one on the spot.

Naunet knew he was the better fighter between the two of them, but that was only if he could keep Torga from using his stupid strength. Naunet slid under a haymaker aimed at his head, then kicked Torga's torso. If Torga felt it, it didn't show.

While his heads attacked Shabaka and Dragar, Torga chased after Naunet. Each swing of his fist could've torn Naunet's head from his shoulders, which is why Naunet made doubly sure that wherever Torga's fists flew, he didn't stick around for long.

"He's gotten stronger!" Naunet hollered.

"No shit, fuckface! I could have told you that!" Rajah yelled.

"Why didn't you, then!?"

"Because fuck you, that's why!"

"Shut up and move!" Naunet hollered again.

Naunet dodged out of the way as Torga hurled the five-hundred-foot body of Dragar back at him.

"We need to keep him still! The spell is almost complete!" a yellow-colored god yelled.

"That's easier said than done!"

"Well, if you'd stop complaining and *focus* maybe it wouldn't be!"

"Oh yeah? Swap places with me then!"

"Are you crazy!? He'd kill me!"

"Then shut the fuck up!"

Naunet charged at Torga, while Rajah and Amatzin used their magic to slow him down and Sereath waited for the right moment to strike. She only had one chance to pull her spell off, and if she missed, Torga wouldn't give her another chance.

Torga swung his fist at Naunet, but it seemed to just pass right through him as Naunet twisted his body slightly to the side and slammed a palm into Torga's stomach, with nary a grunt from Torga. "That didn't happen the last time we sparred," he said.

Torga's eyes flared, as did his temper. It was a gamble pissing him off, but Naunet needed something to keep him occupied while the gods finished their preparations. Suddenly a serpent head came out of nowhere and sunk its teeth into Naunet's shoulder.

Naunet screamed in pain as the acid venom poured into his system. "You son of a bitch!" Naunet hissed. "Now, do it now!"

Rajah grabbed Sereath and threw her onto Torga's back.

Naunet pulled Torga's head down to keep her away from his fangs and Sereath gently placed her hands on either side of his head.

"Sleep," she ordered.

Despite Torga's will, his eyes slowly closed and within moments, he was asleep.

"It's done! Hold on everyone!"

Every living person on the branch was suddenly teleported away.

~ ~ ~

I opened my eyes to see a gray-tiled ceiling and a fan slowly rotating.

"Where—am I?" I asked.

"Oh, thank God you're awake!"

I recognized the voice. Even after all these years, that was the one voice I remembered above all others. I blinked the sleep from my eyes and quickly sat up in bed. "Sarah?"

A blonde-haired bullet slammed into my chest, knocking me onto my back, and began sobbing into my shirt. "Don't you ever do something that stupid again, do you hear me?"

"What did I do? What happened?" I asked. I couldn't remember doing anything bad. Actually, I couldn't remember much of anything at the moment.

Sarah sat up and glared down at me. "Pretending not to remember won't save you."

I gave her a blank stare.

"You remember, don't you? You saved that boy's life and got hit by a truck in the process. You've been in a coma for two weeks."

"Oh..."

Sarah leaned down and gently kissed me on the lips. "I'm glad you're back."

~ ~ ~

"I'm glad you're back," repeated Sereath as she stood in front of Torga with her hands on his head and her eyes closed.

"Sounds like he's having a pleasant dream," Naunet said.

"If all goes well, it'll be a dream he'll never have to wake up from," the violet-colored god replied. "I assume your master will hold up his end of the bargain?"

"Watch your tongue, and do not doubt my master. He will always do right by his allies," Naunet sneered.

"Hey, Naunet, old buddy, old pal, how's it going?" Rajah asked, a manic smile on his serpentine face.

"Shut up."

"Aw, don't be like that. Can't you just let bygones be bygones and forgive me? You've gotten yourself a new broad, after all."

"Do not speak of her!"

"Boys, enough. Your voices are making it incredibly difficult to keep him under."

Naunet wisely shut his mouth at Sereath's warning.

For the next few hours, the only sound they could hear was Sereath whispering sweet nothings into Torga's ear and the gods chanting.

"Jealous yet?" Rajah whispered.

"Shut. Up."

"Yeah, you're jealous," Rajah snorted.

"I'm going to kill you when this is over."

"You'll have to find me first."

"Boys!"

Naunet and Rajah's mouths snapped shut and the silence returned.

Several hours later, a whirlwind of magic appeared outside the circle of pillars. The magic slowly turned into a massive black Hydra with eight heads and eight tails. Each of the heads had an oriental helmet made from

Yggdrasil's wood with a long-forgotten language inscribed onto it, and each tail was lined with spikes.

All sixteen of Orochi's eyes opened at once and looked down at the gathering. Then, almost instantly, the Hydra was replaced with a fifteen-foot-tall man with sixteen arms. The gods, Naunet, Rajah, and Amatzin all "kneeled" at Orochi's feet while Sereath nodded her head.

"Finally," Orochi sighed.

"Sire," Naunet began.

"Now, Naunet. Is that anyway to speak to your older brother?"

"Right," Naunet said contritely. "Hello, brother. It's good to see you again."

"Oh ho," Orochi murmured as his eyes landed on Sereath. **"Who might you be?"**

"My name is Sereath, Sire. I am the current Lamia Queen."

"Interesting." Orochi eyed her up and down. **"What of Sharlaska—does she still live?"**

"Grandmother? Yes, she lives."

"Grandmother, eh? You hear that, Naunet? Sharlaska is her grandmother."

"I'm aware, Sire," Naunet replied, clearly uncomfortable with Orochi's statement.

"Excuse me, Orochi?" the violet-colored god interrupted. "We have long researched ways to free you from your prison and, as you can see, we were successful. By anchoring a serpent of similar power to you here, we can trick the enchantments into believing you are still trapped, and—"

"I do not care for the specifics, godling. Just get on with it."

"Er—Right away." The god gave out orders to the other gods, then got back to work while Orochi walked over to Naunet's side.

"She your woman?" Orochi quietly asked, never taking his eyes of Sereath.

"Unless Sire wishes to claim her."

"No," Orochi chuckled. **"She's all yours, dearest brother. Consider it my gift for releasing me."**

"You're too gracious, Sire." Naunet managed to reply without venom coloring his tone. It would not be wise to upset Orochi now.

~ ~ ~

Approximately five hours later, the gods finished setting up the ritual to bind Torga in Orochi's place and the serpents were preparing to leave, as their parts in this plan were over.

The first to go was Orochi, as he had a meeting to attend with the mother of these godlings.

However, before Naunet could activate the spell to send the rest of them away, he spotted Rajah hanging off of Torga's shoulder.

Since the day prior, Sereath had locked Torga within his dream where he was free to rest. Neither she nor anyone else was close enough to stop the insane bastard from whispering who knows what in Torga's ear.

"Rajah, get your ass over here!" Naunet called.

Rajah held up a clawed digit, then continued whispering into Torga's ear.

Suddenly Torga's eyes snapped open and everything went straight to hell.

A burst of aura exploded out of Torga's body and instantly absorbed everything within arm's reach, including Rajah.

Most of the gods and serpents managed to escape this fate by teleporting away, but Amatzin wasn't so lucky. Naunet and the other survivors were now several hundred feet away and were staring in mounting horror at the wave of abyssal blackness creeping towards them.

"What about the spell? Did it work?" Naunet asked the violet god.

"Yes, it worked! He's trapped here!" he yelled back.

"Then we need to leave! Now!"

Out of the blackness echoed a voice that would haunt Naunet's dreams for the rest of his life. **"You can't escape me. No matter how far you run or how well you hide. I will find you."** Two glowing orange eyes appeared out of the blackness and stared at Sereath. **"You. I'd like to thank you for what you did to me. Thanks to you, I got to spend time with my wife again. For that, you've earned a quick death."**

Naunet grabbed her arm and pulled her into his chest. "You won't touch her, Torga. I'll die before I let you touch her."

"Naunet, my friend," an ominous laugh echoed from deep within the cloud. **"I'm coming for you first."**

Naunet and Sereath teleported away as the wave suddenly sped up and devoured everything in sight.

~ ~ ~

For ten *years* in the dilated zone, my aura devoured everything it touched: the twin stars, the old neutron star, every part of Yggdrasil within the system, and everything else both large and small were devoured just as fast. When nothing else remained within the time dilation, my hunger turned on me and consumed everything except for my consciousness, leaving me to float endlessly through space as a void of darkness and hunger.

Ding!

∞∞∞∞∞∞∞

You have unlocked a hidden evolution!

From dirt and leaves, to monsters and trees. You have consumed everything on your path to power. Through great trials and tribulations, what started as a burden has become your greatest strength. A new body must be forged from fires of your will: Would you like to ascend?

∞∞∞∞∞∞∞

"Y—E—S."
Ding!* Ding!* Ding!

∞∞∞∞∞∞∞

Congratulations!
Through your own power and force of will, you have ascended to the realm of the divine as a minor Dark God.

Name: Torga

Race: Quasar Serpent/Gluttonous Dark God of Hunger and Gravity

Minor

Classification: Tier 10(+1)

Level: 100(?)

Experience: N/A

Kenneth Arant

Titles: Destroyer of Asgard, The Dark Serpent, The Unwavering One, Royal Serpent, Free, The Devourer of Worlds, God of Hunger, God of Gravity

Stats:

- Physical

    - Strength: ∞

    - Endurance: ∞

    - Dexterity: 1,051

    - Speed: 1,583

- Mental

    - Intelligence: 74

    - Wisdom: 51

    - Charisma: 31

- Resistances

    - Elements: 90%

    - Divinity: 90%

    - Mental: 60%

- Immunities

    - Mind Control

    - Illusions

    - Disease

Skills: Major Stealth, Heat Detection, Absolute Gluttony, Absolute Growth, Greater Petrifying Gaze, Superior Acid Venom, Detect Concealment, Energy Breath, Fly, Magic Enhancement, Elemental

Manipulation, Omnipotent Control over Hunger and Gravity, Shapeshift, Aethereal Form, Size Control

Traits: Dark Gluttonous Aura ∞, Growth +1,000, Forever Growing, Indomitable, Absolute Regeneration, Ageless, Oxygen Independent, Self-Sustaining, God of Hunger, God of Gravity

∞∞∞∞∞∞∞∞∞∞

My aura flared out around me, and I could suddenly move again. After ten years of being locked into one position, I was free. "I'm coming for you all..."

Interlude: Birth of a Monster

Chaos filled the streets as every god's worst nightmare became reality. Orochi's prison was broken, the Serpent King was free, and judging by the power he'd used to break out, he'd gotten *much* stronger after his imprisonment.

No one knew what to do. When the older gods sealed Orochi ten thousand years ago, it was with the promise that neither he nor his brother would ever be able to escape. But with that promise broken and the original sealers nowhere to be found, what were they supposed to do!?

"Attention everyone, can I have your attention please!?" Ytyx, current de facto "king" of this branch of the Golden City gods yelled from his balcony.

All motion and sound within the area ceased as every citizen turned their sights on the king himself, or on his holographic projections littered throughout the city.

"Ahem, thank you. Now, I know what you're all thinking: 'Orochi's free from his prison, so he must be infinitely more powerful than before' right?'"

Chaos and chatter exploded in the streets.

"Quiet!" All sounds once again ceased. "Please, listen to my words until the end." When no one objected or started to panic, he continued. "As I was saying, yes, it would *seem* as if Orochi has gotten more powerful. However, I have just been informed by the captain of our wonderful royal guard, the Seraphs, that a plot to free Orochi has been uncovered, and they seemingly failed to stop it. But do not worry, my subjects. The captain has been executed for his incompetence and a task force has been created to slay Orochi once and for all!"

Cheers erupted and a new kind of chaos ensued.

"Sire, you do know what will happen if we're wrong and Orochi escaped under his own power, yes?" Haskill, Ytyx's loyal vassal, asked from his position behind the king.

"Of course. But if I'm wrong, then we're all dead anyway. So why should I let my citizens destroy my beautiful city before Orochi can? It will take time for Orochi to make his way here. Time that I fully intend to enjoy."

"As you say, sir. Shall I send in some goddesses for the lord to enjoy?"

"Yes, three should be sufficient. Thank you, Haskill."

"Of course, sir."

~ ~ ~

"What have we done?" Naunet stared wide-eyed at what *used* to be Orochi's prison and the star-sized orange eye glaring at them.

After escaping Torga's wrath, they were finally back together and could live their lives as they wanted, or so he thought. Lacking the magical power necessary to teleport them to a planet connected to the Bi-frost, Naunet and Sereath were enjoying flying alongside each other when *it* happened.

A sound akin to breaking glass echoed throughout all of Yggdrasil. Naunet's eyes widened and he looked back the way they'd came. He saw a titanic wave of green mist with two star-sized orange orbs staring down at them.

"Well, look who it is. Fancy meeting you here, Naunet."

"Damnit! Run!"

"How is he free already!? It's been less than ten hours since we sealed him!"

"I don't know, but I'm not sticking around to find out!"

Suddenly the branch beneath them lurched, causing them to lose their balance and fall. Naunet looked back and saw a great green-scaled hand formed from the mist wrap around the branch. It was pulling the entire thing towards the eyes.

"You're not getting away this time."

"Like hell we're not!" Naunet wrapped his arms around Sereath and started to leap as far and as fast as he could from the ominous orange eyes. However, before they could jump more than twice, a green-scaled humanoid was suddenly standing in front of them. It was clearly male from the rather obscene thing hanging from its pelvis. It stood around six feet tall with an above average sized body, short black hair, and almond-shaped *orange* eyes. The snake-man appeared to be inspecting himself and wasn't paying Naunet and Sereath any attention. Well, until they tried to jump again and an intense gravitational pull slammed the two of them into the branch.

"You know I don't make false promises, Naunet."

Naunet struggled to lift his head and look Torga in the eyes. "H—How did you escape?"

"Don't worry about it, "friend," Torga sneered

While Torga was speaking, Sereath managed to twitch a finger and send a spike of the branch towards his back. But the branch disintegrated before it came anywhere near him.

Torga just made an annoyed sound and glanced at the offending digit. "It appears that's not going to work anymore." He reached down and grabbed Sereath's hand.

Naunet screamed, and he begged Torga not to hurt her.

Without looking away from Naunet, a burst of aura traveled down Torga's arm and surrounded Sereath.

"I promised you a quick death, and I'm a man of my word." Before either of them could react, Sereath just—vanished, as if she'd never been there at all. "Now, it's your turn." Torga grabbed Naunet's arm and squeezed. Pain unlike any Naunet had ever felt coursed through him as his arm was instantly consumed and a creeping blackness raced up his arm until he could no longer tell if he even still *had* an arm.

"It would seem I can control what I eat and what I don't with more precision than before. For example, I just ate every nerve, muscle, and tendon in your arm while leaving the hide behind. Isn't that neat?"

Naunet's eyes glazed over as his mind was overloaded with pain.

Torga "lightly" slapped him a few times to wake him up. "Now, now, you can sleep all you like when you're dead."

Naunet's eyes refocused.

"That's better." Torga lifted him by the throat and smiled at him. "I want you to know I take no pleasure in this, Naunet. Believe it or not, if you'd done what you could to help me instead of betraying me as soon as you got what you wanted, I would've let the both of you go on with your lives."

"You—You bastard! I'll kill you! You hear me!? I'll fucking kill you!"

Torga suddenly released Naunet and allowed him to fall to the branch. Then he took two steps back and appeared to concentrate for a moment.

With the gravity gone and Torga no longer suppressing him, Naunet dashed towards Torga with the intention of ripping his face off. But a sudden hunger pain tore through him and he collapsed against the branch.

"What did you do to me!?" Naunet clawed at his stomach in a vain attempt to relieve himself of the pain.

"I gave you only a tiny portion of the hunger I've felt over the years." Torga crouched down in front of him. "The pain you're feeling right now? That's what I felt after not eating for only two hours."

The pain in Naunet's stomach tripled and he screamed.

"Let's see how long you can handle the pain I've felt all these years."

~ ~ ~

The whole time Naunet cannibalized his own body, I looked on with a feeling of complete and total apathy. Naunet succumbed to his own self-inflicted injuries after making it to the seven-hour mark.

You were a good man, Naunet. A good husband. It's a shame you were such a shit friend. I sighed and with a wave of my hand, Naunet was reduced to ash.

I jumped into the air and my body exploded into green energy particles, then I began to swim through space while following the branch towards whatever planet it was connected to. Luckily, in my current form at least, there didn't appear to be a limit to how fast I could move. My new form was also much more intuitive than my body ever was; every one of the skills I used required little more than a thought to activate. Using magic was as easy as breathing and happened near instantaneously.

The best part of it all? Because of my Self-Sustaining trait, I was no longer hungry. Not even a little bit. Even after ten hours of flying, I felt nothing. Not one spark of hunger, not one iota of thirst, and It. Was. Glorious! I took to flying around in my snake-man form, so I could enjoy being normal, for a change. Well, maybe not normal, but closer than I'd been in a long time.

Unfortunately, my fun was cut short when an explosion of lights flashed all around me and a mob of gods appeared to block my path. I jerked my head back and flipped to avoid flying into one of the more brazen members of the pack.

Okay, I really need to learn how to teleport.

"Captain, it would appear we've managed to stop Orochi before he could escape." A small hobbit looking man said to a tall cat-man.

"Orochi? Wait, I'm not—"

"Save your excuses snake-king. We know who you are. Your form doesn't fool our eyes."

"Look, as much as I'd like to stand here and argue, I'm kind of in the middle of something, so—"

"Under the order of Lord Ytyx; God-King of Yggdrasil, you, Orochi; Serpent King, are hereby sentenced to death."

"I'm telling you, I'm not Orochi."

"Our intelligence says otherwise. Kill him." A group of five overly large and muscular men charged after hearing the order.

"Your intelligence, much like my patience, is nonexistent. Now, would you kindly get out of my way?" A burst of aura wiped out every god caught in the blast. The lucky few who were too far away managed to teleport at the last second, saving them from their comrades' fate.

"Everyone! Regroup and attack at range, on my mark!" The gods began manipulating their domain. Most created gigantic balls of elemental energy, others began using time, space, and destruction magic to slow or otherwise debilitate me.

But, before any of them could get a shot or a spell off, I raised my right hand and the full weight of a star slammed into each and every god still in my way, crushing all but the most durable into a bloody mist. Then I released another burst of aura and wiped out everyone but the lone captain amongst them.

"Now that the meat-shields are out of the way, you're going to teach me that little teleporting trick. Got it?"

The cat-man visibly swallowed and replied in a quivering voice, "And if I refuse?"

"Eh, I'm sure an 'intelligent' man such as yourself can figure that out, all on his own."

"If I do this, you'll let me go?"

"Sure, I'll let you go." I showed the god a friendly smile and internally added, *straight to hell.* But I couldn't say that last part out loud. No, the teleporting trick was too neat to pass up. So, I'd wait until after the god taught me how to do it before sending him into the great beyond. Ayla, Findral, and the rest could afford to wait a few more hours for my return.

Chapter Twenty-Seven

AYLA LEANED BACK AND PROPPED HERSELF ON her elbows while she stared into the moonless night sky. Ever since her father left almost a week ago, she'd taken to hanging out on the deck of Gungnir to watch the stars and to get away from Taranis, the bustling city the Asgardians had claimed as their new home.

However, on this night, she was not alone.

"You know you're not supposed to be out here unattended."

Ayla rolled her eyes and turned to look over her shoulder at the intruder. "Alone? It seems like that's become a foreign concept lately. I've been surrounded by guards and maids for so long I can barely remember what being alone feels like."

"Can you blame us for being cautious? You *did* almost die a few days ago."

"Yes, and you and Findral did a great job of ensuring that did not happen." She huffed and turned away from him.

A few moments later, she heard his light footsteps as he came nearer, then she felt movement just behind her as two strong arms covered in a thin white fabric wrapped around her waist and pulled her closer until she was practically sitting in his lap. Luckily, she was wearing trousers, or this could have been a very problematic position to be in.

"I'm sorry," he mumbled into her back.

She jumped in surprise and turned in his arms until she was sitting sideways with her head facing him. "What're you apologizing for? It's not your fault I was attacked."

"Yes, actually, it is. We finally got the would-be assassin talking and..."

"And?"

"It was a warning. It was her way of letting me know that she knew about you and she wasn't happy about my—trespasses."

"What in Yggdrasil do you mean? Who's warning you and what trespasses are you talking about?" Her eyes narrowed in consternation at the uncomfortable look on his face. She turned to fully face him and grabbed his head between her hands so she could look into his eyes. "Thor, I won't be able to understand unless you explain it to me. "

He leaned into her hands and the uncomfortable look changed to one of sadness. "Before we met, I was already engaged to someone else. She found out about you and sent the assassin as a warning to me. 'Stay faithful to your family's promise or else,' or something along those lines."

Ayla's face went blank as she attempted to process what Thor said. Eventually, she grew tired of sitting so close to him, so she slid off his lap and sat on the ground beside him.

"Did you love her?" she whispered. Almost as if she were afraid of the answer.

"Gods no!" Thor spun to fully face her. "I swear on my family's honor, Ayla. I wanted nothing—nothing to do with this engagement."

"Then why agree to it?"

"That's—It's complicated."

"Try me."

Thor sighed and fell back onto his butt.

"My father made a deal with the Greek king Zeus to prevent a full-scale war between our peoples. I was to wed the youngest of Zeus' daughters to seal the deal, as it were."

"And it was this fiancé of yours that sent the assassin?"

"Unfortunately." Thor allowed a sardonic laugh to escape his lips, which was echoed by Ayla only moments later.

"Ha. Why can't things just be simple, for once?" She sighed and pulled her knees into her chest.

"Who says they can't?"

"Hmm?"

"Be simple, I mean. What if we left and didn't tell anyone where we were going or even that we were leaving?"

"Don't be ridiculous, Thor. We can't just up and leave. What would your parents say? What would my *father* say?"

"Who cares what they'll say?" He got on his knees in front of her. "I was serious when I asked you to marry me, Ayla. Please, run away with me."

"Do you realize what you're saying?" she asked as she stood up and started walking away. "You'll be giving up your kingdom, your family, your—"

"But I'll have you." He gently grabbed her waist and turned her to face him. "And that's all I want."

"You're set on not making this easy for me, aren't you?"

His response was to roguishly grin and pull her closer to him. "Well, I am known to be quite vexing when I want to be."

"So, I've noticed." She sighed and placed a hand on his chest to slightly push him away. "But you know this can't last forever."

"We don't have to run forever. Just until we're free to be together without all of this holding us back."

"And what if that never happens? What if this," she motioned to the two of them, " isn't what fate has in store for us? What then?"

"Then we'll make our own fate. We'll decide our own destiny and to hell with the fates."

"That's impossible." She pushed him away and turned from him. "No one can deny their fate, Thor. Not my father, not my grandmother… not my biological parents." She whispered with a hitch in her voice. She took a few deep breaths to calm down and started walking off.

"Ayla, wait!"

"Don't touch me!"

Thor jerked his hand back as if he'd been burned.

"Sorry I—I just need to be alone for a little while. I'll meet you back at the castle later, okay?"

Thor's mouth opened and closed several times while he tried, and failed, to come up with something—anything—to say to stop her.

"Okay."

᷈ ᷈ ᷈

"Okay," Thor said softly.

"You idiot," I whispered from a position high above them. I'd managed to teleport, after an ungodly number of failures, to the last place I remembered seeing before my departure. But after arriving and spotting Ayla and Thor on the deck of the Gungnir, I'd decided to stop by and say "Hi."

What a colossal mistake *that* was. Now I was stuck floating above the couple while my instincts pulled me in two different directions. On one hand, I could sympathize with Thor. I understood his feelings and the truth behind his words, because not long after I started dating Sarah, I'd asked her the same question, for mostly the same reason. On the other hand, this was my daughter Thor was pursuing and I wanted to protect her.

But was that truly the right thing to do? Without the monstrous hunger I'd been barely able to suppress, I was able to think clearly. And for the first time since my reincarnation, I could see the effects my actions had on the two mortals—two *people*. Which meant there was only one thing I could do. Nothing.

I decided then and there that the best course of action was to simply let the two handle this on their own. Whatever came of this would be entirely of their own making.

It was time they had someone in their corner.

"No, Ayla, it *is* possible to forge your own fate." I shifted into a six-foot-long pale green snake with miniature suns for eyes. *And this old father of yours is going to make sure that no god interferes with your ability to do so.* I teleported away from the area in a flash of pale-green light.

~ ∴ ~

Ayla didn't return to her room until just before dawn the next morning. After passing through the canteen and somberly greeting the guards stationed there, she made her way through the overly opulent halls of the ship to her room.

However, just before she could open the door and enter, she heard a loud crash and several bangs coming from inside. She threw open the door and rushed in, only to stop short at the sight of her six-foot-long Jormungandr slowly spinning as it floated just above the floor.

"Mom! Help me, please!" the serpent aspect on the head of the staff hissed.

"Oh, stop complaining! You're the one that jumped me in the first place."

"Wait, Dad!?" Ayla yelled after recognizing the voice and spotting the six-foot-long serpent lounging across her bed.

"Howdy."

"You're back!?"

"Nope, I'm Dad."

"How!? Since when!?"

"Well, when a mommy snake and a daddy snake love each other very much, they—"

She stared at him in confusion until his surprise appearance finally wore off and his words clicked inside her head. "Oh, ha ha ha, very funny! Can I please just get a serious answer from you, for once?"

Torga grinned at her. "I finished my trip and got back last night. I figured I'd wait for you in here, but that odd looking staff over there decided to jump me when I flew in through the window."

"It's not my fault, Mom! He scared me and I just—reacted."

"So he says," Torga huffed and laid his head back down on Ayla's pillow. "Ohh," he moaned. "You have no idea how much I missed this feeling."

"Um, Hello! Can you please explain what the hell happened while you were gone!?"

Torga let out a deep sigh and painstakingly lifted his head off the pillow again. He moved to the end of the bed and slowly blinked his eerie orange eyes at her. "Alright, Ayla. You should order two cups of coffee, pull up a chair, and sit down because this is going to take a while."

~ ~ ~

After his conversation with Ayla the previous night, Thor had barged into his parents' quarters and all but demanded they rescind the deal. It certainly took a lot of convincing on his part, but eventually, his mother grew tired of the argument and simply ordered her husband to comply. Which is what led to the two of them, Thor and his mother, plus a dozen or so guards, flying at breakneck speeds across the planet and landing just outside of the Greek kingdom boundary to await a permit for entry.

But the last thing he expected to happen is exactly what *did* happen. Zeus, a truly massive man, stood over seven feet tall. He had tanned skin, salt-and-pepper hair, the heavily muscled body of a warrior, and lightning-colored eyes. He was accompanied by his royal guard and Athena, a beautiful young woman with tanned skin, rose-colored hair, and turquoise eyes—and she was Thor's soon to be ex-fiancé.

They landed twenty feet behind the Asgard-Greece border and climbed off their Pegasus mounts, gleaming white horses with manes and tails of the purest blue and birdlike wings. The party that greeted them were all wearing the standard outfit of Greek royalty, which consisted of snow-white robes, leather sandals, and a lightning bolt shaped pin just above their right breast.

However, instead of coming to greet them, the Greeks stood beside their horses and waited for them to make the first move.

"They're waiting to see what we do," Thor said to himself.

He knew that if they crossed into their territory without permission, it would be a declaration of war. Which is what the Greeks ultimately wanted since the two kingdoms had been at war since the time of their ancestors and they were just looking for an excuse to eliminate the Asgardians. On the other hand, the Greeks' pride was preventing them from outright attacking due to the contract they'd sworn to uphold.

The Greeks may have been a paranoid lot, but they were honorable—in their own way. Thor took several steps towards them and stopped just before he crossed the border. "Athena!" he yelled. "I beg of you, please stop these attacks against my fiancé!"

"Are you accusing my daughter of something, young prince?" Zeus asked in a falsely polite tone.

Thor turned to look back at his mother and his eyes pleaded for her assistance. But his mother just gave him a kind smile and a nod of encouragement.

"Lord Zeus, please, you must convince her to stop," he replied after returning his attention to the Greeks.

"I have no idea what you're talking about, Thor," Athena said. The pleasant smile on her face would have given almost anyone else the impression that she was sincere. But not Thor. No, he knew very well the mask she wore to hide her true nature. After all, he used one to hide his nature as well.

"Athena, please, you have to listen to me." He took another step forward, which prompted her to do the same. "This is the only opportunity you're going to get to save your people from a senseless death."

"As I said, Thor, I have no idea what you're talking about."

"Damnit, Athena! There is no chance! Not one opportunity or outcome in which you succeed in this! Now, maybe you do succeed in killing Ayla, and maybe I'm too weak to protect her from you. But in doing so, you will have doomed your people to extinction."

Zeus stuck his arm out in front of Athena and pushed her behind his body. "Are you threatening us, boy? Need I remind you that it was your father that initiated this deal because you were losing the war?"

"Oh, spare me the 'I'm insulted' speech. My father offered me up like some kind of prize to whoever would listen. Just ask the Atlanteans. He offered me to them when I was still just a child."

"Be that as it may, you should watch your tongue, boy. We still have an army that could easily wipe you off the face of Yggdrasil."

"Yeah? Well, my fiancé has a Torga."

"A—She has a what?" Athena asked.

"Torga, I believe, is the name of the elf girl's father," Frigga said as she stepped to her son's side. "And I'm in agreement with my son on this one. If you do somehow succeed in killing the girl, you will have only yourselves to blame when Ragnarök comes knocking at your door."

That's what finally got Zeus and Athena to show some emotion other than disdain, as mild surprise flitted across their faces. And Thor understood why; anyone who'd ever known his mother as more than just "queen" of Asgard, knew she'd never use the term Ragnarök lightly. In fact, she and his father both were deathly afraid of the prophesied end of the world and avoided just the casual mention of the word. So, for her to use it in such a way showed how serious this situation was.

"Then, let us hope your guards are as competent as you brag, or we just might get to see this 'Ragnarök' you so fear," Athena replied after a moment of silence.

"Athena—What have you done?"

"What I swore to do if you tried to back out of our deal."

Thor's eyes widened and his fists tightened until his nails drew blood. "Gods damnit! Tyren, contact father and have him quadruple the guard around Ayla! No one gets to her!" he barked to the captain of the guard.

"Aye, sir!"

Thor glared at the Greeks with unadulterated rage in his eyes. "If you cause her harm, you're dead."

"We'll just have to see about that. now, won't we?" Zeus replied with an infuriating smirk. He mounted his Pegasus and pulled the much shorter Athena onto the horse behind him. Then they took to the skies and within seconds were out of sight.

~ ~ ~

Reina was walking with her companions Donna and Leon. Donna was tall and possessed fiery red hair with white highlights, wide green eyes, and a body most men would die for, as evidenced by Leon's near-constant staring at her ass. She was wearing two diamond earrings that seemed to glow in the dimly lit guildhall. She was also wearing a modest green robe, which looked decidedly un-modest on her. A long ebony staff was leaning against her shoulder.

Leon was a twenty-something-year-old human, slightly over six feet tall, with sun-kissed skin, chocolate-colored eyes, bright white teeth, and short black hair. His chest plate, gauntlets, and pauldrons were all polished to a mirror shine, and his long-sword was inlaid with gold. Overall, he looked like a rich guy with more money than sense.

The three of them were walking through the massive gate that protected Taranis from the outside world, when the sight of someone she recognized brought Reina up short. Sitting at a little table in front of what appeared to be a modern-day cafe was Findral, the dark-skinned elf with demonic looking horns that was traveling with Ayla the last time she'd seen her.

"You two go on ahead and find some lodgings for the night."

"What're you going to do?" Leon asked after taking the proffered bag from Reina's shoulder and adding it to his own, which he carried on his back.

"I think I see an acquaintance. I'm going to go say hi."

"Oh, well, can I come too—"

"Will do, Reina," Donna interrupted and tugged on Leon's arm. "Let's go."

"Aww, but Donna," he whined, "I wanted to go see Reina's friend."

"Which is why we're going in this direction."

Reina just rolled her eyes at the byplay between the two and made her way over to join Findral. She was spotted almost as soon as she neared the table and the dark-skinned elf pleasantly smiled at her.

"Hello, Reina. It's nice to see you again."

"Same to you." Reina smiled back. "So, do you mind if I join you?"

"No, please, by all means," she replied while motioning to the empty chair beside her.

"Thanks." Reina sat down and stretched her legs out in front of her.

Findral took a sip of her coffee and said, "So, Reina, what brings you to Taranis? Are you on a contract or something?"

"No," Reina replied in confusion and shuffled to the edge of her chair so she could pull a piece of white parchment out of her back pocket and handed it to Findral. "This was delivered by a guild messenger a week or so ago."

Findral set her coffee to one side and took the paper from Reina's outstretched hand. After just one glance at the title written in opulent golden ink, Findral groaned and used her other hand to massage the bridge of her nose.

"What is it? Did I miss the wedding?"

"No, it's just that I forgot they'd already sent these out."

"But... isn't it normal to send out invitations before a wedding?"

"Yes, but not when the couple in question have yet to even set a date for said wedding."

"You're kidding! Then who sent out the invitations?"

"King Odin and Queen Frigga most likely." She leaned closer to Reina and whispered conspiratorially in her ear. "But I think it was just the king's doing. He's far more excited about the wedding than the queen is. "

"Figures," Reina sighed.

Findral smiled at her, downed the rest of her coffee in one gulp, then walked over to the counter and ordered an extra-large, extra strong coffee to go. She walked back over to Reina and motioned for her to follow.

"C'mon. Ayla will be glad to see you and I'm sure the master will be too."

"The—master?"

"Ayla's father."

"Oh—OH! I didn't think he would be here since the wedding wasn't happening yet."

"He returned from a trip just last night, actually. You do want to meet him, yes?"

"I mean, sure, I guess. Though I don't know how I feel about a man that has so many servants," she said as she stood to follow.

"Servants?" Findral asked in confusion.

"Well, you do call him 'master' don't you? That makes you his servant, right?"

"Oh," Findral laughed. "No, he actually hates it when I call him master."

"Why do it, then?"

"Because in spite of his unwillingness to admit it, he deserves all the respect and praise we can throw at him. After all, how many men do you know that would search throughout the cosmos for a wife who may or may not still live?"

"Um—What?"

Findral stopped so suddenly that Reina walked into her back and bounced off, hurting her nose in the process. Findral spun around and began checking on her. Once Reina had assured her that she was, indeed, fine, Findral sighed and said, "Please don't mention this to the master. He doesn't like talking about it."

"Sure, I can do that," Reina said after wiggling her nose a few times to make sure it wasn't bleeding.

"Thanks."

Reina just waved her off.

After a few minutes of walking in silence, Reina politely asked, "So—he's looking for Ayla's mother?"

"Hmm?"

"You said he was looking for his wife, right? I just assumed that was Ayla's mother."

"Oh, no, it's not Ayla's mom."

"He had her out of wedlock, then?"

"Nope, he adopted Ayla after the death of her last living relative, her grandmother."

"Oh." Reina was quiet for a few more minutes as they wound their way through the throngs of people. "Does he have any other children?"

"He's mentioned that he and his wife had three children together."

"Are they here too?"

"No, and I've never actually met them either. He very rarely talks about his time before he was taken from them."

"What do you mean? How was he taken from them?"

"Master is a reincarnator. He was taken from his home planet by a god and basically dropped on some backwater planet on the other side of Yggdrasil."

He's like me? She was getting more and more interested in this mysterious "father" Ayla and Findral had told her about.

"What kind of elf is he?"

Findral burst out laughing at the question. Her outburst was so loud the surrounding people glanced at her in consternation.

"Sorry, sorry everyone," she apologized, then turned to Reina. "Sorry, but I'd forgotten that we hadn't told you much about him the last time we met. Torga—that's the master's name—isn't an elf."

"He's not?"

"No. He's most definitely not."

"He's a human, then?"

"No, he's definitely not that either. You know, it's probably better if you just see him for yourself. I seriously doubt you'd believe me if I just told you what he was."

"I don't know about all that now. I've seen some pretty weird stuff in my travels."

"I'm sure you have," Findral said with a smirk on her face.

Just as the two passed through the gatehouse leading inside the castle, an alarm went off and the massive iron gate slammed shut behind them.

"What's happening!?"

"I—I don't know. C'mon, we need to go check on Mistress Ayla!"

"I'll be right behind you," Reina said, nodding.

Suddenly, it felt as if the entire world rumbled and Reina and Findral wound up sprawled on the ground.

"That's not good."

"What's not good?"

"Something must have pissed off the master..."

"What does that have to do with anything—Wait, are you trying to say Ayla's dad did that?"

"Unfortunately."

"But that's impossible!"

"Ha! You'll soon find out just how little that word means in the face of my master's will," Findral said with a grim expression on her face.

"You bastards!" echoed a voice seeped in power. Every syllable caused the world to shake and fear to race down the spine of all who heard it.

An explosion rocked the castle as a wall on the top floor was destroyed and two masked figures in black clothes plummeted towards the ground, while a third leaped out of the hole after them. However, before they could reach the ground and possibly die on impact, their downward momentum came to a halt. Their bodies halted in midair and stayed there as if they were held by invisible hands.

Not long after they stopped falling, a heavily muscled, green-scaled man with short black hair floated out of the hole. The only clothes he seemed to be wearing was a bath towel wrapped around his waist. In a bridal carry held within his arms was the unmoving form of Ayla.

"Who is that?"

"That would be the master," Findral said matter-of-factly.

"That's Ayla's dad!?"

Instead of answering her, massive wings of pure flame burst from Findral's back and she flew up to meet him, leaving Reina to gape after her.

The hulking snake-man floated to the ground, accompanied by Findral and the still unconscious Ayla, which caused all of the surrounding humans to back away in fear.

The snake-man swiveled his head to look at the three would-be assassins and waved his hand at them. Whatever forces were keeping them in the air slowly lowered them to the ground.

They immediately tried to run, but before they could get more than a foot from where they landed, he waved his hand again and a round of sickening snaps rang out, a heartbeat before the three men collapsed to the ground, wailing in pain.

He crouched over them and asked, "Did the Greeks send you?"

The three men remained silent.

"You will answer my question before you die."

"Master, I think they are ninjas," Findral spoke up. The snake-man just stared at her. "Assassins that worship those of the Shinto pantheon?" she hedged.

He just snorted at that and pulled the mask off of the closest man. "More like nonjas," he said in a derisive tone directed at the three men. Then, he threw Findral a reproachful look and said, "And I'm aware of what they are, Findral."

"Then, why—"

"I thought I told you never to call me 'master.'"

"Oh. Right. Sorry."

Torga just sighed and lifted the first man's head so he could look into his eyes with his own glowing bright orange ones as he allowed his anger to show itself again.

"Did you use poison?"

"N—No."

Torga's eyes narrowed in suspicion and suddenly the man's left eye seemingly evaporated into black mist. "You're already on my shit-list, so lying to me isn't helping your case."

"Heh, I knew I was already a dead man as soon as we were caught. Why should I bother telling you a damn thing?"

"Simple. Because I can make things so much worse for you."

"I can find out for sure," Reina interrupted.

Torga let go of the man's head, finally noticing that Reina was standing there. He soaked in her appearance, spending a particularly long time on her body suit—

"Are those—guns?" he asked while pointing at the mana launchers on her hip. "Sorry, that was rude. Do I know you?" Torga asked as he reached behind him and tightened the towel.

"Your name?" he asked again, this time in a more polite tone.

"Reina. I'm a friend of Ayla's."

"Interesting…" he muttered.

Reina once again averted her eyes from the heavily muscled torso of the man claiming to be Ayla's father. *No, down girl! You're happily married and he's searching for his wife. You don't have time to be drooling over him, so focus!* she berated herself.

However, now that she'd gotten a closer look at his scales, she found that she really wanted to touch them. *Are they as rough as they look or are they soft like a snake's?* She had to shake the thought from her mind, so she could focus on the task at hand.

"There appears to be some form of mild anesthetic in her blood stream. Not enough to fully paralyze her, but enough to make it difficult for her to move. I'm also detecting traces of dendrotoxin in her system. My guess is the anesthetic was used to hide the symptoms of the toxin. Very clever. "

"Can you remove it?"

"I can flush out her system, but we'll need somewhere quiet so I can focus, and she'll need plenty of fluids afterward."

"Right." He scooped Ayla into his arms and began floating a few inches off the ground, which made his already tall form tower over Reina even more. "Findral, find the others and tell them what has happened. I want them to report to Ayla's room in no less than ten minutes."

"Understood." Findral nodded and took to the skies.

Then he held out his hand for Reina to take. "You coming?"

"You know, normally, I'd make a guy buy me dinner before I went home with him." She reached out and grasped his hand, which caused her body to slowly lift off the ground until she was able to look into his bright orange eyes.

"I'll be sure to make it up to you later."

The three of them smoothly lifted into the air and went into the hole Torga had made earlier.

Hours later, after an exhausting use of her magic to flush out Ayla's system and ensuring the girl would live to see the sun rise again, Reina awoke to find herself in an ornate bed with plush pillows and incredibly soft sheets. When the smell of a spinach omelet, raspberry jam covered toast, and coffee hit her nose she leaped from the bed and practically devoured every morsel. It was her favorite breakfast meal, after all.

A soft knock on the door alerted Reina that she had company, so she hurried over to the door while taking that last bite of toast with her. When she opened the door and saw Ayla's dad standing there wearing a baggy white shirt and black trousers she almost choked on the toast.

Torga just smiled at her.

"Good morning."

"Oh, um—Morning."

He leaned in and peaked around the door to see an almost clean plate and the smile on his face grew even larger.

"Enjoyed your meal, did you?"

"Yes, you can give my thanks to whoever made it."

"You're welcome." He shrugged, then motioned towards the door. "Mind if I come in?"

"Sure, I guess, but what do you mean 'you're welcome'?"

"I did say I'd make it up to you, didn't I?" he replied with a polite smile down at her.

"Wait—*you* cooked it!?"

"I'll take that as a compliment towards my cooking skills and not an insinuation that you believed I couldn't cook." He laughed as he made his way over to the lone table in the room and sat down.

"What, pssh, of course, I didn't think that." Of course, that was exactly what she'd thought, but she wasn't going to tell him that. She moved to join him, but before she could sit down, he stood up and pulled a chair next to him out and turned it towards her.

"Thank you?"

"Of course," he replied as he easily pushed the chair closer to the table and retook his seat.

"So… What's up? Did you want me to check on Ayla again?" She asked to fill the awkward silence that followed.

"No, she's fine. Thanks."

"Oh- of course."

"Mind if I ask you a personal question?" He asked without looking at her.

"After that breakfast? You can ask me anything you want," she joked.

He grinned at her. "Are you married?"

The smile she'd been wearing all morning was instantly wiped off her face as a memory of her husband flashed through her mind. The memory was like a bucket of cold water and quickly sobered her up.

"I am."

"Do you love him?"

"That's a stupid question. Of course, I love him."

"When was the last time you saw him?"

"That's none of your business, is it?" she said sharply.

"Please, humor me."

"Fine!" she yelled. Then, after a brief moment of hesitation, she said, "It's been a while."

Torga just quietly watched her with those golden-orange colored eyes of his.

After a full minute of silence, Reina couldn't take it anymore and pushed her chair back so she could stand up. As she was walking over to the bed to grab her gun belt so she could leave, Torga spoke up.

"Are you a reincarnator?"

"What?"

"Were you reincarnated into Yggdrasil?"

"What if I was?" she snapped. She snatched up her gun belt and fastened it around her waist. But she soon had to take a step back as Torga was standing in front of her.

"Sarah?"

Her head jerked up and she glared at him. She drew her pistol and aimed it directly at Torga's face.

"How the hell do you know that name!?"

A golden liquid seemed to pool in Torga's eyes as he stared down at her. "It is you," he whispered.

Reina pulled back the hammer on the gun. "Answer me!"

Torga slowly reached up and wiped the liquid from his eyes. "I know I look different than you remember, but c'mon, don't you recognize me?"

"What're you talking about?"

"Jeez, and to think you used to complain about *my* memory," Torga said in mock consternation.

"Again, what the hell are you—you—Huh?"

The gun fell from her hand as the dots connected themselves. Her eyes widened and she tried to take a step back in surprise, but she tripped over the bed and fell onto her back.

Which caused Torga to genuinely smile at her in a way that made her heart skip a beat.

"I've missed you, Sarah. More than you could ever know."

"A—A—Albert?"

"I've gone by Torga for a little over a century now, but yeah, it's me."

"A century?" she whispered.

"You've been gone a long time, Sarah."

"But it's only been ten years!" She climbed to her feet and glared at him.

"For you, maybe. But for me? Well, you died when I was thirty-six, right?"

"Yeah."

"I was eighty-seven when I died."

Reina collapsed to her knees and unshed tears filled her eyes. "No—No, that's not possible. I wasn't gone that long. It was only for a little while," she whispered to herself. "Please, tell me you're lying? Tell me I didn't miss out on my babies' lives. Tell me I didn't leave you to raise them alone."

"Hey, I think I did a great job raising them, thank you very much," he joked.

She just stared at him.

"I'm sorry, Sarah."

"Were they happy?"

"They missed you, of course. But yeah, they were happy."

"Thank God." Right there, in front of the husband she'd been searching for, she broke down and cried about the life that had been taken from her.

Torga moved around to the side of the bed, sat down, and leaned against the headboard, then pulled her onto his chest.

"It's alright, let it out."

His words made her cry even harder. She spent the rest of the morning crying into Torga's chest and only stopped when she'd exhausted herself and just laid on top of him to watch the clouds outside of the window.

"So—" she sniffled. "What happens now? Are you going to just leave me here to go find your wife or can I come with you?"

"You know," Torga said after a moment of silence, "for a doctor, you can be really stupid sometimes."

"That's mean. I just wanted to know if—"

Torga pulled her onto his lap and kissed her as deeply and passionately as he could without hurting her. And he didn't let up until Reina was gasping for air.

"You were the one I've been looking for, you dummy. I've waited for damn near two centuries for you to be in my arms again and I'll be damned if I let you go that easily."

"Oh—" she panted.

"Now, if you'd told me earlier that you no longer loved me? Well, I probably wouldn't have said anything and just would've stood back and let you live your life. But now that you've told me? I'm not leaving your side for anything."

He picked her up and sat her on his lap.

"In fact, you'll be lucky if you can walk after I'm done with you."

"What do you—" She felt something poke her in the butt and her eyes widened in surprise. "Ohh, so that's what you meant," she finished with a sultry smile as she leaned in to kiss him again.

EPILOGUE

SOMEWHERE OUTSIDE OF YGGDRASIL'S BRANCHES, a ball of white flame the size of a star floated. With only empty space surrounding it, it was a wonder it managed to exist at all, let alone grow to such proportions. But this was no ordinary flame, oh no. These flames were the remains of a goddess of life.

Her body and followers destroyed by the one she called brother. This goddess laid dormant while her body healed. At least, that was her original plan. At some point during the healing process, her mind also began to heal from the scars of the past.

Without the pressures of being a goddess weighing on her, she was finally able to grieve for all that she'd lost, and in peace. But with the peace of mind her isolation granted her, also came the guilt of her actions.

The murder of innocents, the betrayals of those she considered friends, and the way she treated her brother. The guilt of these actions slammed into her damaged mind with the weight of a black hole.

"So, the princess finally decided to pull her head out of her ass. Eh?"

A swirling mass of gray light began to form in front of the flame. From this light, a skeletal hand holding a long black cane emerged. Immediately after, a tall skeleton in a red tuxedo stepped out.

"Amaar—what do you want?" A tired feminine voice echoed from within the flame.

The skeleton's teeth twitched upwards and his pitch-black eyes showed a clear sign of humor within them.

"What? Can't an old skeleton come see his favorite pigeon without cause?" he asked with false hurt in his voice.

A deep sigh drifted out of the flame. "Amaar, I'm in no mood for your games. Just tell me what you want, then be gone."

Amaar reached up and pulled his top hat off. **"Hmm—No."** He slicked back his hair and twirled his mustache, then placed the top hat back on his head.

"You've been on your high horse for a bit too long, and this just so happens to be the best time to knock you the fuck off." Amaar slammed the cane into the gray light he was standing on. This caused a dome of gray to expand and cover the entirety of the star-sized flame.

"What're you doing?" the feminine voice yelled. The shock of being enclosed within Amaar's power blew away any trace of exhaustion from her voice.

"What I should've done when I first noticed your fall from grace, and were it not for my sister—your patron's request, I would have." The gray sphere began to rapidly shrink, causing the flame to shrink with it."

"No! I've learned my lesson. It won't happen again!" the voice shrilled.

"Oh, I'm aware," Amaar said in a dull monotone.

"Then why do this?"

A skeletal hand reached up and pulled the top hat down over Amaar's forehead, casting an ominous shadow over his already intimidating eyes as a faint red light shined within them.

"Because, my dear. Regardless of your current emotional or mental state, you made one Very. Big. Mistake."

"Tell me and I'll fix it. I swear!" the voice begged.

"You disturbed my nap with that explosion a few years ago," Amaar said in a completely serious voice.

"Um—What?"

The gray sphere immediately shrunk to the size of a marble and flew into Amaar's hand. He held it up to his eye and stared at it for a few seconds while a tiny voice raged from within it.

"You kiss your mother with that mouth?"

He rolled the sphere around a few times, then drew back his arm.

"What do you think, Turkey? Pinball, pool, or bowling?" he asked with a "smile."

"None of the above—" the tiny voice started.

"Pinball it is!" Amaar snapped his arm forward and sent the marble flying at speeds much faster than light.

The gray sphere protected the planets and stars from the impacts while it bounced back and forth across the known galaxy. Until finally, after two years of bouncing, it slammed into the forehead of a young elf. The impact propelled the elf onto the ground and resulted in a quick, painless death.

The goddess, who'd long since been knocked unconscious, was sent even further into unconsciousness while the gray sphere pushed her flame into the elf girl's head.

"I think it's about time the gods remembered what it was like to be mortal. Don't you,

Forna?" Amaar's voice echoed through the girl's body as her soul was pushed out by Forna's.

Amaar turned to the tiny soul floating next to him and gently pulled it towards his face.

"I'm sorry you had to suffer through that, my dear," Amaar said sincerely.

"I won't hurt anymore?" the spirit asked.

"No, the sickness is gone."

"Would I have died soon anyway?"

Amaar nodded his head. **"Unfortunately."**

The spirit was quiet for a while, then a tiny giggle escaped from it. "It's alright, I forgive you!" it chirped.

Amaar smiled at the tiny soul. **"Go on, then."**

He pushed the soul into the sky and used his power to guide her into the cycle, the afterlife for the people of Yggdrasil. Minutes after the soul departed Amaar turned his attention back to Forna. **"I'll see you soon, Forna. May you learn from this experience and come out better for it."**

～ ～ ～

It was a dark moonlit night and a young elven girl was being chased by a dark figure clad in black robes. She ran through the dark forest wearing nothing but a tunic that had a large blood stain on the front, just below her collarbone.

"You know you cannot escape me, little bird. Come home willingly and you won't be punished," a venomous voice said to the elf's back.

"No-No-No-No-No, he's dead! He's been dead for millennia!" the elf frantically thought as she glanced over her shoulder at the figure.

"Dead?" the dark figure asked, as if it could hear her thoughts. **"Did you really believe you and your pet lizard could truly kill me?"** The cold voice laughed humorlessly.

"We did! We killed you!!" she yelled, her eyes widening in fright as she realized the shadow was gaining on her.

"No," the voice chuckled. **"His power may have temporarily destroyed my form, but I am deathless. or did you forget that without his power to keep me from regenerating, nothing can kill me?"**

"No-No-No! It's just a dream! It's just a dream!" the elf yelled as she tripped and landed hard on her face. She quickly flipped onto her back and crawled away from the form that suddenly towered over her.

"Unfortunately, you are correct little bird. This is a dream, but I am real, and I'm coming for you." The shadow reached out and gently lifted her face to his. **"You are mine. You have always been mine, and you will always be mine,"** the shadow harshly whispered as it roughly smashed its cold lips to hers.

The elf violently shoved the shadow away, climbed to her feet, and ran away to the sound of cold laughter.

"And soon you will be back where you belong— by my side." Sixteen glowing red eyes raced after her, gaining on her with every passing second.

~ ~ ~

The elf girl shot up in bed. Her heart was hammering away in her chest and cold sweat covered her body. She sucked in a ragged breath and desperately tried to calm down before she woke her roommates.

She was lying in a dark three-person tent that she shared with two other elf girls; sisters if she remembered correctly.

She glanced down at the bedroll she'd been sleeping in and moved to get up, when she accidentally placed her hand in something wet. *Is that... blood?* the elf girl wondered as she lifted the woolen blanket to her nose and sniffed.

Yep, definitely blood, she decided as she thought back to her nightmare. She gingerly lifted her other hand and placed it on her chest, just below the collar of her gray tunic. She pulled away a bloodstained hand.

With a sigh, she focused on bringing her magic to the surface and whispered, "Vokrii Hass—"

A faint white light surrounded her hand and she pressed it to her wound. She hissed in pain as the magic took effect and pure life energy flowed into the wound, causing her body to accelerate the healing process, clotting the blood, knitting together the muscles, and finally sealing the skin. When all was said and done, only a faint white scar in the shape of a sun remained.

She sighed in relief as she climbed out of the bedroll, folded up the blanket, and headed for the tent flap.

Hopefully, I can get this cleaned before they wake up—

"Bad dream?" the person in the leftmost bedroll asked.

Too late for that, apparently. The elf girl sighed and turned to the voice.

"Yes, I—I had a nightmare," the elf girl admitted.

"Want to talk about it?"

She shifted uncomfortably, "No, it's over now and—and I'm fine." She tried to play it off as nothing, but her voice sounded weak even to her own ears.

The other elf girl was silent for a few moments then said, "Okay, well I'm going back to sleep. Wake me if you want to talk about it."

"Will do." She quickly agreed as she turned and fled the tent.

Outside, the elf girl glanced briefly at the surrounding tents, then made her way to the nearby river. It was about two hundred feet from the camp—close enough to be useful, but far enough away that no one would mistakenly fall into it in the middle of the night.

The elf exhaled a sigh of disappointment as she knelt on the grass and shoved the blanket into the cold water.

"Gaar sos," she whispered while concentrating on the blood stain. After a few seconds, the blood began to release its hold on the blanket and drift away on the gentle current. *Oh, how far I've fallen,* she snorted to herself as she pulled the blanket from the water and placed it on the grass to dry. "An upper tiered life goddess reduced to cleaning bloodstains with cheap parlor tricks." She laid on the grass and looked up at the stars. "What happened to me?"

"You mean besides you becoming a power-hungry bitch and ruining lives?"

The elf girl rolled her eyes and looked at the skeleton leaning against his cane a few feet away.

"Amaar," she mumbled and made a sour face.

"Birdbrain," he replied.

"What do you want, Amaar? You've already given me a fate worse than death, so what more could you want from me?"

"Worse than death?" He smirked. **"You would've preferred I simply wipe you from existence?"**

She shrugged. "Don't I deserve it?" She stared into his abyss-colored eyes. "I—I've done horrible things in the name of justice. I let my rage blind me to the fact that I—for all my good intentions—had become just like him."

Amaar watched her with narrowed eyes. **"How mature of you to finally admit that you were a hypocritical piece of rhinix excrement."**

She glared at him for a few seconds—then cautiously let her eyes drop. "I suppose I was," she mumbled.

Amaar walked over and stood at her side, causing her to flinch in anticipation, but he just sat down cross-legged and chuckled. **"While I am glad that you seem to have finally come to your senses, I'm curious what brought this on?"**

She shrugged, "Being stuck here, in this body, with these people I—I've had a lot of time to think about it." She sat up and slightly turned to him. "When you first sent me here, I was so angry. Angry at myself, at the gods, at Niabus." She threw him a glare. "And most definitely at you."

He smirked. **"Join the club. I hear they give all new members a jacket and the donuts are delicious."**

She stared at him in bewilderment, then shook her head. "Yes—Well—Be that as it may, after spending a few years with these people I—I don't know. I guess at some point I just realized that it was no one's fault but my own and I guess I got over it?" she said with confusion clouding her eyes.

"Got over it?" he asked.

She just nodded her head and fell onto her back.

"Yeah, it surprised me too."

"I guess this vacation of sorts has done you some good after all," Amaar said, breaking the silence after a few minutes.

"Vacation? Is that what this was supposed to be?"

"In a manner of speaking, yes."

She hopped to her feet and stared down at him.

"Does—Does that mean I get my powers back!?" she asked excitedly.

"Hell no," Amaar snorted. **"Making progress, you are. But fucked up, you did. Yes, hmm,"** he replied in a weird accent while stroking his chin.

She frowned. "So, I'll never be a goddess again?"

"As you were, no," he said while continuing to stroke his chin.

She narrowed her eyes in annoyance and growled, "Amaar, stop talking in that stupid accent. This is my life we're talking about here!"

He stopped stroking his chin and frowned at her in mock consternation. **"Hey, don't disrespect the accent! A long time ago on a far, far away branch of Yggdrasil, this accent was used by a very wise man-thing."**

"Yeah, whatever you say," she said while rolling her eyes.

She stood up and gathered her now barely damp blanket into her arms and said, "Goodbye, Amaar. Since I won't be getting my powers back, I hope to see you again only after I die," she said coldly and stormed off towards camp.

"That may be sooner than you think, Forna," Amaar chuckled, then vanished in a gray light.

Books, Mailing List, and Reviews

If you enjoyed reading about Torga and the rest of the gang in *A Snake's Path* and want to stay in the loop about the latest book releases, awesome promotional deals, and upcoming book giveaways be sure to subscribe to our email list at:

www.ShadowAlleyPress.com

Word-of-mouth and book reviews are crazy helpful for the success of any writer. If you *really* enjoyed reading *A Snake's Path*, please consider leaving a short, honest review—just a couple of lines about your overall reading experience. Thank you in advance!

ABOUT THE AUTHOR

Hello, everyone. My name is Kenneth Arant and I like to pretend I'm a writer in my spare time. A bit about myself: I'm a retired martial artist with fourteen years' experience, six of which I used to teach others how to not knock themselves out with a pair of nunchucks.

Currently, I'm a full-time night owl with a minor caffeine addiction and a penchant for letting my imagination run wild. My dream is to write awesome books that people will enjoy for years to come.

BOOKS FROM SHADOW ALLEY PRESS

If you enjoyed *A Snake's Path*, you might also enjoy other awesome stories from Shadow Alley Press, such as Viridian Gate Online, Rogue Dungeon, the Yancy Lazarus Series, War God's Mantle, American Dragons, Dungeon Bringer, Full Frontal Galaxy, or the Jubal Van Zandt Series. You can find all of our books listed at www.ShadowAlleyPress.com.

James A. Hunter

Viridian Gate Online: Cataclysm (Book 1)
Viridian Gate Online: Crimson Alliance (Book 2)
Viridian Gate Online: The Jade Lord (Book 3)
Viridian Gate Online: The Imperial Legion (Book 4)
Viridian Gate Online: The Lich Priest (Book 5)
Viridian Gate Online: Doom Forge (Book 6)
Viridian Gate Online: Darkling Siege (Book 7)

VGO: The Artificer (Imperial Initiative)

Kenneth Arant

<<◇>>

VGO: Nomad Soul (Illusionist 1)
VGO: Dead Man's Tide (Illusionist 2)
VGO: Inquisitor's Foil (The Illusionist 3)

<<◇>>

VGO: Firebrand (Firebrand Series 1)
VGO: Embers of Rebellion (Firebrand Series 2)
VGO: Path of the Blood Phoenix (Firebrand Series 3)

<<◇>>

VGO: Vindication (The Alchemic Weaponeer 1)
VGO: Absolution (The Alchemic Weaponeer 2)
VGO: Insurrection (The Alchemic Weaponeer 3)

<<◇>>

Strange Magic: Yancy Lazarus Episode One
Cold Heatred: Yancy Lazarus Episode Two
Flashback: Siren Song (Episode 2.5)
Wendigo Rising: Yancy Lazarus Episode Three
Flashback: The Morrigan (Episode 3.5)
Savage Prophet: Yancy Lazarus Episode Four
Brimstone Blues: Yancy Lazarus Episode Five

<<◇>>

MudMan: A Lazarus World Novel

<<◇>>

Two Faced: Legend of the Treesinger Book 1
Soul Game: Legend of the Treesinger Book 2

<<◇>>

Rogue Dungeon: Rogue Dungeon Series Book 1
Civil War: Rogue Dungeon Series Book 2

A Snake's Path

Troll Nation: Rogue Dungeon Series Book 3
Rogue Evolution: Rogue Dungeon Series Book 4

eden Hudson

Revenge of the Bloodslinger: A Jubal Van Zandt Novel
Beautiful Corpse: A Jubal Van Zandt Novel
Soul Jar: A Jubal Van Zandt Novel
Garden of Time: A Jubal Van Zandt Novel
Wasteside: A Jubal Van Zandt Novel

<<<>>>

Darkening Skies: Path of the Thunderbird 1
Stone Soul: Path of the Thunderbird 2
Demon Beast: Path of the Thunderbird 3

<<<>>>

Death Cultivator: Death Cultivator 1

Aaron Ritchey

Armageddon Girls: The Juniper Wars 1
Machine-Gun Girls: The Juniper Wars 2
Inferno Girls: The Juniper Wars 3
Storm Girls: The Juniper Wars 4

<<<>>>

Sages of the Underpass: Battle Artists Book 1

Gage Lee

Hollow Core: School of Swords and Serpents 1
Eclipse Core: School of Swords and Serpents 2

Kenneth Arant

Chaos Core: School of Swords and Serpents 3
Burning Core: School of Swords and Serpents 4

Shadowbound: Ghostlight Academy Book 1

J.D. Astra

Zero.Hero 1
Zero.Hero 2

Morgan Cole

Inheritance: The Last Enclave Book 1
Redemption: The Last Enclave Book 2

Kenneth Arant

A Snake's Life: A Snake's Life Book 1
A Snake's Path: A Snake's Life Book 2

Mark Stallings

The Elements: Silver Coin Saga Book 1

Books from Black Forge

Aaron Crash

War God's Mantle: Ascension (Book 1)
War God's Mantle: Descent (Book 2)
War God's Mantle: Underworld (Book 3)

Denver Fury: American Dragons Book 1
Cheyenne Magic: American Dragons Book 2
Montana Firestorm: American Dragons Book 3
Texas Showdown: American Dragons Book 4
California Imperium: American Dragons Book 5
Dodge City Knights: American Dragons Book 6
Leadville Crucible: American Dragons Book 7
Alamosa Arena: American Dragons Book 8
Alaska Kingdom: American Dragons Book 9
Wyoming Dynasty: American Dragons Book 10

Barbarian Outcast: Princesses of the Ironbound 1
Barbarian Assassin: Princesses of the Ironbound 2
Barbarian Alchemist: Princesses of the Ironbound 3

Raider Annihilation: Son of Fire Book 1

Kenneth Arant

Kraken Killjoy: Son of Fire Book 2

<<<>>>

Boss Build Book 1

Nick Harrow

Dungeon Bringer 1
Dungeon Bringer 2
Dungeon Bringer 3

<<<>>>

Valhalla Virus: Ragnarok Rebels Book 1

<<<>>>

Witch King 1
Witch King 2
Witch King 3